The Butterfly Garden

The Butterfly Garden

Annette Blair

Five Star • Waterville, Maine

First Edition, Second Printing

Published in 2005 in conjunction with Tekno Books and Ed Gorman.

Set in 11 pt. Plantin by Ramona Watson.

Printed in the United States on permanent paper.

Library of Congress Cataloging-in-Publication Data

Blair, Annette.
    The butterfly garden / by Annette Blair.—1st ed.
        p. cm.
    ISBN 1-59414-314-5 (hc : alk. paper)
    1. Custody of children—Fiction.   2. Single fathers—Fiction.   3. Amish women—Fiction.   4. Midwives—Fiction.   5. Widowers—Fiction.   6. Amish—Fiction.   7. Ohio—Fiction.   I. Title.
    PS3602.L333B87 2005
    813'.6—dc22   2005043218

Dedication

To Lisa Norato, writer and friend
for
Supper plotting and dessert brilliance
Book stores and brainstorms
Father Christmas, Sexy Vicars, and Designer Witches
Your turn next.

Chapter One

Walnut Creek, Ohio, 1883

Amish Midwife Sara Lapp stopped at the base of the farmhouse steps and tilted her head, as much to keep the autumn wind from stealing under her black wool crown-bonnet as to meet the eyes of the man towering above her on his porch.

Adam Zuckerman stood taller and more forbidding than usual in the eerie pitch of night, even barefoot and unflinching on a cold porch floor. One suspender crossed his open-throated union suit, the other hung in a loop at his side—an oversight that should make a man seem vulnerable. But Adam Zuckerman was as about as defenseless as a grizzly.

Sara swallowed and raised her chin, determined to say what no one else dared. "Abby should not be having another. You're killing her with so many babies so close."

Adam Zuckerman reared back as if struck, raising the hair at the nape of Sara's neck, skittering her heart.

Even the wind howled a wild lament.

A moment of fury claimed the taciturn man, another of rigid control, before he raised his lantern high, and examined her, inch by slow insulting inch. "What know you, Spinster Sara," said he, "of such things as should or should not happen between a man and his wife?"

A hit, dead center. Mortal—or so it seemed. Spinster

Sara. And if she called him mad, like the rest of the world did, how would he respond?

Mad Adam Zuckerman, whose scowl could stop a man cold, whose presence could turn children to stone, even his own . . . especially his own. Why had this self-chosen outcast, of all people, called her to tend his laboring wife, despite the community's stand against her?

No one could figure him out.

No one tried anymore.

Sara climbed to the porch, despite his defiant stance. "Time I looked in on Abby."

But Abby's husband stepped in her path. "Get out." That flash of emotion appeared again and vanished again.

She was the lesser of evils, Sara knew. None of her people—man or woman—wanted a man around during labor and birth, doctor or no, but without care, childbirth in their Ohio Amish community was too often deadly. "If you have no need for my skill as a midwife, why did you send for me?"

"Skill or no, the right to judge is not yours."

Given the accuracy of his statement, the catch in Adam's voice disturbed Sara. "But the right to save lives is," she said. "Leave Abby alone for a while after this."

His eyes went dark and hard as flint, making Sara look away, and pull her cape closed against a sudden chill.

A newborn cry rent the air, forcing their gazes to collide, Sara's born of shock, Adam's of regret. "Move aside and let me in," Sara said, but Adam turned, entered and let the door shut in her face.

Raising an angry hand, Sara shoved it hard and smacked him good, taking no solace from the hit. Stepping into the farmhouse kitchen, she was assaulted by the lingering scents of smoked ham and cabbage. A kerosene lamp on the scarred oak table flickered and hissed, hazing the perimeter of the room, but Sara knew her way and made straight for the stairs.

"Wait!"

She stopped and rounded on him. "For the love of God, Abby could be bleeding to death!"

Adam paled, defeat etching his features with an unforgiving blade until emotion dimmed and none was left. "She's not." He hooked that forgotten suspender over his shoulder with slow, even precision.

Not his words, but his misplaced action and calm voice gone brittle held her. Sara shivered. "Did you deliver the baby, then? Before I came?"

Adam did not move so much as a muscle, yet Sara watched, mesmerized, as he struggled to tear himself from some agonizing place. "She delivered it."

Despite the blaze in the hearth, cold assaulted Sara with knife pricks to her skin. "Then how do you—"

"She's gone."

Her denial as involuntary as her sob, Sara grasped a chair-back for support, but none was to be found. Her pounding heart took over her being.

The babe's cry came again. Louder. Angrier.

The old walnut regulator clock grated in the silence—the commencement of eternity marked in counterpoint to the commencement of life.

As if from nowhere, and without acknowledgment, a grudging if temporary amnesty flowered between Mad Adam Zuckerman and Spinster Sara Lapp. She read it in his eyes as clearly as she knew it in her soul, and she was shaken, because deep in a place she tried to keep sealed, Sara feared she had been altered.

But panic was not to be tolerated. There was death to

deal with, and life. She took the stairs at a slow pace, no more prepared for one than the other.

As she approached Abby's room, Sara saw inside where a row of pegs lined the wall. One of Abby's dresses hung beside Adam's Sunday suit. If marriage had a picture, this would be it. On the floor below, an aged walnut bride's box sat open, baby clothes spilling out.

The babe in its cradle had fallen into a fitful sleep. Sara covered it with a second blanket and it sighed and slept on. When she stepped to the big bed, a second unfettered sob rocked her.

Tired. Even with her pain-etched features relaxed in death, Abby Zuckerman looked too tired to go on. Sara smoothed hair the color, scent and texture of stale straw off her only friend's cool brow. "Time to rest, Ab."

Abby's bony arms above the quilt contrasted sharply with her swollen, empty belly beneath. Even as a child, Abby had been thin, but her skeletal form looked so much in keeping with death, of a sudden, that Sara wondered why she had never noticed it before.

Swallowing hard, whispering a silent prayer, Sara squeezed her friend's work-rough hand for the last time.

Just like Mom, Sara thought, ignoring the pull on her heart.

If only there'd been a midwife for Mom.

If only she'd been sent for earlier tonight. If only. . . .

Sara looked up, far beyond yellowed ceiling plaster and slap-patched roof, farther even than dark, scudding clouds gravid with snow. "Miss you, Mom. Meet Abby Zuckerman. Be friends."

A sound from behind caught Sara's attention. Adam must think her daft as him. Everybody knew her mother died with her brother at his birth fifteen years before. She raised her chin and turned to face her nemesis.

"A man needs sons to help on the farm," he said, and waited, seeking understanding, Sara knew, but she did not have it to give. And after too long a time to be comfortable, he grunted and turned away. "Got to go milk. See to the babe."

From the top of the loft ladder, Adam Zuckerman gazed down at the little midwife whose passion for things beyond her control was greater than was good for her. Sometimes life cost dearly, he thought, too dearly to be borne. Spinster Sara had not yet learned this. He almost hoped she would never have to. His girls could use some of that passion.

He, however, had learned, for good or ill and at a very early age, that in life there were no choices, no control, none. It was the hardest lesson his father had ever taught him, and the most painful.

Adam descended the ladder at a plodding pace, postponing the inevitable for as long as possible. He'd plotted his course before sending for Sara, yet to give his plan voice, set it in motion, was infinitely more difficult than he expected. This was another of life's non-choices, however, and he *must* move forward with his plan.

He'd heard once that a man raises his children the way he was raised, and once was enough.

No choice. None.

Adam wended his silent way to the house, the would-be midwife's disapproval stabbing between his shoulder blades.

In the dawn-lit kitchen, somehow emptier for the loss of its mistress, Adam turned to face the woman who would never be a midwife if he had his way.

"The children will be awake soon," he said. "When they

are, you take them." His voice cracked with the words—words that would both save and damn him. Impatient with himself, he cleared his throat. "Keep them."

Spinster Sara, never at a loss, stilled.

Time stood as if suspended.

"The children?" she asked. "Your children? Keep them?"

A lump—scratchy, choking, and big as a hay bale—caught in Adam's throat. It swelled and tightened his chest. He could barely draw breath. For the sake of his children, he could not turn back. The nod he gave her was weak, but strong enough, because for the first time in his memory, the rebellious spinster looked as if she did not have all of life's answers.

"What are you talking about?" Even her voice trembled.

Sending his children away was the only way to protect them; his father had taught him that at least. And it had not taken half the punishment the devil doled out for him to learn it.

Just remembering brought a measure of sanity. Adam shifted and squared his shoulders. "Take them home with you. Raise them."

Sara's flash of almost childlike wonder turned so quickly to shock, Adam doubted seeing it, but even the possibility gave him hope. "I'll pay you."

"*Mein Gott,* you are mad."

"So they say." Madness, he believed, ran in his family.

"You can't mean till they're grown."

Forever, he prayed. "For a while . . . until I can make other arrangements." Until you cannot bear to let them go, he thought. It would happen. He knew it would. He only hoped Sara's strength and determination—misplaced though it was with midwifing—worked in his children's favor, rather than in her ability to part with them.

12

"If this is grief," she said, "you have an odd way of showing it. Those children are yours. You're their father."

"Abby wanted you to have them." Adam hated the heat of embarrassment that consumed him—for the simple lie, yes, but more for the canker that created the need for lies. He wasn't getting away with it, though. Sara's expression demanded more. He sighed. "They need you," which was truer than she would ever know. "They don't need me and I don't need them." Not wholly true, but close enough so it didn't matter.

"Right. They're just babes, not good for much. They can't help on the farm."

"That's so." Adam turned to hide the agony clawing at his belly and climbed the stairs to his bedroom. He was aware that Sara followed, because that knife slid deeper between his shoulders.

He watched her wrap the babe tighter and lift it from the cradle, the mighty hand of fate squeezing his chest, forcing the breath again from his lungs.

Abby would have been pleased to die giving him a son, but she would have thought she failed otherwise. He had not had the heart—beyond ascertaining that the swaddled babe in his dead wife's arms lived—to discover whether Abby had died fulfilled.

"What is it?" he asked.

The woman touching a tiny hand to her lips, the one who thought she could save the world, looked sharply up and all but hissed. "A babe. An innocent."

Another he could not love. "A girl," he said, covering defect with indifference. "I guessed as much." He was almost glad. A boy would have made Sara stab him with the question of whether a son was worth the cost of his mother's life.

It was not.

Adam knelt by his wife's bed, lifted her thin, work-rough hand and turned it to stroke her callused palm with his thumb. When emotion threatened to swamp him, he reminded himself that grief and punishment must wait. Urgent matters needed settling.

Abby had promised to protect the children. Now he needed someone else to do it. Someone willful and single-minded to the point of stubbornness, someone strong— stronger than Abby. Someone who would fill their lives with butterflies and sunshine.

Spinster Sara.

Adam whispered a prayer for the dead and was surprised to hear Sara recite it with him, surprised she was still there. When he finished, he allowed his gratitude to show, but he could see she didn't understand that he was grateful for so much more than her prayer.

Sara watched Adam stroke Abby's cheek and turned from a sight too intimate to witness, her anger tempered by bafflement, her embarrassment by yearning. She had sometimes secretly longed for a husband's touch, though never from such a husband as this.

"You think I killed her," he said, surprising her, forcing her to gaze, again, upon the sight of a man grieving for his beloved wife, but Sara was too bewildered to answer.

"I think you're right," he said, and Sara knew, not the satisfaction she might have expected, but an astonishing need to offer comfort. Rather than give it, she reminded herself that this was the man who would give away his children.

Adam threw aside Abby's blanket and cringed at so much blood. "Why? How?" he asked, his gaze locked on the gruesome sight, his question filled with torment.

Choked of a sudden with remorse over her earlier accusation, which now appeared horribly prophetic, Sara raised her hand toward Adam's back. But she lowered it again without making contact. A man such as he would not welcome solace, not from anyone, but especially not from her.

She saw no sign of the afterbirth. Abby had bled to death. "It wasn't—" Sara swallowed to soothe her aching throat. "Sometimes—" She shook her head. "I'm not a doctor, just a midwife. It might not . . . I mean it can happen with the first or tenth, close together or not. I am sorry for your loss, sorry for judging. I was wrong."

As if he had not heard her feeble attempt at absolution— as if she had a right to give it!—Adam lifted his wife in his arms.

"What are you doing?"

Again, he seemed surprised by her presence. "Get out," he shouted for the second time that night.

Her involuntary step back seemed to recall him to his surroundings. He shook his head as if to clear it, looked back at his wife, touched the sleeve of her bloody gown and sighed. "I need to wash and dress her for her final journey. Roman went for the casket after he fetched you."

Sara stilled. Roman had dropped her at the end of the drive and kept going. Had he received the request for a casket before he fetched her? Had Adam sent for her after Abby died? It made no sense. No, she must be mistaken, as she could very well be about this man. Abby had once implied as much.

Adam placed Abby back on her bed. "Dress and feed the girls," he said, sounding suddenly tired. "I hear them stirring."

"Let me wash Ab. The girls will need you."

"No! By God they won't!" His fury was back with a ven-

15

geance, but it was nothing to his aversion. If he disliked his children so much, they would be better off with her. Was it because they were girls? Boys, he had wanted, to help with the farm.

"Go to them." This was an order, and Mad Adam Zuckerman issued orders to be obeyed.

"I cannot take them." Sara wondered why she refused to accept what she'd wanted forever: children, a family—however temporary—a treasure she had almost given up hoping for.

One of the two suitors in her life had said there would be no children for her. She was as bossy as a man, he said, too bossy to bed. The other had not been as kind.

Four little girls. Oh, Lord, she wanted them as dreadfully much as she wanted to be a midwife, but she could not take them. She could not.

They were his. Not hers.

"It's because you'll have to give up midwifing if you take them, isn't it?" Abby's angry husband asked. "Giving up would be hard for a stubborn one like you." He looked her up and down in that icy way of his, and Sara wondered how a look so cold could make her so hotly aware of her own shortcomings. "Well, what is it to be, Spinster Sara?" he asked. "Children of your own? Or a life of watching others bear fruit while you wither on the vine?"

Another hit, more direct, more painful. Sara squared her shoulders to hide the hurt. "Even if I could take them— which I cannot—I would not give up delivering babies." Sometimes she felt as if she could do anything. Most times she knew better. But taking Abby's girls away from their father was wrong. She could not help noticing that a barely-discernible discord existed between Mad Adam Zuckerman's words and his actions, between what could be seen and heard, and what could not. Ab would have told her she wanted her to take the girls in the event something happened. Besides, Sara sensed that deep down Adam Zuckerman did not want to give away his children. So why was he?

Perhaps this was why they called him mad.

Adam sighed, in defeat or weariness, Sara could not tell. "Take them till after the funeral then. Please."

Adam Zuckerman, pleading? "Why me?"

He considered for too long, she thought, as if he were choosing and discarding a series of possible answers. "You have no one," he simply said. "No one."

Unable to bear the pain in that truth, Sara silently took the newest Zuckerman to her fast-beating heart and into the kitchen to wash, and when the babe opened her big Zuckerman eyes, Sara was lost.

Before long, the mite was clean and soft in Sara's arms, her tiny heart-shaped mouth pursed in sleep, her full head of chestnut hair a fluff of wayward curls.

Sara shut out the pain and absorbed the pure and simple pleasure of human contact. She rocked, hummed and savored, until four-year-old Lizzie, ranked-and-professed big sister, barefoot, hair in her eyes, dress on backward, entered the kitchen from the enclosed stairway and came right to her. "Hi Sara, what you got?"

Before Sara could answer, from the enclosed stairway came a bit of whining and some childish Penn Dutch chatter. Then three-year-old Katie, all smiles, curly hair and big eyes, dragged Pris over. Two-year-old Priscilla, eyes downcast, pouting as usual, companion-blanket in hand, stepped behind Katie.

Sara reached over and tugged on the blanket, drawing forth the shy, sullen Zuckerman who had just been displaced as baby of the family. Pris looked, not at Sara but at the floor. Sara lowered her head to see Pris's face, and with a whine, the child lowered hers even more.

This continued until Pris was on all fours, whining for all she was worth, brow touching the floor. What had always seemed a game to Sara disturbed her more than she would like, though she'd never followed it through to this sad conclusion before.

"Pretty Pris," she said, not daring to touch those dark curls. And she would be pretty, Sara thought, if she were not so sulky.

With nut-brown hair and storm-gray eyes, they were, all three, the image of Adam Zuckerman. Lord, and weren't they the most beautiful little girls in the world. Sara wanted to gather them up, hug them tight and protect them forever.

"Where's Mommie?" Lizzie asked.

The pain in Sara's heart might have come from a blade, it cut so sharp. They had no Mommie anymore. They had no one. She shook her head in denial and determination. Even if she didn't take them home with her, they had her now. Sara held the baby forward so they could see her. "Look what you've got. A new sister."

"What's her name?" Katie asked.

"I waited for you to wake up so we could name her together. Let's each say a name, then pick the one we like best."

"Noodle!" Katie shouted on a giggle.

But Lizzie was, as usual, serious and wise. "Can we call our baby Hannah? Mommie said Hannah, if we got another sister." She ran across the kitchen. "I'll go ask her." But Lizzie stopped in her tracks and stood stiff-backed and unmoving, because her father suddenly filled the entrance to the enclosed stairway.

For each of Adam's steps into the kitchen, his oldest took one backward, never removing her gaze from his.

Sara feared he'd tell them their mother was dead in his cold, harsh way. But she needn't have worried; he didn't tell them anything, he just passed them by.

Katie ran after him, "Datt, Datt. My got a baby. My want Mommie, Datt. My's hungry."

He ignored his high-spirited daughter, the only one who did not seem afraid of him. "Sara will feed you," he growled.

"We named the baby Hannah!" Sara yelled at his back as the door slammed behind him. She was right. He didn't care.

With Lizzie's help, Sara got Katie and Pris dressed and fed, her need to weep having less to do with not knowing how to care for the girls and more to do with the joy Abby would never know.

Stooping down, Sara bundled Lizzie in her cape and bonnet to send her to the barn. "Go ask your Datt for a lambing bottle so I can feed Hannah some milk. I'll watch you from the window."

Shaking her wise little head, Lizzie placed her hands on each side of Sara's face, as if she must pay strict attention. "No, Sara. Mommie will feed Hannah with her Mommie's milk."

Sara swallowed hard and blinked to clear her vision. She covered Lizzie's small hands against her face with her own. "We're going to try the bottle for Hannah. Cow's milk will make her strong."

That must have made sense to Lizzie, because she nodded and skipped off on her errand.

As Sara watched the child approach the barn through the window, she touched her cheek to baby Hannah's and let her tears fall. Behind her, Katie giggled and Pris whined.

★ ★ ★ ★ ★

In the lower level of his huge bank barn, Adam paced.
Cows lowed. A mule kicked its stall. Ginger ran to and fro,
barking needlessly. Even the sheep in their pens bleated;
the stupidest animals God created, and even they knew
something was terribly wrong.

Why had he let Abby talk him into trying again for a
boy? Yes, he wanted sons. A man did need sons on a farm.
Everyone knew that. But not at such a cost.

Dear God, Ab, what have I done?

She might have been content with the girls, but she
thought giving him a son would make him love her. He never
did succeed in making her understand that he couldn't love
anyone, for their own good.

"I do this because I love you." He could hear the words
in his father's voice, words he could not, would not, say to
his children, not to another soul, for the cruelty doled out
in their wake was not to be borne. Love. He could never
dare feel it.

Abby had known and said she accepted it. She had
known enough to protect the children. Now she was gone
and it was his fault. He hadn't let himself love her, and still
he destroyed her.

Adam punched a hay bale, over and over, until his
knuckles bled. He wanted to hit something bigger, harder,
throw his whole body into the fight, but he couldn't. Not
yet. His punishment for killing Abby could wait until after
her girls were settled.

He couldn't keep them. Not alone. Not without somebody who cared enough to keep them safe. Without
Abby, no one was left who knew why but him, and he
wanted to keep it that way. Neither he nor Abby had
family. Ab had said that together, with their children,

they were a family, but what was a family with no heart?

Broken.

Only one person in the district whose heart he knew, because she was the only one ever came close enough . . . Spinster Sara.

Sara visited Abby—not often—but when she did, usually when he was away, Abby chattered on for days after about Sara.

She'd damned near leveled him with a barn-board at Zook's barn-raising, and that was the first time he set eyes on her. At fellowship meals after service, Sara often served him first. Looked him right in the eye, she did. Wasn't afraid of anybody, that one. Spoke her mind.

Lord, she drove people crazy with speaking her mind. She was fractious all right. He'd often thought she served him just to prove she could handle anyone. Look at her trying to become a midwife. She was in for a fight with that. The whole district was set against her.

Spinster Sara. Midwife Sara.

Scrapper Sara, more like.

Bad enough she'd been earning her own living for years with her salves and remedies. Now she was trying to learn doctoring, something no woman should. Worse, she was going about it all wrong. Spending weeks in the company of the English doctor . . . it was scandalous, immoral, a man and a woman tending to the intimate needs of a woman in labor, sometimes overnight. Adam clenched his fists and gritted his teeth.

And, Sara, unmarried on top of it.

He'd once lost his temper over her foolishness, and Ab had laughed at him and—Adam stopped pacing, struck in an almost physical way with shock and remorse. Here he stood, consumed with fury at another woman, when his own wife had just died.

Ah, and here, in loud and rattling reproach, came the cabinet-maker with his spring wagon bearing Abby's casket. His father was right. He was worthless. He'd failed as a son, and now as a husband and father. He was defective, body and soul. His children didn't need him. They needed Sara. Already he'd seen her give them a mother's smiles.

Sara would take good care of Abby's girls.

When she'd drawn them to her, without extending so much as a finger, and let them name their sister, he knew he'd been right to send for her.

And Sara was right too. He'd killed Abby as surely as that empty casket sat waiting for her body. God, he could still hear Ab weeping for a son. He'd hated himself for his weakness, had vowed if she weren't pregnant after that one time, she would never be again. But she was.

And now she was gone.

"Datt?"

Adam looked down, toward the barest whisper of sound, and wondered when his oldest daughter had arrived to stand before him. Lizziebelle.

He fisted his hands at his side to keep from reaching for her.

"Why can't Mommie feed Hannah with her Mommie's milk?"

Adam leaned against the lambing pen, seeking balance in a careening world. Guilt. Hard. Raw. He swallowed and forced himself to take a breath, and needed two more before he could speak. "What did Sara say?" he asked in a voice that did not sound like his own.

"That you would give me a lambing bottle and we would feed Hannah cow's milk to make her strong."

Adam nodded and turned his back on his motherless

child, because for the life of him, if he did not, he would gather her up and . . . condemn her to the punishment love enforced.

The girls played quietly in Abby's sewing room while Sara rocked baby Hannah and fed her milk from the boiled bottle and nipple.

Abby's body would soon be carried in an open box from her bedroom into her best room.

At the very thought, the sharp claws of anxiety clenched Sara's every muscle, holding her captive in the same way it had fifteen years before.

Her mother's labor had gone on for more than a day. Her father had set off in an ice storm for the doctor . . . and died in a ditch with a broken neck.

Sara had been fifteen when she'd taken that lifeless baby boy and placed him in her mother's weak arms. Fifteen, when she'd pushed wadded towels between Mama's legs to stop the blood . . . but watched her life drain away, instead.

The next morning, in a house gone silent, Sara had stepped into the best room to see three caskets—two large, and one too tiny to bear. Crude boxes with covers to smother.

She'd had trouble breathing then.

She had trouble breathing now.

Once again, panic rushed her. Abby's girls were too young to see such a sight. But Sara couldn't take them, not from their father. It would be the greatest cruelty to lose both parents at once; no one knew that better than her.

And yet, with such a parent?

Her mind scrambled for an answer, examining and discarding every possibility, until. . . .

If she took the girls . . . for a time . . . and taught their father, somehow, to know and love them. . . . It seemed an impossible task, and yet Abby said there was something worthy hiding deep inside Adam Zuckerman, something he wanted to keep buried. Sara thought she had glimpsed a shadow of that something today. She was almost certain of it. Besides, what choice did she have?

She wasn't sure which would be more difficult, re-forming Mad Adam Zuckerman or letting his children go once she loved them. Except that wasn't even a consideration, because she loved them already.

Sara rose and went to the window. The clouds were dark and angry still. She sought guidance from beyond the firmament, but neither faith nor entreaty would come, only anger, and in her heart, she gave it voice. I won't let them lose both parents, she informed He who seemed to have abandoned them, almost expecting thunder and lightning in reply. Then she admitted that she could not do it alone and whispered, "Help. Please." But neither comfort nor response was forthcoming.

"Fine then," she snapped. "I'll do it myself. And this time I won't fail."

Sara hurried to the bottom of the stairway. "Adam," she shouted, angry with God for not listening, and with Adam for . . . everything. "Adam, come down here, now!"

Like a mule team spooked by a jackrabbit, he came, but he stopped when he saw her, his face pale and taut, his breath short.

"I'll take them," she said. "Until after the funeral," she added in a rush. "And if I'm called to deliver a babe while I have them, I'll go if I have to take them with me."

Adam hesitated then nodded once, his relief so apparent, Sara thought she might have imagined the wretchedness that preceded it. "Shut Abby's door," she said. "I'm taking them upstairs to get their things. I'll tell them about Abby later. It's best they think of their mother smiling and happy in heaven, not cold and silent in a box."

Another single nod, a hard swallow. "I won't show her till you're gone."

Chapter Two

Through her yard, Sara chased Abby's daughters, the two oldest shrieking almost as much as her. And though Pris wasn't excited, or even smiling, it seemed as if her eyes almost danced . . . until the girls rounded a corner and came upon their father by his buggy in the drive. Then everything stopped—sound, movement, joy. Sara came up behind them and touched each small shoulder in turn, telling them without words that she was there.

Adam absently looked them over, then he stiffened: anger, fear, transforming him. "Where's the baby?" he shouted.

No hello. No mention of his reason for coming. And Sara panicked. Not because of his bellow, which was normal, but because she expected he'd come to tear her heart from her flesh.

Two days and already she couldn't bear the thought of giving his children back. But for some reason, she sensed she could not let him know how much she wanted to keep them, so she masked her dread and pointed to her porch. "Hannah is there, in her cradle."

"*Mein Gott,* she'll freeze to death!" Adam marched right over, as if he expected to find proof of his foolish accusation, and found a swaddled infant instead, her chubby apple-cheeked face peering up at him with huge gray eyes exactly like his. Hannah gurgled and cooed when she saw him, swinging her arms in her excitement, for all the world as if she knew him.

Sara tapped the tiny pink nose and got a bubble for her effort. "She likes it out here. We all do. We don't stay long. Just a few minutes, to use up energy and get fresh air. It's cold for autumn, yes, but. . . ."

Adam looked away, and Sara guessed he was no more displeased than usual. "Can we go inside?" he asked, with as near to manners as Sara had ever seen.

She offered the girls cookies and cocoa, and they got in line for plates and cups to bring to their small table by the hearth. She was pleased they were doing as she'd taught them and looked to see if Adam noticed how well they behaved, but he wasn't even looking at them.

Adam took in every aspect of the tiny cottage, finding it difficult to ignore Sara's bed, with that bright flower-garden quilt covering it, as if the sun shone down on her even in sleep. He shifted, uncomfortable about invading what amounted to a spinster's bedroom.

He hadn't realized she had only the one room. He'd have to get her a bigger place . . . if he convinced her to keep the girls longer, until after the funeral . . . and after that to keep them till harvest, then until Christmas, then spring planting, and longer still, until she loved them too much to let them go.

Adam didn't let his gaze linger on the girls. They were fine. No more or less happy, it seemed, than before, which was as good as could be expected, he supposed, after the loss of a mother. Though it had taken Pris a minute to remember to pout, which raised his spirits for some odd reason.

Sara placed a cup of chocolate and a plate of cookies in front of him; then she sat across from him. He'd never seen such a small kitchen table as this one, with barely room for the two of them. He had to turn sideways to keep his knees from touching hers.

The girls were nibbling cookies at a child-size table, Katie chattering, Lizzie listening and Pris staring into the fire.

"My father was a carpenter," Sara said. "He made me the table and chairs when I was small. Mom and I used to have cookies and milk there. The girls like it. I think they're doing well, considering. . . ."

Adam grunted, wondering if she'd already taken to doing those "mothering" things with them. He didn't remember his own mother doing such things, but then she had always been too busy looking over her shoulder.

Adam cleared his throat and leaned close, afraid the girls might hear. "You told them, then?"

"Not yet," Sara said. "Do you want to tell them together, now?"

"No!" Adam cringed inwardly. His cowardice, he got from his mother's side of the family. All gazes were now turned his way, nobody moving, not even Spinster Sara. Adam shook his head. He hadn't *meant* to frighten them that time. "I brought you money," he said, taking a small leather pouch from his pocket and shoving it toward Sara.

She regarded it with a scowl, then ignored it to watch the girls.

"Pride is a sin," he said, reading her and making her prickly mad, which he had once found sporting, like baiting a line or a trap. "It costs to feed them," he said. "You have no time to earn money for food while you're caring for them. I take care of my own, Sara."

"Oh," she whispered, leaning forward, brows arched. "So you remember they're yours?"

With a growl, Adam pocketed his cookies and stood. "I

brought meat and vegetables too. They're in the buggy. Come." At the door, he turned. "Lizzie, watch your sisters."

He led the way outside, trying to hide his nervousness. The girls' future depended on his success right now, yet seeing them made it difficult to keep to his purpose. He wanted to pack them in his buggy and run away with them, which might be laughable, if it wasn't so sad.

Scrapper Sara stopped before him, hands on hips. "You didn't bring me out here for food. This had better be good, Adam Zuckerman."

He felt as if he were ten again, waiting for a knuckle-rapping from the teacher—half dreading the pain, half glad he'd got her attention. Adam shook his head, turning from Sara's sassy scowl to lead her around his buggy. Lifting the back flap, he indicated the crates. "Potatoes, squash, winter beets, ham, turkey. I'll help you take it in before I go." He was stalling, he knew; she knew it too. And they both knew he'd brought too much food for a few days. He was trying to turn her up sweet, but it was no use. Spinster Sara could be sour as pickled cabbage. "Sara, I need a favor."

She raised only one of those winged brows this time.

Adam sighed. The woman didn't even need to speak to sass him. No use putting it off anymore; there was no softening her, so he forged ahead. "I . . . the girls need you to keep them a bit longer."

To Adam's surprise, Sara bit her lip, blanked her features and looked beyond his shoulder. No sass. No scrapping. Probably planning her next jab. But when she faced him again, there seemed to be no more fight in her. "How much longer?"

Hope. He heard it in her voice, and his own hope soared. But he needed to be cautious. He had to act as if he planned to take them back, while making it seem more and more impossible to do so. "Well, I . . . can't work the farm and take care of them at the same time. I mean, it's coming on harvest. Winter vegetables have to come in soon." He felt his face heat for the way he'd reacted to the baby being outside. "Even bundled up warm, like you had them, I can't keep them outside for as long as chores take."

"What about relatives? A mother, an aunt, a sister? Isn't there anyone who could come and help you with the girls?"

Adam hadn't thought much about his mother and sister in years, except to think how lucky they were. "My mother and sister are dead. A carriage accident . . . or so *he* said."

"He? Who is he?"

Adam could not believe he had voiced the old doubt. Heat climbed his neck. "I was five when they died," he said. "I have a child's confused memories. I did not mean to . . . you have an annoying way of. . . . You disarm me, Spinster Sara."

"And you, Mad Adam? You worry me."

Adam folded his hands behind his back. "No, no mother or sister. Guess I need to find a woman to come every day or to live-in." Adam feared for a minute Sara would offer, which was not what he intended. Would he never get this right?

Something was bothering her too, because she was worrying her lip enough to tear the tender flesh.

"I hoped you would keep them until . . . say. . . ." He'd go for a later date, knowing how contrary Sara could be. "Say, until after spring planting."

Again, hope lit her eyes, but she snuffed it like a candle. "That's months away," she wailed, sounding almost helpless.

Sara, helpless?

"Adam, I can't."

"They like you, Sara." And why that should hurt her, he did not know, but it surely seemed to.

"They belong with you, Adam, and that's all there is to it."

"Till after harvest," he bargained, hoping, given his reason for the lie, that it could be overlooked. "Just till then."

Sara sighed and closed her eyes. When she opened them, they were bright with unshed tears, as if pain hovered, but she fought it bravely. "I need to think about it. I'll tell you in a couple of days, after the funeral."

In the grabhof, the Amish cemetery, silent mourners, flanked by plain time-bruised stones, saw the sun shine down one last time on Abby Zuckerman's face, her features serene in death in a way they had never been in life.

Truth to tell, Sara could barely see her friend through her tears. Sorrow. Guilt. She was grief-stricken at Abby's death, yet she felt such joy at having the girls.

More than anything, she wished Abby were alive to care for them. Barring that, she wanted Adam to take them . . . except that she wanted so very badly to keep them.

Rather than pray for the repose of that sweet, sweet soul, in the way the solemn men and women around her were doing, Sara prayed for the strength to do what was best for the girls, no matter the cost.

When Adam and Bishop Weaver lifted the top of Abby's casket, to close her inside forever, Sara nearly shouted for them to stop. Instead, she sobbed and promised Ab she would love her girls forever.

Serenity filled her of a sudden, and Sara believed that Abby's spirit soared free, perhaps for the first time ever, even as her neighbors tossed dirt on her casket.

Peace, it was called.

Sara was especially glad, in that moment, that Jordan—Doc Marks to the community, teacher and friend to her—had surprised her this morning by coming to stay with the girls so she could attend their mother's funeral.

When she had arrived at Adam's house earlier, one of about fifty or so of their neighbors, Adam had questioned her with his look from halfway across the kitchen. She hadn't been certain if he was surprised she was there, or if he wanted to know whether she would keep the girls. She'd wondered how she could give them up when she was barely strong enough to let go of their mother. But she had tried to say with her look that everything would be fine, which she sincerely hoped it would, and Adam had relaxed, as if she succeeded in reassuring him.

Now, beside his wife's grave, he stood taller than most, broader of shoulder as well, and solemn, as always, as he turned his broad-brimmed black felt hat round in his huge, capable hands, as if he could not bear to remain still.

A bear, many called him, a grizzly. Brooding. Silent. Mad.

He was all those things, yes, but Sara was beginning to suspect he was more. And while feeding baby Hannah during the sweet silence of the night just past, Sara had promised herself she would uncover that part of him he concealed from the world. She might bring him and his children together more easily if she could, if she became the live-in helper he said he needed for them, though she supposed he would have asked her, if he thought so.

Did she want to move into Abby's house to care for her girls? Yes. Did she want to move in with Mad Adam Zuckerman? No. Yes. Perhaps. Sara sighed. She supposed she'd go or live anywhere, if it meant she could raise the girls. With Adam around, she wouldn't have to worry about them, either, if—when—she was called to deliver a babe.

Spending time with the girls each day, watching them grow, teaching them the things all little Amish girls should know, could fill her days—her life—with purpose. And if she could also midwife—even if that meant putting up with Mad Adam Zuckerman's growls and scowls—her life would be more fulfilling than she could ever have imagined.

Abby had not thought Adam was so terrible to live with. Sara had mentioned his gruff once, and Abby had smiled such a secret smile, Sara thought she must be thinking about that part of marriage. What must the intimate side of marriage be like, when even a man like Mad Adam could bring such a smile?

Sara raised her head when she realized where her mind had wandered, and warm with embarrassment, she thrust her wayward thoughts aside.

As everyone began to leave the cemetery, Adam came to stand beside her. Funny how good that made her feel, even though his reason had solely to do with getting her to keep his children. Even so, it felt almost as if she were something of a friend to him. Without Ab, neither of them had anyone.

Before long, they were alone in the graveyard, both of them staring at that dark, rich mound of dirt, missing the woman at rest beneath it. Sara bent to smooth the earth, almost as if she could make Abby more comfortable. She plucked a few stones from the moist soil, tossed them and patted the disturbed sections back into place, begging Abby's guidance as she prepared to answer her husband's request.

Again, peace filled her, and Sara knew what she must do. "For Abby," she said, not looking at the silent man beside her. "For her, I will keep the girls until after harvest."

Then she would bring them back to their father and stay

to help, whether he asked her to or not. And teach him to love them, by God. And when they needed her no more, she would lay herself down and die too.

No. Sara stood. No, she would not do that. She would become the best midwife Walnut Creek had ever seen. Safe deliveries. No more dead mothers. No more dead babies. She would do it for Mama. "For Abby," she said.

"Danke," Adam whispered, his voice hoarse.

Chapter Three

"Looks like he fell hard. About twelve feet from the top of that ladder." Roman Byler shook his head as he gazed at Adam Zuckerman's unconscious form. "Dead drunk, like he's been for months. Dead inside too, I think. Always has been, far as I know. Noticed that the first time I saw his eyes, and we were only kids then. But with a father like his, who could blame him?"

"I never met his father," Doc Marks said. "But I've noticed the same thing about his eyes."

Yes, Roman thought, the man most people avoided was as good as dead inside. Only once in past years had he seen a spark in Adam's eyes—Schmidt's barn-raising, when Sara Lapp had raised her chin and served Adam first, joking about his appetite matching his size. Roman remembered thinking, even then, that most men wouldn't sport with Adam Zuckerman about his size. Yet that slip of a woman had dared, and with a twinkle in her eye, as well.

"What do you think, Doc?"

Kneeling, Doctor Marks examined Adam's bloody thigh and shook his head over the jagged piece of bone piercing it. "I think he needs a swift kick in his hind end."

"I know that," Roman said. "I mean about his injuries."

"Smacked his head a good one. Broke in a few places—his arm, maybe a rib or two, but it's his thigh I'm worried about. Seen more than one leg have to be taken after a break this bad."

"Adam's way too stubborn to let that happen," Roman said.

"With the right care, it might not come to that."

Roman shook his head. "Can't imagine who'll do it."

"I can imagine."

Roman considered the possibilities, and there weren't many. It wasn't that their neighbors disliked Adam, exactly. He was always first to help in time of crisis, and Roman was pretty certain Adam was the nameless man who always sent money to their neighbors in need. No, they didn't dislike him, but his odd, silent ways, his carved-in-stone frown, made them uneasy. They simply did not understand him, so they avoided him, which suited Adam fine. Worse, since the districts had been re-divided, only one person visited the Zuckerman house. Roman regarded the doctor. "Sara Lapp?"

"Who else?" Doc Marks asked. "Well, there's you, since you're as close to a friend as Adam ever had, but between raising your niece and nephew and your mom and pop being sick and all. . . ." The doctor sat back and slapped his thighs. "No. Sara's the one."

Roman shook his head. "I don't know, Doc. The Elders aren't going to—"

"It would get his children back where they belong. Sara's supposedly got them until Christmas now, right?"

"Ya, until he changes his mind again."

Doc Marks nodded. "It's about time somebody took a hand in that."

Roman raised his brows, doubt filling him. "Us?"

The Doctor pointed up. "Him."

Roman whistled. "You think God did this?"

"Who else?"

"A drunken sot, that's who." A man who thinks he deserves to be punished, Roman thought.

"I don't think the Elders would want to see a man suffer, Roman."

"There's all kinds of suffering, Doc. And sometimes the Elders mistake one of them for redemption."

The doctor grinned. "I take it you don't always appreciate their . . . interference."

"Interference can be a good thing. Sometimes. I suppose."

"Right," the doctor said, looking around. "Help me unhinge a door, so we can get him inside. After I try to put that bone back where it belongs, I'll go get Sara and the girls."

In the old sewing room off the kitchen, in the bed where Abby used to put the girls when they were sick, Adam sat propped by a mound of pillows, his head wrapped and pounding, his right arm in a sling and his left thigh afire and lashed to a splint.

Where the blazes was the blasted *English* with the foolish cure he'd promised? Some doctor.

Adam couldn't imagine a cure that wouldn't hurt more than the need for it, but things couldn't get much worse.

The kitchen door slammed and a commotion of voices and shuffling followed. "Brought you a nurse," The *English* yelled from the kitchen.

A nurse?

A babe's wail. A giggle. Katie? Elation. Despair.

A whine. Pris. Oh, no.

Adam's heart beat at a run, yearning and fear fighting so hard inside that nausea rose up to choke him.

A shadow marred the sun's path through the room, beating its owner to his side by moments. Spinster Sara.

Joy and dread warred within Adam, until the deep breaths he was forced to take couldn't catch up to his pounding heart or calm his roiling stomach, which made his head reel the more. He needed another drink. He needed to rage—at God or, at the least, at Sara. But when he opened his mouth, his stomach cast up its contents in greeting.

Sara's shock lasted less than a second. "Damn it, Adam, my clean Sunday dress."

"Don't cuss around the girls," he rasped, pulling up the corner of her apron to wipe his mouth.

Her eyes widened. She began to speak, stopped, tried again and failed; then she shook her head and poured him a glass of water.

When he finished drinking, she placed her hands on her hips. "Stupid drunk." She turned and walked away. "I'll get you something to settle your stomach," she threw over her shoulder.

While she was gone, Adam tried to figure out how to get Sara to take his children away again, and fast, before having them here sliced open his heart and bared it for the buzzards. But before he could, Lizzie was walking toward him, one slow, well-placed step after another, both hands holding a glass of milk, and with so much concentration that watching her tensed him right up.

She stopped and looked into his eyes, her big gray ones so beautiful, hopeful, like Abby's, it made him want to weep. He coughed and cleared his throat.

Considering it was the first time in weeks Lizzie had seen him, she didn't seem to be as affected as him. He supposed that meant he'd done the right thing. He supposed he should be glad.

If only he hadn't damned near broke his neck.

If only he'd broken it for good.

"Mommie's gone to walk with God," Lizzie said, the blow to Adam's midsection unexpected and sharp. "In heaven," she explained. "She's a treat, Sara said, to make God smile."

Adam's heart thumped against his broken ribcage, and his gut took the punch badly, but considering its recent disgraceful behavior, things could be worse. "You miss Mommie?" Had he actually given voice to the tormenting question?

Lizzie's eyes filled and her lip quivered—this blow sharper than the last—but she gathered herself together in the exact way he'd seen Sara do. "We have Sara now," she said. "And I love her. . . ."

"But she's not Mommie," Adam whispered.

Lizzie nodded, stopped, then shook her head.

Adam guessed that meant she agreed with him. A sudden and unfamiliar force, powerful and compelling, to protect this little girl from hurt—his little girl—fired Adam with more pain than all his broken limbs put together, and he gasped, "Tell Sara I need a drink." He'd spoken harshly, but Lizzie didn't stiffen as she used to. This was not good. She should be afraid of him. She must.

"I brought you a drink. See?" With both hands, Lizzie raised the glass she was carrying higher. "Milk." She took a couple of slow steps closer.

"I want a different kind of drink," Adam said, fisting his hands, once again to keep from reaching for her. "Sara'll know."

Lizzie shook her head. "This is all the drink you're getting and it's more than your sorry self deserves . . . Sara says."

A completely foreign urge to laugh assaulted Adam with such force, and turned so fast into a need to weep, he had to scrub his face with a shaking hand to gather control.

Sara was here. His children were here. Half of him wanted to rant, the other half wanted to exult. Now he'd gone and proved everybody right. This was it. Adam Zuckerman had gone stark, staring mad.

A good twenty minutes after Adam sent Lizzie to fetch Sara, the pushy woman came charging into his room . . . yes, she definitely charged.

But if a body could ignore her narrow-eyed scowl, then the way she looked in that fresh purple dress, cinnamon curls escaping her white kapp, and those wide green eyes in a face that was one of God's finer creations, a body might wonder why she had never married.

"Well," said she, hands on hips. "What do you want now, clumsy?"

"It's because of that smart mouth you're a spinster."

Sara stepped so close so fast, and with such determination, Adam would have backed away if he could move.

"Listen," she said, poking him in the chest, "I did not want to come and tend your ornery self, but nobody else would, so here I am. Now what do you want?"

"Go away then. I don't need you. I don't need anybody."

"I should go, just to prove you wrong, but since I wouldn't abandon a wounded rodent, you're stuck with me."

Was she calling him a rat?

Despite the affront, Adam had a problem. He had sent for her a quarter hour before to give her a piece of his mind, but his needs had changed, and they were desperate. "I need that jug over there."

"Adam Zuckerman, you're not to be calling me in here every two minutes. And no more whiskey!"

"Damn it, Sara, that's my pissin' jug. Now, give it to me or change the bed." He had to hand it to her; she hardly blushed as she went for the jug and handed it over, none too gently. But for some reason, she just stood there after that.

"Well," he said, after a minute. "Long as you're gonna stay, either hold the jug or aim. It's hard to do both one-handed."

She quit the room so fast, Adam experienced, for the second time in his life, a need to laugh that was so sharp, it made him want to weep. He swore instead.

Wishing he had a drink to blank his mind, and stewing over his damnable situation, kept Adam awake half the night. But despite that, he woke with a feeling the world was in order, which made him wonder if an infection had set in.

Fortunately for him, Sara had left his jug near the bed, so there was no need to shout.

A few minutes later, as he was about to give in and call for breakfast, he heard Roman Byler in the kitchen. Then Roman was at the door to his room. "There's an Amish couple from a settlement in Indiana over at Sussmans'. The wife's in labor," Roman said. "And Doc Marks isn't back from Akron. Woman's already lost a babe in childbed and she's scared to lose another. I'm taking Sara over there, Adam, and don't you be arguing."

"Damn it, Roman, it's dawn and freezing. She can't take the baby out—"

"Here we go," Sara said, carrying Hannah into the room, followed by Lizzie, Katie and Pris. The three oldest climbed up on his bed with him, making him see purple and blue lights for the pain in his limbs.

41

Whining all the while, Pris settled on the far corner, her back to him, her arms folded. Then Sara tucked the baby into the crook of his good arm. "Get used to it, Datt," she said as she patted his aching head.

"What the devil do you think you're doing?" he shouted.

"Getting you settled, so I can go deliver that baby."

"You can't mean to leave me here? With them?"

"Why? They won't hurt you."

Adam cringed. Didn't she understand? No, of course, she didn't. How could he tell somebody as strong and perfect as Scrapper Sara how defective he was?

Maybe she was the wrong one to care for the girls, after all. If she was going to be so careless with them, they'd be better off with . . . him? The thought made him feel less helpless and more furious. "I forbid you to go!"

Sara stiffened at the same time Roman's bark of laughter filled the room. "Now you've done it," Roman said, making Adam want to erase his former friend's smirk with a forbidden fist.

Sara pierced Adam with her look. "Get up and stop me, why don't you?"

Trying not to laugh, Roman cleared his throat. "Before she agreed to go, Sara made me promise I would come back to help you."

Sara shot Roman a look that said, "Shut your mouth," which, under any other circumstance, would make Adam want to gloat.

"Ask Lizzie if you need anything while I'm gone," Sara said, scowling at him, but her face softened as she bent to kiss Lizzie's head, the smile she gave his eldest bright enough to rival the sun.

"She's a big help, is Lizzie." When Sara turned back to him, her smile vanished. "I've let you put me off long enough. I've been weak, but no more. Christmas is nearly here. You may as well practice."

"Adam Zuckerman," Roman said with a grin, "your eyes look—"

"Mad," Sara said, as she passed Roman to leave the room.

Roman chuckled. "Alive, I was going to say. They look alive." Then he too was gone.

"You're an old busybody, you know that, Roman Byler?" Adam shouted after him.

"Ya, a busybody," Roman countered from the kitchen. "But younger than you."

And before Adam could think of a response, the kitchen door slammed, then Roman's carriage passed his window.

Being alone with his children like this hurt worse than the pain in his limbs, though that was pretty bad too, 'cause Katie had taken to bouncing on her knees beside his broken leg.

One thing the girls had in common right now, even Pris who'd turned to give him a scowl; they were staring at him as if he might want to have them for breakfast.

So if he wanted them to fear him, why did he feel as if he was letting them down?

Baby Hannah, who'd grown to be a wiggling handful in the past two months, took to demanding her breakfast in tones that Sara might be able to hear from the Sussman house. And when Adam looked to Lizzie for help, he saw something he had never noticed. She was a person—a little one, but with knowledge beyond her years in those wide doe's eyes of hers.

He nodded at her, because for the life of him, he couldn't speak beyond the lump in his throat. And Lizzie nodded back, just before she took the bottle that had slipped between him and the baby and plugged it into that noisy little mouth, cutting the sound mid-wail.

"Thank you," Adam said, but the words were such a croak, he had to nod again to make her understand. And her smile was so easy and so wide, that lump in his throat got bigger.

"My's hungry, Datt," Katie said, and Lizzie, bless her, performed another miracle. She pulled a fassnacht from a cloth sack he'd just now noticed and gave it to Katie. "Doc Jordan calls these 'dough nuts,' " Lizzie told him on a giggle. Then she handed one to Pris, who pulled her blanket close and turned her back on him to eat.

As if the jolting statement that Sara had had the English doctor at her house hadn't been made, his girls started eating their foolish breakfast, spreading crumbs over him and the bed, watching him all the while.

When Katie held her fassnacht to his mouth, Adam stopped frowning. To say he was surprised was a mild account. He looked at Lizzie to see what he should do, and it was her turn to nod, so he took a bite. But all that did was make that lump downright impossible to swallow.

For the life of him, Adam didn't understand why he wanted both to throttle Spinster Sara Lapp and embrace her at one and the same time.

The sound of Baby Hannah draining the bubbles from an empty lambing bottle brought him back to his impossible situation and he stared at the babe as if there might be an answer in that tiny flailing fist.

Lizzie touched his arm, breaking the taut rope of unease holding him motionless. "Better burp her or she's gonna be mighty cranky."

"If I knew how to do that," Adam snapped, "I'd be your mother, not your—"

Lizzie's eyes filled and Adam clamped his mouth shut. He didn't know if it was his fury or his mention of her mother, but Adam felt as if . . . as if he'd crushed her fingers in a door. Yes, that's exactly how she looked—betrayed—and in more pain than she could bear.

That he didn't know how to soothe her was a hard pill for Adam to swallow, harder even than having her here. "Lizziebelle, I'm . . . sorry. I . . . I don't know how to burp her," Adam said, ashamed for so many reasons, not the least of which was the absurd excuse he offered.

"My do it," Katie said. And darned if Lizzie didn't take the baby right out of his arms, give her to Katie and help the giggling child perform the task. And that tiny mite of a baby girl burped louder than he did when he'd guzzled enough whiskey to fell an ox.

For a minute, Adam feared the baby might return the contents of her stomach, but God, who'd been handing out some nasty punishments of late, decided Hannah would just settle down to sleep. And Lizzie returned the baby to his care.

"Why'd you give us to Sara, Datt?" Lizzie asked. "Is it 'cause you didn't know how to do burpin? 'Cause Sara can teach you; then we can stay."

Adam looked toward the ceiling and frowned. *Ah, you did have worse in mind.* He turned to Lizzie. "Wouldn't you miss Sara?"

"Sara could stay too," Lizzie said, which got the other two to jumping: Katie with glee, and Pris with her pouting face directed at the bed, not at him. Which woke baby Hannah, and made Adam's stomach feel like his fassnacht was dancing its way back up his throat, when it had only just got past it.

When it seemed they'd settled down and Pris might fall

asleep, baby Hannah got to making some grunting sounds, filling the room with a smell that brought a curse to Adam's lips at about the same time it brought a giggle to Lizzie's.

Three trips to the kitchen by Lizzie and Katie—Pris gagged the whole time—and a load of towels later, and Hannah was sweet-smelling and sleeping again. And Adam was certain, when Sara returned, he was going to jump right off the bed—broken bones and all—and strangle her.

Mercy Bachman was forty if she was a day, and she hadn't lost one baby, she had lost nine over thirteen years.

Abby all over again, she was all bones and angles, with so much heart and hope—and fear—Sara had to bite her lip and plant her feet just to keep herself from running away.

She'd not been this frightened during her brother's birth. She hadn't been smart enough yet to know how fierce an adversary death could be.

Mercy's work-worn husband, Enos, sat in a rocker in the kitchen, staring into the face of the Sussman baby in his arms as if willing it to be his.

Roman waited outside, likely afraid he would miss something.

May Sussman boiled water while her husband, Cal, chopped wood; she said he could average a cord or more during a good labor.

Sara smiled but her heart pounded. Mercy's labor was proceeding slowly. Too slowly.

Sara helped the ungainly woman don her robe and took her into the best room to pace. There Mercy told Sara the story of each and every lost child, until a pattern emerged. Stalled, overlong labors, exhausted mother and baby. After as long as three days of labor, each child had been born whole but weak, which none overcame beyond the first few minutes or hours.

Sara encouraged Mercy to walk faster and sent May's husband to Jordan's house to wait for him. She told Cal he could chop wood there, if it would help, but he must wait and bring the doctor back. She set Roman to escorting Mercy around May's best room while she prepared a tea of Gossypium root bark to induce stronger contractions. She remembered Jordan saying it was good for labors that started and stopped. She added wild ginger to the tea to increase Mercy's energy, and through her, hopefully, her child's.

For the first half-hour, Mercy sipped tea as she walked, then her labor took off and Sara feared she had used too much root bark. When Mercy was ensconced in bed, her husband started to whine and panic, which distracted Mercy, made her tense and slowed her labor. Sara ordered Enos outside and May Sussman to keep him there.

Sara gave Mercy more tea and ordered her up again for a sponge bath and a change of gown. Before the bath was finished, Mercy was doubled over in pain, but Sara made her walk some more.

Mercy begged to lie down but when Sara explained that if her labor progressed quickly, the baby would still have strength left after it was born, Mercy picked up her pace.

"For heaven's sakes, Mercy, I didn't say to run."

Mercy stopped in surprise and they laughed together.

Sara invited Roman to entertain them with his stories, and though he faltered with every one of Mercy's gasps, he talked about everybody in the district, including Midwife Sara and her care of Mad Adam Zuckerman and his children.

A half-hour later, when Mercy wanted to push, Sara let

her lie down. And when Sara caught the rhythm of labor, she knew it was nearly over. She put her hand on Mercy's belly to feel the child, and a great yearning for a miracle like this of her own welled up in her. Knowing it was impossible, Sara pushed yearning aside to concentrate on her patient.

Between pains, while Sara prayed for guidance and Mercy lessened her grip on the sides of the bed, Sara saw Roman peek in from the far reaches of the kitchen, and realized that he had never gone back to help Adam. She pushed frustration aside. Adam needed this time with his children, and Mercy needed her full attention.

Finally, Sara saw the baby's creamy scalp and touched the lively pulse there. She nodded with relief and smiled. "Your baby seems strong, Mercy. Let's bring it into the world, shall we? Push. Now."

Mercy's scream made Roman bolt, Sara saw out of the corner of her eye. Then the baby's face emerged, and as Sara made to ease the child's way, the mite slipped into her hand, sleek, bloody, beautiful, and swinging her arms.

Sara knew two things in that moment, with undeniable certainty. She had never been so frightened in all her life and she had been born to be a midwife.

She had no more than cleared the mite's mouth and turned her to slap her bottom than the baby girl was crying for all she was worth . . . Mercy too. Sara too. She grinned at Mercy. "Lungs like these are gonna' make a lot of noise for a long time, Mercy. Here, hold your daughter while I cut the cord."

While Sara cut and tied the cord, she became aware of her surroundings. May, in the bedroom door, Roman, a few paces behind. Mercy's joy as she gazed at her child, her husband Enos pounding on the outside door.

"Let the new papa in as far as the kitchen, May." Sara took the baby, wiped her tiny face and wrapped her in a blanket. "Let Datt hold his new daughter in that rocker near the stove, until we have a chance to wash her proper. Mercy is going to be busy while we deliver the afterbirth."

When all was said and done, after more tears and hugs, Mercy said Sara had their gratitude for life. But Sara was the grateful one. Little Saramay was her first delivery without Jordan, and she would always be grateful that Mercy had given her the chance.

Saying goodbye, finally, made Sara think of losing Abby. In one afternoon, Mercy had become a special friend, but they would never see each other again.

In the end, Mercy promised to keep in touch.

It had taken less than three hours.

Sara returned to the Zuckerman house, still shaking inside, despite her elation, to find a collection of soiled towels frozen in a heap by the back door.

In the bed where she'd left them, Adam was sitting up, head thrown back, snoring fit to wake the dead, baby Hannah asleep in his arms. Katie was curled against him, and behind her, Lizzie and then Pris, like spoons in a kitchen drawer.

As Sara began to back from the room, Adam raised his head and looked straight at her. And Sara didn't think she could have imagined the bite of his silent fury.

Foolish her. She had imagined that an afternoon with his children would soften him. But it didn't take her long to realize that now Mad Adam Zuckerman would be harder, madder and more disagreeable than ever.

Chapter Four

Tomorrow for the first time in a dozen years, Sara would not be alone for Christmas. She would be with the children she loved and the man she wanted to beat black and blue . . . except that Adam was twice her size and most of him was already that color.

The children had been asleep for an hour when Sara set Christmas treats in their plates for morning. Along with some sweetmeats, nuts and an orange, the three oldest would each get a faceless Amish rag doll. Sara had discovered them at the bottom of Abby's sewing basket, a slip of paper pinned to each naming the child for whom the doll was intended, almost as if she knew. . . .

Sara had denied the possibility and cut out three small quilts and pillows to go with the dolls. Stitching them became particularly relaxing on those evenings when the mystery of how to make Adam love his girls kept her awake.

Mad Adam Zuckerman. Brooding. Angry. Puzzling. Perhaps he didn't like children. Perhaps he'd never wanted any. Perhaps . . . he already loved them.

Sara frowned. Perhaps she was as mad as him.

She'd been in his house five long, frustrating days. Days of arguments, silences, growls and curses—though never within hearing of his girls, she noticed. Days when she and Adam dared not look at each other for some unseen force crackling between them, a kind of two-sided . . . aversion, more hot than cold. Invisible lightning was the only way she

50

could think to describe it, and heaven help either of them if it actually struck.

Long days with long evenings, during which Adam's glances—of warning or anxiety—seemed almost a plea, but for what? Evenings like this.

Sara filled a pitcher with hot water and gathered soap and a razor, and mentally braced herself for the battle she intended to win. She raised her chin to display the kind of mock bravery she always needed around men—except for Jordan, who did not count among the males who knocked her knees and tied her tongue.

But Adam Zuckerman was something different and everything Doctor Jordan Marks was not. Male to his marrow, Adam stood too tall, too wide, too hard and too imposing—body and spirit—for Sara's peace. He was, in fact, the most disquieting man it had ever been her misfortune to stumble upon.

For a year, she had tried, with little success, to conquer her mind-tripping confusion around Abby's husband. In the attempt, she had served him and joked with him. But now she had no choice but to conquer her uneasiness, for if she failed in this task she set herself—to teach Adam to know and love his children—he would best her in their nameless battle, the loss of which four little girls would suffer.

Wits sharp, Sara hoped, bravery in place, she approached her quarry, and saw the exact moment stubbornness transformed him. Though not by so much as a blink did he move, he mentally folded his arms in defiance. When the snarl came, Sara was so prepared, she surprised them both with a laugh, lessening the tightness in her chest as well as the certainty in his look. Good.

To bolster her swelling confidence, she took a breath and squared her shoulders. "I am going to shave you and give you a bath," she declared, trembling inside at the thought of touching his warm skin with all that hard muscle beneath.

Adam's eyes narrowed even as his pupils grew larger.

Feeling alarmed, as if she should not be close enough to notice, Sara trembled to her kneecaps but stood her ground.

His caught breath hitched her own. "Don't need a bath," he said.

"Tell my nose that!"

For a blink, the set of his mouth softened, a rare smile hovering, but Adam masked the slip with a curse. "Damn it, Sara, I'm clean enough. I'll wash when I can wash myself."

"Tomorrow is Christmas. You'll wash today."

"Give me the cloth, then." He tore it from her hand, splashing water in his lap, sending the bar of lye soap skittering across the floor. He cursed again.

Sara sighed and fetched the soap. She was going to give the ornery bear a bath if it killed them both, which it just might do.

She brought the washstand closer and filled the basin with hot water from the pitcher; then she lathered the cloth until she was ready to face him.

When she did, she nearly gave up. Stubborn mouth, firm lips. Male. Thick brows shadowing hard eyes gone soft but wary still. Pain she had read in them the night Abby died, though she'd not been able to read much more than fury there since.

Hands huge and callused. Male. Hands capable of controlling a team of six Belgian horses with a flick of the wrist . . . of washing and dressing his wife for her final journey.

"It makes you cry, this chore?" Adam's words wrenched

Sara from the image of him sponging blood from Ab's legs, the grief in his eyes so plain, she had gasped. He'd hated her for walking in on him then, for catching him at a weak moment. When he'd handed her the baby clothes she had gone to fetch, he looked as if she saw his soul, read its secrets . . . as if he would never forgive her for it.

"It's the stink makes my eyes water," she said, wiping them with the back of her hand. "You smell worse than usual."

When indignation narrowed his own eyes, and she could tell from the spark in them that he was about to argue, Sara slapped him in his big mouth with the soapy cloth. And while he spit suds and cursed a blue streak, she gave his face and neck a vigorous and thorough wash.

Adam had never felt anything as blessedly wonderful as that warm cloth against his sweaty skin. He needed a bath so bad, he itched in places he couldn't reach to scratch, and it was driving him crazy. "Long as you're gonna keep up that fool scrubbing, might as well wash my hair."

Sara stilled like a doe in lantern-light, Adam thought, then she nodded as if she'd given herself a talking to, and lathered his hair.

Heaven. He had gone to heaven. And when Sara reached over to lather the length in the back, and her breasts filled his face, so close he might touch a pouting nubbin with his lips, his body agreed. In fact it made its wholehearted delight known in a blatant and uncomfortable fashion.

Adam could not cross his leg for the splint, never mind the pain, so he bunched the blankets in his lap, as if by accident, which was not easy, since they were wet from the spill, and he had only one good hand after all.

Fortunately his embarrassment tempered his body's betrayal and he was able to relax a bit. After Sara rinsed and combed his hair, he was grateful for a shift in position as she washed his back and unbroken arm. She spent a long time washing where God's good earth had etched his callused palms and lined his knuckles, and she was gentle, almost soothing in her ministrations, where his nails were misshapen and scarred.

Adam wondered how a hand-washing could make him want so much. Then she started on his chest and he came face to face with a hunger that made all needs previous seem weak, an urgency bordering on pain.

Sara must be as aware as him of the shift, because for once, she did not scold or lecture. And when their eyes met, where moments before hers had seemed just plain green, they were now more like a forest at dusk, flecked in brightening gold. Adam read need there, the likes of which he had not thought any woman capable.

For the life of him, he could make no sound. He could barely breathe. He did not like seeing Spinster Sara's need, despite the odd sense of satisfaction it brought. But his aversion did not last, because as Sara worked her way from his chest to his belly, with those slow, warm strokes of hers, she washed everything but the physical from awareness, his eager body pulsing in blatant expectation.

"I'll take it from here," Adam croaked. But it was too late, for Sara had stopped to gaze in fascination at where he stood the sheet erect. "I said, 'I'll take care of that!'"

Eyes big and round, she looked at him, and as quickly looked away. Face red as the setting sun, and probably as hot, she turned her attention to washing his big clumsy feet, another pleasure as keen as the hand-washing, though infinitely more humbling. When she washed his broken leg, he felt as if she were piercing it with a pitchfork, though her touch was light as butterfly wings.

But her gentleness did not last, and Adam about died when she turned him to wash his backside. And when she lost the cloth and grazed him with her hand, he nearly jumped from his skin. But she was as quick and silent as she was rough, and before long, she handed him the lathered cloth and fled the room.

Hard as a pikestaff, he thought in disgust when he began his task, and it did not get any better for imagining Sara performing it for him. Despite his trying to ignore it, when he was so aroused he was in pain worse than he ever remembered being, even as a randy boy, Adam knew he was in big trouble.

If Spinster Sara kept giving him baths, she was gonna be a whole lot wiser than most spinsters, because he was gonna spill his seed every time she picked up a wash cloth.

His father was right. He was a stupid, worthless piece of farm dung. He could not stay on a ladder without breaking half the bones in his body, when he should have broken his pizzle instead. His wife dead four months, and here he sat, aching for another woman.

"Sara," he called, noting the thread of forbidden yearning in the word, almost as disgusted over his physical reaction to her as over the rest of his sorry life.

She was paler and calmer when she returned, but as she cleared the washstand, he touched her hand and she jumped like a scared cat. "You have to take them away again." He hated begging, but if it would get her the blazes out. He looked straight into her eyes, hoping she could see his desperation. Yes, for once, he hoped she could read him. "For their good. And yours," he added.

Sara stiffened and shook her head. "If you're talking about your children, I can't. I can't go until you're better. They belong with you, Adam. I'm leaving them here when I go. So it's best that I stay till you're better."

"Get somebody else to take care of me."

"Idiot." Sara's expression revealed a struggle Adam did not understand. "You've scared everybody else off," she said. "And don't tell me you did not know you were doing it. Sometimes I think you're ornery on purpose."

Adam chose not to reply to such a clever remark. Damn the sassy scrapper, anyway. "All right, blast it. If getting better will get you out of here, I'll be walking again so fast, The *English* will think he performed a miracle."

"Call him Doc Marks or just Doc, but don't call him The *English* like the others do. You may be more surly than the rest, but I don't think you're as ignorant, for all you pretend to be."

That bit of wisdom surprised him as much as it worried him. Scrapper Sara was a whole lot smarter than anybody gave her credit for, him included, though he would not make that mistake again. "And you're bossier." He cleared his throat to keep himself from revealing his admiration for her strength, noticing that his comment seemed to cause her pain, which frustrated him further. "You have to take them . . . as soon as I can walk."

"If not for that leg, I'd be returning them to your care the day after tomorrow. I said I'd keep them until Christmas, and you'll have them returned to you as soon as you're up and about, so you had best learn to care for them while I'm here to help you. I'll not be taking them away again."

"Sara—"

"If you want to discuss this, Adam, then behave tomorrow." She regarded him for too long. "I want to see joy on those babies' faces tomorrow, not sadness. Just one day, Adam. Christmas Day. Be nice. And later, I'll listen to what you have to say."

Sara had never bent the truth in her life, not until lately. She'd told Adam she did not want to come and care for him, when she knew very well she considered it a God-given opportunity to teach him to love his children. She'd tried to give him the impression she wanted to leave the girls with him, when what she wanted was to raise them herself. She told him they'd discuss her decision, when there was nothing to discuss. She would not change her mind.

The next morning, Sara dragged furniture around, so she and the girls could eat their Christmas dinner in Adam's room with him.

She hoped that since today was the most holy day of the year, that He whose birth they celebrated would help her find the strength she would need to give Abby's girls the father they deserved.

During dinner, Katie was too taken with her doll to eat. She even ignored her favorite cinnamon pears, so Sara suggested her doll be put down for a nap. Katie slid off her chair and trotted over to her father, where she lay the doll beside him, covering it with her new little quilt. Then she kissed the doll, and to her father's shock, she kissed his hand.

With his kissed hand shaking, Adam speared a bite of turkey, but not before Sara saw the raw fear in his eyes, and she stilled. Big, bad, Mad Adam Zuckerman, afraid of his children? More afraid than they were of him? But why?

Adam did not much like Christmas. Never had. Neighbors visited on Christmas, which, as a boy, meant he'd had to stay inside, under his father's steely eyes, where, for some reason, he made one mistake after another, and paid dearly later for each.

No. He did not like Christmas.

Especially not this one.

Before Adam could register the sound of carriage wheels on the drive, someone was opening the outside door. And before Sara could rise, that interfering English doctor was entering Adam's room.

The *English* smiled at Sara in a way he had no right to do, while he rubbed the cold from soft hands with trim fingernails, hands that had never worked the sweet, moist earth. "Ah," he said, unbuttoning his coat, examining their Christmas meal. "In time for dinner. Just as I planned."

Sara laughed and stood to take his coat. "As you always plan."

Adam's growl did not begin to express his anger. Not only did The *English* embrace and kiss Sara, but Lizzie, Katie and Pris jumped from their chairs and lined up for kisses too. His girls.

Adam bristled. "What do you mean by—"

"Thanks, don't mind if I do," The *English* said with a wink, making Sara giggle.

Adam could not believe it. Practical, determined, headstrong Spinster Sara had giggled. "Sara, you know how the Elders feel about your consorting with The *English*," Adam said. "Mind, now, no good will come of such a friendship, nor of that midwifing nonsense, either."

The *English* laughed.

Sara did not.

Adam guessed it would take more than his threats to turn her away from the man. Adam's stomach tightened and what little appetite he had, fled. She must really like the doctor, then.

"I taught Sara midwifing, Adam, and we became . . . friends." The *English* cleared his throat, looking embarrassed, and Adam enjoyed his discomfort, though he did not care to examine it. Was there something more than friendship between them?

"It was Sara who talked me into settling here in Walnut Creek," The *English* went on. "So the community would have a doctor."

"Except they won't call him for birthings," Sara said. "So I became a midwife."

"They won't call you either," Adam muttered. "Except Roman, for strangers, and everybody knows he's—"

"You called me," Sara said, "for Abby."

"I did n—" Adam swallowed. "Roman talked me into it." Adam did not want her to know that he'd thought of calling her only after Abby died. Yes, he should have called her to deliver the baby, but how was he to know Abby would need help after three easy births? If only she'd told him she was in trouble; he had been right outside her door. He shivered, thinking of Abby's miscarriage the year before, which she had made seem so natural and unimportant.

He would have called Sara if he realized, but ifs were poor and painful company, he knew very well. And why Sara should have a good opinion of him, he did not know, because that was already water over the dam.

Sara shook her head as if Adam's silence was proof of his witlessness and her low opinion. "Jordan, do sit down and share our Christmas dinner."

Adam grumbled about people with no more sense than to barge in on dinner, and after Sara told him to be quiet, he brooded while the girls took turns showing The *English* the dolls Abby had stitched and the quilts from Sara. He was surprised when Lizzie said the cloth in Sara's little quilts was from Mommie's dresses, sorry he hadn't noticed that himself, and ashamed for the first time ever that it was not to their father his girls flocked, but to a stranger with city words and gold buttons on his coat.

Sara called their little blankets "memory quilts" and asked each of his girls to tell a "smiling" story about their mother that the cloth squares made them remember. While they did, Adam had to remind himself why they could not come to him, that Spinster Sara must leave and take them with her—for their own good.

Having Sara around was confusing him, poisoning his resolve. "When can I get out of this bed and get on with farming?" Adam demanded of the man who was rocking a fussy baby girl he had no right to soothe. "And when can Sara take my girls home?"

The *English* raised a brow. "Your girls are already home." The medical man shook his head gravely. "You'll need Sara's care for weeks and weeks."

"Weeks!" Adam and Sara shouted together, and with the same troubled pitch.

The *English* seemed to struggle with a smile, but he grew serious too quickly to be certain. "That leg's got the worst kind of break," he said, which Adam knew to be true. And yet, in his rioting gut, despair was the least of his emotions.

He closed his eyes, almost dizzy. Sara was staying. She was staying. His girls were staying. For a while, at least. Weeks. A long time. Too long.

Not long enough.

They heard another carriage come into the yard, and everyone, even The *English,* stopped to listen. This time, as should be, Sara was allowed to go to the kitchen door and open it. Then Bishop Weaver was entering Adam's room. *"Guten morgen,"* he said. "Blessed Christmas."

The first thing the Bishop did was give Lizzie, Pris and Katie a handful of wrapped treats. "Christmas sweets from Mrs. Weaver," he said. "Mondel schnits and peanut mojhys."

A raised brow from Sara, and the girls put the candy by their plates and went back to their dinner. Adam could not believe Sara made them mind with just a look when Abby had always needed to shout.

Bishop Weaver rocked on his heels and surveyed the room with an eagle eye. Adam imagined a dozen breaches of their rule of life. Non-attendance at Christmas Service for a start. Consorting with The *English*. Remaining in bed when chores called. Worse, an unmarried woman in the room with him in bed. Adam hardened his features and thought about . . . the baths.

The Bishop nodded. "You are broken in many places, Adam, the good doctor tells us. But not your head, says he. That's too hard to break. So you need a nurse." The Elder looked at Sara.

She swallowed and gave a weak smile. "He is a cranky patient."

The *English* chuckled and took baby Hannah, who was working herself into a good and loud show of temper, into the kitchen. Adam's girls followed, grabbing their candy before they left. Adam wanted to swear, for many reasons.

Bishop Weaver sat in the rocker Sara indicated and nodded at her. "And how do you manage to care for this big ox?"

Adam fisted his hands. In other words, how closely goes this care?

Sara swallowed. "He needs to eat, of course, to get strong again, so I cook for him and the girls. Someone has to bring him his food when it's ready. Sometimes I feed him, if it's soup. He can't balance his broth and hold a spoon at the same time. Sometimes the girls help with that. He cannot get up to tend the fire or keep the house warm, as you can see, so I do that too. I mix unguents for the cuts

61

and brew teas for the pain and swelling. I change his bandages and fetch him the Bible and *Martyrs Mirror* to read."

Adam grunted. His reading tastes had not run to the holy books; farm catalogues and newspapers, more like.

"Sometimes, he asks me or Lizzie to read—"

"Sara, you are unmarried," the Bishop said, interrupting her. "So I beg you will not be insulted by my question—"

The Bishop hesitated and Adam thought, here it comes. . . .

Their high holy leader encompassed them both in his stern look; then he narrowed his gaze on Adam. "Who tends to your more . . . er . . . basic needs, may I ask?"

You may not. Might as well ask if Sara took care of his hard need, damn him. Silence held Adam hostage for more beats than he cared. A glance at Sara and she at him, and without a blink he made a decision she approved, and how he knew, he wasn't sure, but he did. Adam shrugged. "You know Roman. He's here every day. Mostly so nosy he can't stay away, but a good and generous neighbor all the same. He does what he must."

Bishop Weaver chuckled. "Ya, I know Roman. Into everybody's business, but a good heart." The Bishop slapped the arms of his chair and stood himself up. "Well, got to visit the rest of the afflicted. See you on Second Christmas."

Sara didn't even see the Bishop to the door. She stood staring at Adam, him staring back, while The *English* said their goodbyes for them and let the high Elder out.

The doctor playing host angered Adam, but right now it hardly mattered. He had as much as lied to his Bishop, and Sara had gone along with him by not correcting the impression. They had lied, sinned, together, and in complete knowledge of what they were doing. "This is best," Adam said.

"Yes," Sara whispered.

The *English* returned, not the least bothered that another man's daughters trailed him like ducklings to the pond. He grinned and rubbed his hands together. "What say we go sledding to celebrate Christmas?"

Adam was annoyed by the ducklings' delighted whoops.

"Sara too?" Katie asked, jumping up and down.

Sara's glance left him, to be turned toward The *English*, and Adam mourned the loss, hating that the doctor's smile brought Sara's.

She turned back to Adam. "I'll stay with Hannah," she said, and he chose to attribute the loss of her smile to her uneasiness over their shady alliance. They had done more than lie, after all. With a word, she could have dispensed with the intimate side of his care, but uncomfortable as the episodes had become, Spinster Sara did not want them to end any more than he did. And that made him wonder what else the scrapper might want, though nothing could come of it. Ever.

He had killed one woman. He'd not kill another the same way.

"Hannah will be fine with her Datt," The *English* said, stopping Adam's heart and tying his tongue.

She will not, damn it. Adam feared The *English* would place the baby in his arms, and he could not bear to hold her again. The day Sara delivered the stranger's child, he had experienced a need to protect Hannah that nearly broke him—rich, when it was him she needed protecting from. Which was exactly why he had never held any of the others.

"Put her cradle near his bed," The *English* said. "Looks like they could both use a nap. She'll wake him, if she needs anything."

Before long, the sound of squeals and laughter—the

girls', the doctor's and Sara's—carried to where Adam lay. Awake. Mournful. Jealous?

He wanted to be with them. No, he did not.

He wanted Sara out of his life. Did he not?

Adam sighed. He craved freedom from Sara in the same foolish way he craved it from crisp winter frosts that nudged the trees to bud and the sap to flow. Like the elements so vital to life, she nipped at fingers and toes for a time, but the buds and blossoms she encouraged were worth the price.

He wanted to die, but here came his strangest denial, because for perhaps the first time in his sorry life, he wanted to live . . . which just about proved him madder than ever.

Adam bent toward the cradle and allowed his new daughter to curl her tiny hand around his finger: another first for him, a dangerous one.

"Sweet Spinster Sara," he said. "What have you wrought?"

Chapter Five

Five weeks, three days, two hours, twenty minutes . . . and eleven baths. That's how long Sara had been living with him.

But who was counting?

Adam was, ever since the day Roman walked in on one of those baths Adam liked too much, though it was innocent enough. His body could not be blamed for "warming up" to the experience. But Roman had read Adam as clearly as today's newspaper and knew exactly what the experience did to him. Which reminded Adam that his time with Sara, his baths, must come to an end before he began to like having her around, if that were possible.

Or was it already too late?

When Roman came in on that bath, Sara had been washing his chest. And with his eyes closed, Adam had been imagining a different caress, but Roman's cough opened Adam's eyes wider than was comfortable as he regarded Roman's grin. Roman knowing something that no one else did was dangerous, and always temporary; everybody knew it.

"Ya," Roman had said with a hearty chuckle. "Way more alive. Chores are done," he'd added, whistling his way back outside.

Sara had been stunned by the interruption, and Adam took her hand—Lord, she was soft—and told her not to worry. They stayed that way for a long minute, her hand in his, before he'd growled and told her to finish; he was catching cold.

Since Sara brought his children back, he'd been living in hell, with a taste of heaven thrown in for a teaser.

His splint was still secure and the area around the thigh wound—black, blue, purple—festered more often than not, but Adam wanted the leg healed, so Sara and the girls could go . . . most of the time.

He wanted to be alone . . . some of the time.

He'd survived a daily visit from The *English*, who played with his children, which they loved, and who made Sara laugh, which Adam hated. He'd tolerated regular visits from Roman, who seemed to be enjoying his plight, despite the fact that it doubled the foolish man's chores.

Sara's fussing and scolding made life seem . . . interesting, at the least. His girls sang silly songs as they jumped on his bed most mornings. Their giggles when he growled; this too was new and different, and it bothered him . . . somewhat. Adam thought he bore it with good grace . . . ill-grace, if you listened to Sara, though he tried not to.

What had been a surprise—and not a good one—and still worried Adam, were the Church Elders who'd come the day before yesterday. Oh, they had an excuse. Preacher Schmidt was moving his family to Illinois and wanted to say goodbye. But they had asked too many questions, one of them concerning the location of Sara's bedroom, of all things, which had made Adam downright nervous. Still did.

And now, as if his worry conjured the problem, Adam realized, with a start, that Bishop Weaver must be right there in the kitchen. He had totally missed the sound of a carriage, but there was no mistaking the Elder's hearty Penn Dutch chatter and grandfatherly chuckle, which relaxed Adam a bit . . . until Sara shrieked.

Bolting from the bed, Adam hobbled into the kitchen, prepared to save her, but the stoic Bishop's chest stopped his forward surge and the pain in Adam's leg caught up with him and damned-near felled him.

He took the chair Sara offered and tried not to pass out. When he recovered, he saw Roman, looking like a fox caught in the hen-house, turning his hat with nervous fingers, standing somewhat behind the Bishop. This was not a good sign.

When stars stopped dancing before Adam's eyes, he examined both men's faces. "What did you say to Sara that would cause her to shout so?"

The Bishop placed his hands behind his back and rocked on his heels, seeming to seek guidance from a source far above them.

Adam broke into a sweat.

"Adam Zuckerman," the grave voice intoned, speeding Adam's heart the more. "It has been decided by the Elders that you and Sara should be brought before the District on church Sunday next."

Adam shot to his feet—a stupid move. He sat again and willed the kitchen to stop spinning. "What rule do you imagine we broke? I'd like to know, by God."

"Besides blasphemy?" the Bishop asked, a shaggy white brow raised for emphasis. "For living under conditions that could become an occasion for sin."

Adam laughed—a rusty sound—surprising everyone, even himself, as he pinned Roman with his best scowl. "Who incited this foolish charge?"

Roman made straight for the back door. "Wasn't me," he said before he scooted out, but Sara managed to whack him with her broom all the same, which gave Adam no satisfaction at all. Neither Sara, if her look was to be believed.

★ ★ ★ ★ ★

At dawn the following morning, Adam removed his splint and hobbled into the barn, ignoring the searing pain in his thigh, and took great pleasure in throwing Roman Byler out. Didn't even bother to thank him for six weeks' worth of chores.

Ornery, that's what he was today, Adam thought, more so than usual, and he knew it. He'd been fighting a war inside himself, which made it difficult to be neighborly. Should he make Sara and the girls leave before Sunday meeting—as if he could make Sara do anything—or should he let them stay till Bishop Weaver said they must go?

He wanted them to go. He'd wanted it for weeks. So when had it stopped being uppermost in his mind? And why did he feel downright bleak at the very thought?

Because he had no answer, he said nothing, and by virtue of his silence, he let them stay.

But he was not happy about it. He was not.

He and Sara spoke little during the next week, but Adam sensed that she, too, struggled for answers. They had become, in some undefined way, united in their common disgrace, their forced alliance strong and frightening.

Adam watched Sara sometimes, and when she looked back, it was almost as if a . . . connection, which gained strength and substance as the hearing grew nearer, might snap them apart one minute or pull them together the next.

Once during that time, at a moment when that invisible connection became hot and tight, Adam reached out, and Sara reached as well. But their fingers had barely touched before they parted.

Adam knew what it was like, after that, to be branded.

★ ★ ★ ★ ★

Church Sunday—the alternating Sunday that service was held, and the day he and Sara were to be brought before the Elders in Hostetler's barn—dawned crisp and finger-cold. His buggy team blew visible puffs of mist in the frosty air as they cantered, heads high, gaits stately.

Very much aware of Sara sitting beside him, Baby Hannah noisily sucking Sara's trailing kapp-ribbon, Adam drove as if he sat alone, gazing forward, saying nothing. Katie, between them, placed her head on his leg, as if she were reluctant to be separated. From him? Adam straightened in his seat, but he could not bring himself to push her away, because he was not up to her inevitable chatter, he told himself.

Sara saw that Adam was uncomfortable with Katie leaning on him, but he bore it silently so she let Katie be. A few weeks ago, she thought he might have shouted for Katie to move. But what did she know? She had never really seen or heard him shout at his children. The worse she had seen was him pretending they didn't exist, like he was doing now.

As they drove toward a fate neither of them dared voice, Sara felt compelled to break a silence, heavier than their problems. Since worry was not a topic to uplift them, she chose foolishness, instead. "Lizzie says you call your horses Titania and Tawny. I never heard such names."

Lizzie smiled. "Silly, Sara. Those are butterfly names."

Sara questioned Adam with a raised brow, and he grimaced. "For the Tawny Crescentspot," he said on a sigh, as if he had no choice but to answer, "which is attracted to asters. And Titania's Fritillary which favors azaleas. Butterflies. Like my smart Lizzie said."

Lizzie perked up at his words and regarded her father

with awe, and Sara wondered if he realized he'd both claimed and complimented her in one rare statement. That, and his knowledge of the delicate, colorful, almost frothy creatures, caught Sara's imagination. "There's more to you, Adam Zuckerman, than anyone knows," she said.

Silence became foremost after that, except for the beat of Sara's heart, which she was certain everyone must hear.

After a time, Adam cleared his throat. "Sara," he practically whispered, which got her attention better than a shout might have done. "You must take them and leave . . . or else."

Or else she could stay with him . . . against the Elder's wishes? Is that what he was suggesting? It was the first thing that came to her mind. And impossible.

Yet the facts of her life kept intruding. No man for her. Not for Spinster Sara. No children. Too bossy to bed.

If she left Adam, she could have the children, yes, but they did not belong to her, not really. No matter what Adam said, they were his. Only one thing could make them hers—marriage . . . to him.

The disturbing thought straightened Sara in her seat. Impossible.

Marriage. A forever bond, dissolvable only by death. Could she bear to allow death to break her again? She mocked herself with a silent laugh. If she married, at least she would know she had lived.

Oh, she'd come alive with learning to midwife, and even more so with taking the girls. But when she'd come home with them, to a clumsy, ornery giant who fought and growled at every turn, the sun had all but taken residence in her heart.

She felt complete.

Silly Sara, as Lizzie would say. As if Adam's home was

70

hers, anyway. But that was how she felt. Only because he was a challenge, she thought. She'd always warmed to a challenge.

Still, could she now shut the door on the sun and accept a winter heart once more? Oh, life would never be bleak with the girls, except that Adam would always have the right to take them back, and the threat of it would hang above her like a cloud dimming the sun.

Besides, she'd promised Ab, as they lowered her coffin into the ground, to do her best by the girls. So, wouldn't raising them with their father be the best? He wasn't having anything to do with raising them alone, now, was he?

Sara thought about that a long time and about how Adam seemed to be suffering somewhere deep inside himself. Almost as if . . . he wanted to lay himself in a wooden box and close the cover. Hadn't he tried with the drink?

Sara's composure cracked then, and she forced herself not to reach for his hand. "I know," she said, "that there seems to be no choice. But I believe you and the children need—"

"I know you believe it. But Abby could not. You cannot either. It is best for them." He nodded at his children.

Sara understood that Adam believed it was best his children be separated from him, but. . . . "I do not believe that. Tell me why."

"Better you do not know."

Jealousy surged inside Sara and she was ashamed. Jealous of a dead woman whose children enriched her life; this was wrong, and yet she could not seem to stop herself. "Did Abby know?"

It was clear from his look that Adam saw her jealousy for what it was. "She had to."

"Then why not tell me? You've set me to do the same

task." She hated begging but needed answers.

Adam looked at her with an expression she could not read. Pity? Concern? Surprise—that she was subject to such a weakness as jealousy? "Ignorance in this will deliver you," he finally said. "I could not save Abby, but I can save you and the girls. Besides, you're stronger than Abby ever was."

"You make no sense, Adam."

"More than you will ever know. This is best."

Sara did not believe it, but, ultimately, neither of them had a choice anyway. "The Elders will tell us to separate," she said. "And we will. Because we want to stay Amish, we will do what they tell us."

Adam only nodded.

"But which of us will get the girls?" she asked.

"You will; I promise you will," he said, giving her the answer she both craved and dreaded.

Adam saw, when they entered the Hostetler barn, that many of their neighbors already sat on the backless benches delivered for this purpose. Rows of hatless, bearded men sat on one side, facing like rows of kapped women sitting opposite. How often had he seen the sight, yet not taken it in?

Why, today, did it seem so new?

Hung on nails, a crazy-quilt array of wide-brimmed, plain-crown, black felt hats covered the rough barn wall beside the men. On the wall opposite hung a sparse scattering of small but identical hats, because the boys sat with their mothers. All the females, no matter what age, kept their bonnets on, because the fire in the barn's pot-bellied stove did little to take the edge off the cold.

As Adam, Sara and the girls stepped into the barn, they became the center of attention, the coo and rustle of doves in the eaves lonely accompaniment to their entry. Adam bristled at the notion. Why did he notice everything today when usually he heard and saw nothing?

Sara sat with the women, Pris on her lap, Lizzie beside her with baby Hannah in her arms, Katie at their feet.

Adam nodded and took the seat indicated, alone in the center. He was to be the one chastised, then. So be it. Better than Sara, he thought. He would not wish that on her. She had been too good to his girls. And to him.

He owed her.

And if he knew what it was he owed her—or what he wanted from her, for that matter—he would be less uncomfortable, he was certain.

Bishop Weaver entered and began preaching.

Added to the usual three-hour service would be two events. The first would be the choosing of a new preacher, necessary as the new district had grown. This would begin right after the Deacon's sermon, and before the foolish hearing over Adam's "occasion for sin."

Roman looked sheepish when those very words were spoken, much like Ginger, Adam's German shepherd, had looked this very morning, when Adam had taken the pups she'd "adopted" and given them back to Sara's dog, Trixie. No matter Trixie's flightiness, those pups belonged with their real—

Adam bristled and wished he had not thought of that. Damn dogs. Damn Roman.

At the Bishop's request, people began suggesting candidates for preacher. Some names came up more often than others. Roman's was mentioned only once, but Adam saw by his look that he did not want the "honor." Well, that was too bad. Adam did not want to be in the center of them right now. He did not want Sara to leave with the girls, either. Well, he did, but only when she was ready—when he was ready, he meant. Except that Roman had interfered—he was certain it was Roman.

Adam crossed his arms and seconded Roman's name for consideration.

Zeb Coblentz repeated it, as did Zack Zimmer.

Just for fun, Adam said it again.

Others took up the call. Seemed many thought that the man turning green in the corner would make a good preacher, town gossip or not.

Adam caught Sara's look. She knew what he'd done. He didn't much like the way he and Sara could talk without words, but he liked that she seemed to approve his action; he liked the twinkle in her eyes.

He shrugged. Pleasing her was a good end to their time together, though the pain the notion brought made him scowl.

Ultimately, four candidates were chosen for preacher, Roman among them. The candidates rose to pass by a table on which sat a row of four Bibles, each man choosing one. Only one man would find a slip of paper in his Bible naming him preacher, signaling him as "chosen by God." That man would serve their Amish community for the rest of his life.

Adam shifted in his seat. Life was a long time to pay for interference, even if it was the kind that could change others' lives. For a minute Adam wished . . . but it was too late, because look who was holding that fateful slip of paper.

Roman knelt before the Bishop to accept God's will and be ordained. And when Preacher Roman Byler rose and regarded Adam, if looks were flames, Adam would be cinders.

Afterward, everyone took a short break for babies to be fed and such, during which time the district women "protected" Sara from his approach. This made him angry.

Where were they when she was all but shunned for becoming a midwife, when she'd entered the house of a widower seven weeks before?

Twenty minutes later, the hearing began with a reading of the accusation. Living in sin. Adam almost laughed. The charge had somehow changed from "an occasion for sin" to "living in sin." If he'd known it would come to this, he would have made the baths count.

As if she read him, Sara's face turned pink, and she put Pris down and took baby Hannah from Lizzie, standing her, almost as a shield, except she kept peeking around her "shield" to look at him. Adam tried to calm Sara with his look, tried not to be captivated by her unconscious game. He also tried not to reveal to the others this odd ability they shared to communicate in silence. But Sara could not be calmed, and it bothered him that it bothered him.

Adam shifted in his seat and saw that the English doctor was there. What was he doing at service?

The man's reassuring nod succeeded in calming Sara and her shoulders relaxed. While Adam was glad Sara had calmed, he did not need such a man to do it. Adam Zuckerman took care of his own. Except that Sara was not his, he had best remember.

The Bishop spoke first, of sin and the rights of marriage, which were not to be given lightly or outside the union.

Sara appeared as if she were . . . bruised . . . by the shame of it, making Adam want to hit their high holy leader.

The Deacon spoke next and suggested repentance and separation.

Roman, the new preacher, standing to speak last, looked straight at him. "An eye for an eye" best described his silent promise, and Adam braced himself as the new preacher suggested marriage.

Adam jumped to his feet, but his shout was drowned by The *English*. "Roman, are you mad? This has gone far enough! We wanted the children back where they belong, but *Sara* does not belong there."

So, it was Roman, and The *English* too, started this. Well then, served The *English* right if he lost Sara because of it. Yes, and serve Preacher Byler right too.

"There's more at work here than either of us realizes," Roman replied. "You said so yourself, Doc. Leave it alone."

Adam liked the idea of The *English* losing Sara. He began to feel as if Roman was right. What did he mean, more at work here?

"Like hell I will," The *English* shouted, making his Amish neighbors gasp. Hell was a serious place with his people, and Adam felt a chuckle rising in his throat, which, as always, hurt his chest and soured his mood.

"It is too late," the Bishop said. "You have no rights here, Doctor Marks. Much as we appreciate you at our bedsides when we are in pain, Preacher Byler is right."

"But I have rights here," Adam shouted. "Sara does too."

The Bishop encompassed them in his high-holy look, which fairly shouted, "You gave up your rights when you broke the ordnung!" Except they had broken nothing. Wishing now that they had, Adam fisted his hands and gave a half nod.

The Bishop returned it. "Marry and you remain among us. Do not and you will be shunned. Go back home, both of you, and consider how you will respond to your Maker's will. I will be by this evening for your decision. That is my final word."

Adam rose and made his rebellious way to his family then, holding every gaze for certain, as service was not half over. He lifted Katie and Pris in his arms, ignored Pris's whining. "Come, Lizzie, Sara," he turned to lead the way out. "Time to go home . . . and don't forget the baby," he called behind, laying claim to his family, Sara included—which about buckled his knees when he realized it.

Doctor Jordan Marks, in his fancy Yankee carriage, followed their buggy all the way home, and the first thing Adam did when they arrived was limp over and punch the fancy man in the nose. So much for turning the other cheek, but what was one more sin among so many?

Sara screamed and Katie and Pris began to cry. Lizzie took out her handkerchief and told the doctor to hold it against his nose, and despite his injury, the doctor laughed, until Sara told him to go home.

"But, Sara, you can't marry that miserable man. The whole district is afraid of him. You're even afraid of him."

"I am not. Adam is hiding under all that gruff."

"Now, wait a minute," Adam said.

"Keep quiet for once, Adam Zuckerman, and take the children inside," Sara snapped, and because, since the day his father died, he'd not been ordered to do anything—no one dared—Adam Zuckerman did what he was told. But he and Katie stayed by the door to watch Sara pack The *English* off with a shove and an annoyed shake of her head. Then she was inside with them, where she belonged.

Sara was shaking, she was so angry . . . with Roman, with the Bishop, with Jordan, the idiot. For the first time in weeks, the only man she wasn't angry with was Adam. "I can stand being shunned if you can," she said removing her cape. Anything was better than leaving. Anything.

She knew Adam did not want to be left alone with the children any more than she wanted to leave them, and as far as she could see, defiance was their only answer. "You have been as close to shunned as can be, without keeping from Sunday service, since Abby married you," she said. "What would be different about this?"

"Why thank you, Sara," Adam said, his voice rising. "That's the kindest thing anyone has ever said to me!"

Sara giggled, a measure of her discomfort, then she sighed and bit her lip. "Sorry. I meant, together we can be shunned and not be alone."

"We cannot be together." Sara saw Adam's hand begin to tremble. "I mean stay together," he corrected. "You have to move back to your house."

"Oh, certainly, it will be easy living in one room again when we have nine now and we trip over each other!"

Adam stepped back and frowned. He shook his head. "If you care one bit about how many rooms you have, I'm the sweetest man ever lived."

Sara laughed; so did Lizzie, but Sara was more shaken than she wanted to admit. "They did not give us the choice of living apart, Adam. They said married or shunned. Period." Suppose she lost the children. Oh God, they needed her; she needed them. Even Adam needed her, though he didn't know it—and wouldn't admit it, if he did.

"We can go live with Doctor Jordan," Katie said, jumping up and down. "He likes to play with us."

Sara caught Adam's horrified, but quickly masked, look and ran with Katie's suggestion. "He did offer. And as long as I'd be shunned, anyway, I should probably consider his . . . proposal. It's likely the only one I'll ever get."

Adam opened his mouth, shut it and paced the kitchen. He looked at her, at the girls, shook his head and went outside—slamming the door hard behind him—and began to unhitch the horses.

Sara calculated how long it would take him to issue an

order. And while she waited, she prayed for that order to be the one she and his girls, even Adam, most needed.

Then she wondered how she would survive if he did.

Chapter Six

It took Adam less than fifteen minutes to come limping back into the house. He hooked his hat on a peg by the back door with so much force, the peg broke with a loud snap. He stood stock still for a minute after that, while the snapped dowel rolled, clacking its way across the linoleum; then he carefully hung his hat on a different peg. He ladled himself a dipper of water, drank and tossed the ladle into the zinc-lined sink, where it hit and spun with a dull clatter.

The only sound after that was Pris whining upstairs.

Sara resisted an urge to giggle as she watched him begin to pace.

Big, bad, mad Adam Zuckerman was nervous.

Tall. Big hands. Big feet. Despite his size and his limp, he looked fit; not an ounce of fat on him. His chest was broad, his waist trim. And his hips were just about. . . .

Good Lord, in her head she had measured the span with her hands, which was . . . acceptable, she supposed. They were discussing marriage, after all. A big step with such a man. An adventure, she thought, as Adam stepped before her, and she regarded his boots. When he reached beneath her chin, she raised her head in surprise, and he proceeded to untie her outer bonnet, which she hadn't even realized she was still wearing. "Foolish," she said.

"I thought so too, at first. But, damn it, Sara, we have to."

"What?"

"Get married."

"Oh, but Jordan thinks—"

"I don't care what your blasted *English* thinks. You're going to marry me, Sara Lapp, and that's the end of it. Let him find himself an English wife. He can't have you."

"To be truthful, Adam, Jordan doesn't want—"

"I don't give a tin whistle what The *English* wants or doesn't want! I thought you cared about the children."

"Of course I do. What has that to do with—"

"Children?" Adam called. "Lizzie, Katie, Pris. Come down here? Now."

Sara stamped her foot. "Damn it, Adam." Heat rushed her for the childish tantrum. "Let me finish a sentence!"

"Hush." He put a finger to her lips, warming her to her toes. "Don't cuss around the girls."

Sara's emotions ran in all directions. This man, who cussed like a heathen more often than not, kept telling *her* not to.

His girls—their girls soon perhaps—innocent and wide-eyed, came running down the stairs in eager response to his rare call.

"Lizziebelle," Adam said, the nickname bringing surprised reactions all around. "You're a wise child. Do you and your sisters need a new mommie?"

"Yes, Datt."

"And for your new mommie, would you like to have rickety old Mrs. Good with four teeth and twenty cats?"

Katie and Lizzie dissolved into giggles, but Pris walked straight into Sara, without ever looking up at her, and buried her face in her apron. "Want Sara," came Pris's muffled voice.

More afraid than he had ever been in his life—that Sara would agree, that she would not—Adam looked into Scrapper Sara's wide, shimmering eyes. "For their new mommie, our girls want you, Sara. They need you," he said, thinking she looked as if she might be as frightened and hopeful as he was.

Taking the final step toward sealing all their fates felt a bit like nailing his coffin shut—the nails made of words: powerful, irrefutable, with more raw, soul-deep need in them than he ever dared reveal or acknowledge before. Without taking his gaze from Sara's, Adam took her hand and placed it over Pris's tiny kapped head, then he placed his own hands over Sara's. "And so you shall have her."

Their wedding day dawned frost-glazed and kettle dark, a warning from above, Adam worried, for a marriage where no love, only need, existed.

Over the past week, he had watched Sara stitch her wedding dress in the color of the spruce trees on the far side of his property, every stitch bringing a new fear in him to life—in her too, maybe.

When The *English* came, dressed slick as a greased pig, to fetch Sara and the girls for the wedding, Adam said he would take his own family, by God, but Sara insisted that it would not look good if he did.

Since he had another errand to run anyway, Adam let her win . . . this time.

"Sara," The *English* said, "on days like today, the sea shines the very color of your dress, though you're a finer credit to God's handiwork than all His oceans put together."

Adam snorted, but Katie giggled and turned in a circle to catch the doctor's attention and show off a miniature version of the same dress and apron. As ever, her wayward curls popped out the sides of Katiebug's tiny white kapp, no matter how Sara tried to tame them, and Katie spun so long, she lost her balance.

The *English* laughed and kissed the top of Katie's head as he steadied her, and Adam crossed his arms and growled low in his throat.

Yes, Sara made the girls' dresses to match hers for the wedding, but this would be the last time they would match, because, between the ceremony and the celebration, Sara would don the black apron and kapp of a married woman. Tonight, she would pack away her wedding apron—for a good long time, Adam prayed, and may he never see her in it again.

The next time she wore her wedding apron, Sara thought, as she smoothed its pleats, would be the day they placed her in her casket. The Amish tradition had jarred her from the day she understood its meaning as a young girl, settling a pall over every wedding she had ever attended, but never more so than today. She, who had decided to triumph over death a long time ago, rejected the reminder of its inevitability, especially on a day when life beckoned with a butterfly heart.

Mother to four beautiful little girls. Wife to Adam Zuckerman—not always mad, but sometimes tender. She would nurture the tenderness, she promised herself, until people forgot the gruff, until he opened his arms to his children in welcome and love. She could do it, Sara thought as she set off on her journey to the Bishop's house where her wedding would take place. She would do it.

As Jordan's fancy carriage with its shiny brass lanterns jolted forward, Sara looked up at the snow-threatening half-bowl sky above them, trusting in the beauty and peace beyond. "Thank you," she said, in her heart, to He whose will she accepted. And then, to Abby, "Help me to heal the man and children you left in my care."

★ ★ ★ ★ ★

Jake Escher shoved a chicken coop into the back of his buggy at about the same time Zeke Schmidt crowed over his winning bid on two sows.

Adam scowled and began to pace when eleven dozen locust poles came up for bid before the manure spreader. He needed that spreader, but if it didn't come up soon, he was going to be late for his own wedding, and Sara would carve and serve him for their wedding supper.

When household goods came up next, he sighed and bought Sara a big fancy iron skillet for five cents. A wedding present would turn her up sweet for certain, no matter how late he arrived. And if he had it all fixed as fine in his mind, why was he sweating over waiting for the damned spreader to come up?

Four dollars he paid, finally, a bargain, of course, because everyone had stopped bidding as soon as he started. Being "mad" had its advantages. Adam coughed to stop the discomfort of a threatening grin, a frequent experience of late, worse since he woke today. Odd how he remembered being downright scared on his last wedding day.

Of course everything was different this time. This was not a November Tuesday or Thursday, as was usual, and theirs would not be one of three or four weddings that day. Tradition was ignored for the joining of a widow or widower—or to satisfy the ordnung, the rules often twisted by meddlesome preachers.

He and Sara were not a couple of children who did not know what was what. They were smarter than to think a few words would improve their lot. He knew life was more riddled with gopher holes than fields; he'd stepped in plenty. Fallen in, more like, backside over ears.

But not this time. Scrapper or no, Sara was going to

learn to follow his rules, and she was going to do so quietly. Adam grunted, scoffing inwardly at his foolish, wishful thinking as he arranged for the manure spreader to be delivered.

Then he slapped the dust from his Sunday suit, climbed up to his buggy seat and gave the reins a flick, sending Titania and Tawny into a quick trot. He was already late, but a wedding could not start without the bridegroom, now could it?

Yes, Adam thought, spotting the Bishop's house down in the valley, his yard full of buggies, Adam knew exactly what he was getting himself into.

In Bishop Weaver's summer kitchen, Sara paced. What was she getting herself into? She had once likened having a husband and family to emerging from a cocoon of lonely darkness. She had imagined that, as a bride, she would step into a world of light and color, but perhaps she had been wrong. If her bridegroom did not care to arrive on time for their wedding, perhaps marriage for her would simply become another cocoon filled with another kind of darkness. Perhaps she had never been meant to embrace the light.

Suppose Adam had run; suppose she never saw him again?

No. No, she did not believe, despite everything, that Adam would desert his children. And since she came with them—to his mind at least—like as not, he would not leave her either. How foolish of her to wish that she should matter to him for her own sake.

Her heavy heart rising almost into her throat, blurring her vision, Sara stepped away from Roman and his niece, sixteen-year-old Lizbeth, attendants she barely knew, to gaze out the window, take a breath and calm herself.

Having strangers as wedding attendants should not bother her.

It had been some time since the districts were re-divided. With her tiny house on the outskirts of the district she'd known most of her life, Sara had become part of this new community, one peopled with strangers, among them Abby Zuckerman, her best and last friend, and Abby's taciturn husband, Adam, now Sara's missing groom.

Adam. The man with whom Sara would spend the rest of her life. The man she would stand beside in trouble and lie beside in bed. Sara placed a hand to her fluttering chest. Lord, and didn't that race her heart?

She wondered how to tell him that she'd rather they share that bedroom off the kitchen, where he'd stayed since he got hurt, than his and Abby's old room, where she'd recently put the girls. She did not expect that he would understand. She could barely understand, herself, or even believe this was happening.

She guessed that tonight, when she hung her dresses on those empty pegs beside his suit—if he ever came to the wedding—that this would all, finally, seem real. Especially as she would undress after that and climb into Adam Zuckerman's bed. Oh Lord.

Sara struggled again to swallow.

Would he be lying there in that bed, already—waiting, watching? Or would he come to her only after she had undressed, washed and settled beneath Mom's old sunshine quilt? If so, would she watch him perform his own private bedtime rituals?

"Lord it's hot in here." The echoing crack in her voice accompanied her opening of the summer kitchen window for a bracing slice of winter air.

Her face cooled and she straightened, shivered and hugged herself, and as her heart calmed, and she turned to speak, Adam stepped into the room.

The air thinned and warmed. The walls closed in.
Elation set her free.

Adam's intense gaze seemed to look deep into her soul,
sending a new rush of blood to lighten her heart and fill her
lungs. Even more startling, his eyes reflected a concern
rarely revealed. Somehow, as a result, a sense of destiny
calmed Sara to the point where she found herself promising
with her look that theirs would be a good marriage, and
Adam accepted and returned the promise with barely a nod.

Roman chuckled, as if entertained by the exchange,
which was annoying to Sara; Adam too, she saw, but
Roman was nothing if not vexatious. He rubbed his hands
together, his grin wide. "Let's get this done. Food's waiting
and I'm powerful hungry." It was always food first with
Roman.

Into the center of Mrs. Weaver's best room, Sara and
Adam walked hand in hand, toward a bench dead center, between facing sections of bearded men and kapped women.

There, beside Lizbeth and Roman, Sara and Adam sat.

Four hymns and three sermons cited the responsibilities
of marriage and the sacred relationship between husband
and wife. Then the Bishop stood before them. "Adam
Zuckerman and Sara Lapp, if you are still minded the same,
you may now come forth."

Sara and Adam stepped before Bishop Weaver. Roman
and Lizbeth, as attendants, stepped behind them.

The Bishop opened his Bible. "Can you confess,
brother, that you accept this our sister as your wife?"

Tears filled Sara's eyes as she looked down at her hand,
small within Adam's huge callused one, a symbol she was
forever to be protected, someday perhaps, even cherished
. . . never to be lonely again. A moment often dreamed, yet
never expected.

A husband for Sara. A family.

"And you, Sara. . . ."

She started as if from a daydream, and paid strict attention, answering properly, vowing with her heart to care for Adam in adversity, affliction, sickness, weakness or faintheartedness. Adam . . . fainthearted?

"I wish you the blessings of God," the Bishop intoned. "For a good beginning, a steadfast middle time and strength until a blessed end. Amen."

Sara and Adam knelt before their high holy leader and he placed one of his hands on each of their heads. "Go forth in the name of the Lord. You are now man and wife."

Spinster Sara, a spinster no more.

Sara stood and accompanied her husband—her husband!—to their seat, as if she walked on a soft, sun-warm cloud, floating in a haze of joy and peacefulness.

Adam's feet felt leaden, almost too heavy to lift, as he tried to place one before the other for the unending walk back to their bench. A pall, like a thundercloud, hung heavy above him, pressing on his shoulders, weighing down even his heart. Though he could almost see a brighter horizon, far in the distance of his mind's eye, he refused to acknowledge it, because he feared it, though he did not know why.

Sara belonged to him now, not to the doctor, a new mommie for his girls, a helpmate for him. A mate. Adam stumbled and reached his seat sooner than expected, most humbly grateful for its firm support.

More hymns, another sermon, silent prayer. This was the longest marriage service ever.

When it finally ended, they made their way to the upper room, a dreadful custom, Adam thought, and wondered why he felt like a yearling in a spring meadow. On Sara's face, he saw a look of wonder as she turned to gaze at him, as if she were a butterfly set free, and he forgot all else. He forgot even to breathe.

Sara gazed into her husband's bright, shining eyes. Every bride waited for this moment, she thought, and no wonder. Though the upper room was nothing more than a room where an Amish bride and groom waited to officially and ceremoniously enter the celebration of their marriage; it was the place where they were closeted alone together for the very first time as husband and wife. It was a first opportunity for privacy, a kiss, a touch. Many a married woman blushed over what transpired in the upper room on her own wedding day, and many a maiden waited, with bated breath, as Sara was near to doing right now, for just such an experience.

Standing beside the open door, watching them, Roman winked. "I'll wait with Lizbeth at the top of the stairs for the signal to go down." He shut them inside with a chuckle and a click.

The Weavers' bedroom was plain, homey. Sunshine gilded the wedding quilt on the high feather bed. The colors in the quilt—cream, sky blue, forest green and deep wine—matched the flowers painted on the ewer and basin atop the dresser. Mrs. Weaver's "Number Five New Remington Sewing Machine," as she faithfully called it, sat open, a colorful spill of twill and percale quilt squares beside it. Above it, a purple sateen scissors-holder hung on the wall, beside a calendar depicting a bright Swiss mountain scene. Everything must have a use, and if every useful item was colorful, so much the better.

To calm the flutter in her breast, Sara examined the room's pristine beauty in great detail. Then she looked into Adam's eyes, deeper and wider, more open than ever, it seemed, and her heart returned to its buggy-careening pace.

I know you cannot love me, she thought, regarding the stillness in him. You love Abby, as should be. "I will take good care of Abby's girls," she whispered.

Adam raised a hand to her cheek. "Our girls." He barely made contact, yet his touch sizzled like water on a hot griddle.

Sara craved more and closer contact, and before she knew what she was doing, she touched his cheek too. And when he did not pull away, she let her fingers glide through his beard.

Adam's face was close, now, though she did not think that either of them had moved.

His hand at her back made her feel cherished for the first time ever. She touched her fingers to the curls at his nape. Sparks prickled along her spine, her limbs. Adam's groan seemed to come from deep in his throat, and with it Sara welcomed the power of a wife.

His lips were not cold and hard, as she expected, but soft, warm, and yielding, consuming her. It was his chest that was hard, his legs, and the strength of his arms sliding around her, pulling her closer. Sara sighed and opened her lips to his, coaxing, answering, seeking a luxury she could not name. She no longer stood on that cloud, but floated above it, Adam now the root and center of her world.

When they were closer than she thought possible, and she, pliant and bending in his embrace, he brought her into a sensuous new world, branding her with his touch. His stroke beneath her breast brought a blaze of heat, hardly bearable, yet deeply fulfilling.

Even lacking experience, Sara knew then that she wanted Adam in the purely physical, secretly intimate way a woman wanted her mate. And glory of glories, he wanted her in the same way. He was as hard as he had been during his baths, and she was warm, ready and open, in the way she had been at those times. But now was different. Now they were man and wife, sanctioned.

Tonight in Adam's big bed, Sara would know. She would know her husband and experience a woman's pain, the one that marched beside ultimate fulfillment.

With a groan that was almost a curse, Adam lay her down on the big bed, and she welcomed the support of the mattress beneath her almost as much as she welcomed his weight along her length. When he slid his hand up her leg, Sara became too heavy to float. Higher and higher he stroked, until he reached her center and learned her moist secret.

Sara had to turn from his probing look. The thrust of his hips, the stroke of his hand—there, where she'd never felt a touch before—heady and wondrous, almost fulfilling in itself, but not quite.

Not quite.

His kisses, on her face, her neck, her breasts, even through the bodice of her wedding dress, kept time with the pulse in her center . . . with the knock on the door.

Sara gasped.

Adam raised his head, swore. "Coming, damn it!"

Roman chuckled on the other side of the door. "Ya, I was afraid of that, but it's time to go downstairs." He laughed again.

Sara knew she should be changing into the black apron and kapp of a married woman, but Adam pulled her attention back to him. He looked straight at her and she at him. It was important, what had just passed between them. They both knew it, yet neither spoke.

Adam took her hand and slipped it into the broadfall flap of his trousers. Only his union suit stood between her and her husband's flesh. Shocked, almost as much by her daring touch as by his size and strength, Sara applied pressure to her grasp.

Adam did the same to her, and their moans merged in the long, slow way her body instinctively craved his.

"It's time to go down," Sara whispered. For the life of her, she could think of nothing else to say. No wonder married women blushed when the upper room was mentioned. She hoped the flames consuming her would cool before she reached the bottom of the stairs and had to face their wedding guests.

"Tonight," Adam said as he released her.

Sara nodded but dared to stroke him once more, and he cursed as he snatched her hand away.

"Ready?" Roman called through the door, not bothering to hide his amusement.

Adam stood and smacked the door a good one from the inside, making Roman roar with laughter. "This is the most fun I've ever had," Roman called. "Thanks for asking me to attend you." They heard his laughter fade as he moved away. "It's now or never," he yelled, likely from the top of the enclosed stairs. "You'd better come now."

Sara's giggle at his frustration turned Adam's mind, and he damn near smiled as he untied her white apron while she removed her kapp. Her neatly coifed hair made him itch to muss it, but he shook his head, denying himself, for now. He took her black apron out of her hands and dressed her, her smile at his attention touching him so deep inside, he ached.

Scrapper Sara, filled with enough passion to fight her community, bring a squalling infant into the world or do battle with a madman. Smiling Sara, with the kind of passion that could make a man her slave, the kind that would get him hard every time he looked at her, that would have her on her back and . . . ripe with chil—

Like a blow, the realization struck.

"Tonight," Sara whispered, taking his hand. "Ready?"

Warmth deserted Adam, the blood left his limbs, chilling him to his marrow, as together, they stepped from the upper room.

Their wedding celebration went by in a haze as he and Sara sat at the *Eck*, the wedding table. There, in the corner of the main room, the bride and groom and their attendants always sat before those who'd come to celebrate with them.

As usual, smiling made Adam uncomfortable, but he did as well as he could, because it was expected. Besides, it involved only his lips, not his heart. That, in fact, sat encased in ice. Adam shook his head at fate. A rare man had a wife who seemed to want her husband's touch, rather than bear it as a chore. Sara was a wife who might make her husband smile, without feeling sick about it. But such was not to be.

He'd best face facts. He had a new wife he . . . cared about . . . in a different way than he'd cared for his first. With Sara, his . . . fondness was almost of the spirit, if that were possible, and different from his need to protect his girls, though that was deep and fierce too.

He did not think he had ever cared for anyone in quite the same way he cared for Sara. Oh, he had cared for Abby as a husband should. And he cared for his girls in a life-giving way—his sister Emma, too, when she was small. It was fitting, he supposed, that he should deny his body for Sara's sake, in the way he turned from his girls for their sake, and in the way he had taken his father's "punishment" in Emma's place. But Sara. . . .

He would not put *her* through the danger of childbirth. He would never cause her harm. What had happened in the upper room had happened for the best. A warning. If they had come together for the first time tonight, he would not have had the sanity to consider the consequences.

Never had he expected Scrapper Sara to have such an effect on him, but he should have. How could he have forgotten . . . the baths?

Sara surprised him by touching his hand, to indicate a footed plate of swirled yellow glass, bearing a cake with icing daffodils. The cake had been baked by Roman's mother; the cake dish was the Bylers' wedding gift.

As if he occupied the body of someone else, Adam stood and accepted Mrs. Byler's good wishes for a long and fruitful marriage. Roman was taking her home now; his father had not been well enough to come and she was concerned. Roman would be back to continue his duties as groom's attendant. Lizbeth would remain, as bride's attendant, Roman said, in case Adam or Sara needed anything.

Adam noticed then that the married couples were leaving, while the young, unmarried members of the congregation were going out to the barn for a frolic. Lizbeth looked wistful, and Adam was not surprised when Sara sent her outside with her friends. Sara always saw people's needs, even those unspoken.

As bride and groom, he and Sara would not be able to leave until midnight at least. What was it now . . . nine, maybe ten o'clock? How many bridegrooms, he wondered, wanted to ambush a few energetic youngsters at about this time?

Just as well they had to stay. Tired was better than randy.

At nearly one in the morning, Adam and Sara, with Roman's help—The *English* had long since gone—gathered their girls from the beds upstairs and took them home.

"Most bridegrooms do not carry their sleeping children up to their beds on their wedding night," Adam grumbled, for the sole purpose of lessening the constriction in his chest, and elsewhere, and of putting off the inevitable. But it was past time for honesty.

After the children were settled, Sara, his new wife, came back downstairs and stood in the middle of the kitchen, much as she had done on the night of his first wife's death, an occasion he must remember now to remain strong. Sara even held the back of the same kitchen chair, though she had been less woman and more scrapper that night.

Wishing with all his heart that she were less of a woman now, Adam coughed and, with a shaking hand, picked up the lantern in the middle of the big oak table. "Here, use this to light your way upstairs. I don't need to see to find my room."

He wished he hadn't watched her so closely, because when she paled, something sharp stabbed him in the region of his missing heart.

"But I thought. . . ."

"What?" he said, turning toward his room, showing her his back.

"Tonight, you said. . . . Today when . . . when we. . . ."

Adam turned. Much as he dreaded the prospect of looking into her soulful eyes, he owed her the courtesy of plain speaking. "I am sorry, Sara. That was a mistake."

"No, Adam. I thought it was . . . that we were so—"

"Foolish. Foolish, we were . . . I was. This is a marriage to satisfy the Elders. We married in name only to fulfill the ordnung. Do not make more of it than it is."

Sara's back stiffened and before his eyes the woman who'd melted in his arms turned into a scrapper again. And though he could see pain hovering just beyond her anger, she made a good show of strength. "You don't need anyone, do you, Adam Zuckerman? Too strong for such nonsense, right? Well, I'll tell you what I think, big, mean, scary man. I think you're afraid. Afraid of a woman. Of me. That's what I think."

She almost lost it then, Adam saw, and prayed she would not. Scrapper Sara damn near cried as she turned and made for the stairs.

If she only knew that big, bad, Mad Adam Zuckerman wanted to howl louder than she did.

Chapter Seven

Too bossy to bed.

The litany ran through Sara's head as she climbed the stairs. It continued as she slipped off her married apron and wedding dress to reveal the breasts her husband had awakened, aching even now for his touch.

Too bossy to bed. Those words, along with her memory of their time in the upper room, haunted her as she slipped into her cold bed. Alone. Lonely.

Spinster Sara Lapp, a spinster no more, yet Sara Zuckerman, wife, mother, virgin still, curled into a ball, hugged herself tight and let her tears fall. Too bossy to bed.

When the cock crowed, Sara snuggled deeper into her dream man's arms, in the upper room, on the big bed where Adam had touched her in the way only a husband could.

She slipped back into unbuttoning his broadfalls, his union suit. Adam opened her dress, until they were both free of their clothes and . . . and. . . .

Katie tried to raise one of Sara's eyelids with tiny probing fingers. Down the hall, Baby Hannah wailed, likely hungry and wet, and near her ear, Pris whined.

Sara caught Katie's wayward finger and managed to open her eyes. "Does this mean it's morning?"

"Ya," Adam said from her doorway, sitting Sara straight up. "Short night, I know." He pointed his chin at the children as he raised a suspender over his shoulder and shrugged. "They don't seem to care. Come downstairs,

Pris, Katie. Give Sara a chance to wake up. Lizzie, go get the baby and bring her down.

"After you're ready," he said to Sara, "I'll go milk. While you dress, I'll start the stove."

"And this," Sara said as she stepped on an icy floor a minute later, seeking her robe against the chill, "this must be wedded bliss."

Married life turned out to be both better and worse than Sara expected.

She supposed she should deny her yearning, even to herself, but she wanted Adam's arms around her again. Who would have thought it? Certainly not her. She wanted his hands on her in more places than she'd known then— wicked, wicked thought.

Did a decent woman feel such things?

Not for the first time, Sara wished her mother had lived. She needed a woman's advice more now than when her first suitor had turned from her, more even than with her second and last.

A surprising part of her new life was her relationship with Adam, which had altered to one almost of friendship. The small changes that brought this about had begun on the morning of their first full day of marriage. Adam had been there when she awakened, a surprise she wasn't certain she liked then. But now. . . .

Just this morning, two married weeks later, she realized as she awakened, before even opening her eyes, that she awoke now with a feeling of hope . . . of anticipation.

As he had been that first morning, Adam was there, pulling up his suspenders and herding the children off her bed to give her a few minutes to compose herself and dress.

The first morning he'd been his sober self, but these

days, especially mornings, there seemed almost a tilt to his mouth, though on one side only, which gave her heart a bit of a skip every time she saw it. And though his near-smile was a weak one, it was an improvement, nonetheless. A "good-morning" to treasure.

Adam had begun to take on his own farm chores that last week before their hearing and wedding, not stopping for the noon meal, preferring to eat breakfast, skip dinner, and eat a large supper. That too had changed the first day of their marriage.

That noon he came in, sat at the table with them and said the prayer. He discussed all manner of topics, from the sheep he hated for a month after shearing to Roman's gossipy ways.

If one of the children spoke, he listened politely, though he rarely responded. But there had been a change in that too. Sara knew instinctively that for perhaps the first time in his life, Adam Zuckerman saw his children, was aware they existed, though he was not always pleased about it, which annoyed Sara no end. To complicate matters between the two of them, he seemed now to see her, the wife he'd been forced to marry, as most times a nuisance, and at others, a wonder. His contradictory reactions, the unexpected shift from one to the other, was driving her daft.

If she wasn't careful, he'd make her "mad" as him.

A few days ago, when he'd been his old growling self at dinner, she'd dared ask why he married her. "Not to keep from being shunned," she said. "I think I know you better than that already." And not for love, she thought, wishing she weren't so certain.

"For the children," he replied simply. "We both saw they wanted you. Needed you. The same reason you married me," he said. "For them."

99

"For them," she whispered now as she watched them screaming and chasing each other, having a wild, spring-lamb romp, despite the carpet of snow and the crisp in the air. They ran under flapping dresses, the colors of spring meadows and blue spruce, morning-glories and corn-flowers, asters and eggplants.

They wore the new frocks she'd made last week in a pur-plish wool leaning so near to red, Sara expected to be chas-tised by the Bishop any day. What a sight. Lines of blazing color against white snow. Three little girls running hither and yon, their black billowing capes flying behind them, dresses peeking out in bright defiance.

Sitting in her rocker by the window, Sara snuggled her face into Hannah's belly. Her kapp got snatched by a pudgy hand, the baby's gasping gurgle so much like a giggle, Sara laughed. Her happiness bubbled forth then, unexpected, wild, and stopping Adam in his tracks.

"It's not dinner time yet," Sara said, her heart thumping when she saw his look. Was he frowning because dinner wasn't ready or because she had been laughing? Or was her heart racing simply from the sight of the man she felt the need to watch at every turn?

Large as he was, Adam Zuckerman looked like a lad tying empty tins to a cat's tail, caught. "Mild out there," he said, turning her thoughts. "The girls like it."

So, he'd noticed them playing.

"Have to go up to the Millersburg buggy factory. Only place I can get a wheel for the market wagon. Want to come?" Adam reddened. "All of you?"

Excitement beat in Sara's breast, but Adam stiffened his spine, as if bracing himself for a blow. Sara was troubled by the image, but anticipation filled her nevertheless. "I think that would be fun," she said, easing the furrow in his brow.

"Fun," he said, testing the word.

What did fun mean to a man like Adam Zuckerman? Had he ever experienced it? Could a woman teach a man . . . a madman . . . to have fun? Perhaps it was time for a wife to try. "When do you want to leave?"

"When you're ready," he said. "Better get them in to . . . you know."

Sara laughed again. Something had shifted in this house and it was big and burly and made lots of noise. Sara would wager all her worldly possessions that Adam had never, ever, paid attention to the potty habits of his daughters.

Ultimately, making the girls . . . you know . . . before they left, mattered not at all, because Katie was so excited by the outing, they had to stop to go to the bushes a dozen times before they reached Berlin, one town over, with thrice as far still to go.

Between stops, the sights they saw along the way had all three girls asking questions, Sara answering them all. They must never have left the farm before, except, perhaps, when she took them to her house.

At the buggy factory in Millersburg, they each got a licorice stick from the owner, which made their mouths black and comical. Sara trying to wash them off with snow caused Pris to screech and Katie to imitate her with an exaggerated, unholy howl. The factory workers, smoking their noon pipes outside, laughed at the show, and the more they did, the louder Katie got.

Lizzie was clearly mortified and tried to shush her sister.

Adam's gaze shifted from the men, to his daughters, and back, with a look akin to wonder on his face, until Sara began to get them into the buggy. There, she parceled out bread and cheese, but only she and Adam were hungry. They stopped at Escher's Mercantile, a general store that sold everything imaginable. Sara was awed, but the girls. . . .

From seeders and corn shellers to udder balm and lamp wicks, they picked up everything and asked what it was. And while Sara rocked baby Hannah in her arms and made sure they did not touch anything dangerous, Adam answered all their questions.

As he did, Sara was struck by two things. Adam displayed an incredible patience in explaining each item to the girls, though he never smiled nor did he touch them. He even bent on his haunches at one point so Pris could examine a sugaring spout. What also struck her was the length of time that passed between each question and Adam's answer. At first, Sara was certain he would remain silent—he often ignored the girls' questions—but today he answered, eventually, speaking with purpose and a complete knowledge of the subject, even keeping the age of his audience in mind.

Adam Zuckerman, she realized then, was not so much cold and aloof, he was . . . contemplative. He, very simply, considered the subject, in order to give a proper and concise response. It was an enlightening and amazing discovery.

Sara could barely breathe, their outing was going so well, so easily, like any normal family trip to the store might . . . until Katie picked up a pair of white cotton bloomers, unfolding them and displaying them like a flag. "What's this?"

Adam regarded Sara, turned the color of sugar beets, and turned away as fast. Then he looked to the heavens. Sara thought he might be praying for deliverance and her giggle rushed up and out before she could check it.

Adam regarded her again, suspicious of the sound, somehow sure it came from her. He looked back at Katie and nodded. "They're for mommies. Put them back now."

Katie did and Sara breathed easier, until Lizzie tugged Adam's jacket. "I want to buy them for Sara."

She and Adam looked at each other then. She knew she stared wide-eyed with dismay, but she saw something new in Adam's expression . . . a sparkle in his eyes, a deeper curve, even, in that near-smile of his. It was enough to make her giddy. Considering the cause, she put her unsteady hand on Lizzie's shoulder. "Thank you, baby, but I don't need—"

"Put them in the bag," Adam told Lizzie.

"Oh," Sara squeaked, "but I don't—"

"In the bag," he said again, warning her that his decision was made. "Lizzie wants them for you. You shall have them."

Stubborn, Sara thought, more stubborn than her, maybe.

He gave her his back, saying the subject was closed. And she followed him into the next aisle . . . where Lizzie was holding a breast pump, which even Jordan had been embarrassed to explain to Sara. "What's this for, Datt?"

And that was the end of Adam's patience and their excursion. "Time to go," he said fishing money from his pocket. "Sara, get them into the buggy."

And Sara thought that perhaps he was more resolute than he was stubborn, and that there were times, like these, that such a thing might be considered good rather than bad.

The girls slept all the way home.

Snow muffled the sound of the horses' hooves, forming a harmony that blended with the jolting movement of the carriage. "We had a wonderful day," Sara said after a while, her words making mist with her breath.

A sound escaped Adam that might have been a strangled

groan. "I never talked to them before," he said, speeding Sara's heart with the admission, making her pray he wasn't sorry he'd done it. "Pris is like Abby," he added after a while. "She whines because she wants something I cannot give her."

Oh, Lord, and what did that mean? And why did the words turn her both prickly cold and panicky warm at the same time? Sara dared not speak, in fear of breaking the spell his words wrought, words freely given, a rare treat.

"You're good for her, for them," he said. "You've got something Abby never had."

Sara was afraid of the answer, but she had to ask the question. "What do I have that Abby lacked?"

Adam was quiet so long, Sara thought he wouldn't answer; then she realized he was considering his answer, as he had in the store. From now on, she was going to give him time before losing her temper or walking away in frustration.

"What did Abby lack that I have?" she repeated after a while.

He looked full at her then, letting that near-smile of his grow, along with an eye-sparkle that made her heart jump. "Bloomers?" he suggested.

That night, he came into her bedroom.

She had just donned her nightgown and let down her hair. And as she stood, surprised and unsure, he examined her, head to foot. "Bare feet," he said. "Bad as the girls. Where are your socks?"

Struck dumb, Sara could only point to the open drawer on her dresser. He picked up a pair and motioned her to the bed. "Sit." When she did, he unrolled her socks and made to put them on her.

"No, I—Don't."

So he nodded and handed her the socks, sitting back on his haunches to wait while she put them on.

She needed to raise her leg to do so, but he was down there on the floor, where he could see, and she was only wearing her nightgown, after all. Frustrated, she threw her socks at his head. "Just do it."

Adam raised a brow and complied.

Funny how such strong hands could feel so soft sliding along her ankle.

"Get in," he said. "Cold tonight."

Sara slid under her blankets thinking, cold or not, there must be a fire around somewhere. She was sweating, and she couldn't decide which way to settle. Sit up? Lie back? Lie facing him?

She sighed and lay on her back, her hands clasped over the quilt, feeling stupid, useless, as if he had the upper hand, towering over her as he was, a feeling she disliked a great deal.

Adam tried to sit beside her on the bed, nudging her legs over to give him room. He stroked one of her fingers, turned the hand over to examine her palm and trace her calluses.

His face was serene, kind even; maybe not as much sadness rested deep in his eyes as she'd glimpsed hiding there in the past. His beard had been trimmed that morning but she liked it shaggy as well, maybe more so. There was a strength about him, a largeness, bending over her as he was, those wide shoulders of his capable of hefting huge sacks of grain or bales of hay. He could carry his girls on his shoulders if he wanted. Would he ever want so simple a joy?

He could carry her. Where would he carry her? Up the stairs? To her bed. She was in her bed. He was here with her.

Sara thought she knew exactly how he must have felt

when she gave him his baths. There were parts of her that reacted so physically to the soft stroke of his hand, she'd be standing the sheet up too, if she had the right parts. As things were, she knew she was ready, eager to cooperate with whatever he might offer.

Should she offer? Did wives do such things, seduce their own husbands? Better than seducing other women's husbands, she supposed, swallowing a bubble of laughter.

Despite her determination not to allow it, Sara's gaze wandered to the flap of his trousers, and she was sorry, because he was as ready as her.

She looked to see if he'd noticed her perusal, but he was too busy watching where her breasts pointed her gown. "Cold," she said to excuse her embarrassment.

"I don't think so." His voice was ragged, his gaze directed there, where he reached to touch one aching peak, almost as if his hand weighed too much to do anything else.

Sara arched, reaching too, and met that hand sooner than he expected. A flick of his fingers, a rasp at the nubbin and Sara could feel herself moisten in anticipation.

Adam's hand trembled, but he continued.

Sara grasped the bedclothes and closed her eyes while he teased her through her nightgown. Both hands now, touching, molding, lifting each breast toward. . . .

Adam leaned over and took her nipple into his mouth despite her gown, and Sara almost came undone. Stretching out beside her, he suckled hard, wetting her gown, pulling delicious shivers from her, with his lips and tongue.

Streams of pleasure shot from the sight of his torture to her throbbing womb. She wanted him there, inside her, filling that empty place, that place meant for him alone.

If she could just touch the heat of him.

Sara rolled against him to get closer, close enough to

touch . . . and knocked him to the floor.

Adam said a word Sara didn't know and sat up, then he hung his arms off his raised knees while he took several deep, unsteady breaths.

Sara was having trouble getting air herself, and she wanted badly to cry.

A sound escaped Adam, strangled again, hoarse. She thought for a minute he was crying, until she realized it was laughter of a sort, hard and rusty. He seemed as surprised by it as her. Mad Adam Zuckerman was laughing, even if the sound did have an edge of hysteria to it.

Sara burst into tears.

That stopped him. He jumped up and took her into his arms to soothe her and rub her back. "Don't cry. It'll go away. The want will pass. It always does."

Sara shoved him. He was torturing her, putting his arms around her while he was telling her to let the yearning go. She rose to her knees and poked his immovable chest. "Adam Zuckerman, you have to be the stupidest man God ever created."

He sobered. "So my father said."

Sara realized, barely in time, that pointing out her frustration over his unwillingness to make her his wife in truth, might not be in the best interest of a successful seduction. She sat back on her feet. "I was crying because I was happy."

"Well, there you go. I am stupid, 'cause I have no idea what the devil you're talking about."

"I never saw you laugh. Abby said you never . . . but you just did. Don't you see? You laughed today. You talked to the girls, instead of ignoring them. Did you see their faces?"

Adam lowered his head. "I saw their faces. And just now, in that bed, I saw yours." He touched her cheek, tucked a strand of her hair behind her ear. "Ah Sara, don't you see, I'm no good for any of you."

"Let us be the judge of that."

He didn't say anything to that, considering his answer again, no doubt. Best she not give him too much time. She lay back and yawned. "I'm tired." She scooted over to the far side of her bed and turned to face him, patting the empty side. "Get in and let's get some sleep. It's been a long day." She pretended indifference, as if it were easy for her to make such an offer, when it was not, and waited for him to make the next move.

Yearning she saw on his face. Need. Want. Despair. "It's not going to happen, Sara. You and I will never, ever, share a bed. And that is the way it has to be."

"Then why did you come in here tonight?"

"Because I'm an idiot, but don't worry, I won't make the same mistake again."

And he didn't, not even the next morning or the morning after that.

A week passed, during which he avoided her room altogether, morning, night and in between. They were back to where they began. Adam Zuckerman was madder and more remote than ever, and Sara was almost as bad.

February turned into the coldest Ohio had seen in recent memory, keeping children housebound and adults ready to scream . . . until two strangers entered their midst.

Two women traveling alone spent a day going door to door looking for the Amishwoman who delivered babies. The Amish kept their mouths shut around strangers, so the search was anything but easy, but everyone wanted to know who would be looking for Sara, when she hadn't a soul in the world.

When Sara opened her kitchen door, two women stood on her stoop, wearing odd brown outdoor bonnets and capes, while their buggy in the drive, Sara noted with shock, was as yellow and bright as the summer sun.

"Are you Amish?" Sara's thoughtless question embarrassed her. "Sorry. Can I help you?"

The older of the women nodded. "Indiana Amish, we are, and looking for the Amishwoman who delivers babies, Sara Zuckerman. But no one seems to know her."

Sara looked at the younger of the two, but saw no sign of pregnancy. "I am Sara Zuckerman. Come inside, please?" She ushered them into her kitchen and shut the door. "Welcome. Can I take your capes and bonnets? The fire will warm you."

Silently, they handed her their outer wear. Their indoor kapps were gray and gathered rather than pleated, their dresses and apron bodices boxy, not vee-shaped, all in shades of grays and browns. Odd about the bright buggy, given all that. "Tea?" Sara offered, indicating the chairs at her kitchen table.

The younger of the women nodded and sat. The older followed her lead.

"Is there something I can do for you?" Sara asked again as she put honey jumbles and crabapple tarts in a plate, but neither answered. The younger looked toward the older woman to respond, but the elder seemed unready, or unwilling, to speak.

Sara brought the kettle and tea strainer to pour.

The older woman smiled and nodded. "We hear you deliver babies and make the Elders mad doing it." The woman's smile, her admiration perhaps, made Sara want to hug her. She smiled, instead. "I am afraid so."

"Mercy Bachman told us," the elder of the two said,

which started them talking about Sara's first patient and her sweet little girl. "Mercy is expecting again," the elder stranger said. "They are planning to return, so you can deliver it."

Sara was flattered and failed to hide her pleasure. "I cannot wait to see her again, but Indiana to Ohio is a long way to come to give birth."

"Mercy waited for years for one living child; she is willing to come a good distance for another. They have even talked about moving here to be near you permanently."

Sara was less attuned to the compliment this time, than to the quiet, young girl, a smile nearly, but not quite, present, so like . . . Adam's. "Have we met before?" Sara asked.

"Ach, foolish me," the older woman said. "I am Lena Zuckerman and this is my daughter Emma. I believe your Adam is my son."

Chapter Eight

Despite the impossibility, Sara's legs trembled as she lowered herself to a chair. "That cannot be."

The woman made to speak, but nap time was suddenly and loudly over and three refreshed and lively little girls flowed into the room, Lizzie carrying Hannah.

"Lena, Emma. Here are . . . my children." She'd almost called them her husband's children, but they were hers now too, and they needed to know she was pleased to claim them. Sara tried to introduce each child by name, but Lena began weeping into her handkerchief.

Emma rose to pat her mother's back and rest her cheek on the woman's head. Sara did not know what to make of them, and neither did the children. Well, except for Katie, who crawled into the woman's lap, bringing a fresh supply of tears. "My's Katie, and my's five," the three-year-old said, holding up two fingers.

Before Sara had a chance to lift Katie off the woman's lap, Adam came in from the barn and hung his hat and coat on the pegs by the door. Rubbing the cold from his hands, he turned, saw the woman and lost the light in his eyes.

His bad leg buckled.

Cursing, half in German, half in Penn Dutch, he regained his balance and, like the night Abby died, he denied whatever emotion gripped him. His gaze riveted upon the older woman, his expression hardened to an uncaring mask. "You are supposed to be dead!"

111

Lena seemed at first frightened, but like Adam, she masked it well. Emma began to scream, and Katie scooted off Lena's lap as the woman rose to calm a daughter who acted as if Adam might eat her alive.

To soothe her, Lena spoke Emma's name over and over, like a song.

"*Mein Gott,* you look just like him," Lena said, regarding Adam from beside her fretting daughter.

"Emma?" Adam's expression closed, but not before he revealed more hope than Sara had ever seen in him. "Little Emma?" He stepped eagerly forward but Emma screamed again, backed away, gaining speed as she went. Then she turned and ran screaming from the kitchen. She dashed through the best room and out the front door.

They could hear her scream fading, as she got farther away.

Adam swore again, in English this time, and the woman scolded him. His laugh was harsh, bitter. "It's thirty years too late. Don't start acting like a mother now, old woman."

Lena really was Adam's mother? How could someone mistake such a thing as a mother's death?

Adam ran out the door as well, no coat or hat, to chase a young woman who shared his inability to smile.

Sara rose, looking to Lena for guidance. "Should I go after them?"

Lena shook her head. "She'll slow down soon enough and he'll catch her, though I can't imagine how he'll—" She stopped speaking, shook her head and turned to the children. "*Kum,*" she said to Lizzie, as if there were no point in continuing what she'd begun. "*Kum, buss grossmutter.*"

The children had a grandmother. A dizzying realization struck Sara; Adam had not needed her to care for the girls. He had not needed to marry her. Except that it was too late to send her away. Marriage was forever. Relief sat her down, her trembling limbs betraying her.

If the woman had come a few weeks sooner. . . . "Oh God."

Lizzie kissed her grandmother as directed. Each of the girls did; then Lizzie placed Hannah in the emotional woman's arms. After Lena kissed Hannah's brow about a dozen times, and cooed and sighed over her, she regarded Sara over Hannah's head. "With you and Adam, ve come to liff," she said. "With my *grossbabies,* ya?"

At the thought of them all living together, Sara's eyes filled, but Lena misunderstood, and rose. "Ve go. Ve go."

"No," Sara said, taking the woman's arm and sitting her back down. "I was . . . It's been a long time since . . . I haven't had a moth—a family for a long time. I'm . . . I—" Sara raised the skirt of her apron to wipe her eyes. "Happy tears," she said on a watery laugh. "A big family. I always wanted a big family."

After a hug, she led Lena, still carrying Hannah, into the best room, toward the window, where they stood side by side staring out at the barren winter landscape for signs of Emma and Adam.

Brows furrowed with worry, Lena patted Hannah's back, while Sara prayed she was correct and Adam would find his sister. They remained there until dusk bruised the horizon and Hannah began to cry.

Sara started supper and fed Hannah. Her new mother-in-law tried to help, but Sara caught her staring out the kitchen window, a fork in her hand, while the frying chicken turned a rusty brown. After she saved supper, Sara walked up behind Lena and touched her arm. "Adam will bring Emma back."

The woman nodded. "I fear he . . . I should have gone.

Emma does not like . . . she is afraid all the time of—"

"She is afraid of me!" Adam shouted, his words tossed at his mother like an accusation.

How could he? Sara thought. How could anyone be angry at a mother who had as good as returned from the dead? Sara was more troubled by this "mad" turn of Adam's than any of the others.

"How can she be afraid of me, after everything?" Adam shook his head, denying the possibility. "I had to get Roman to come and help, but she screamed almost as much when he got near her. Why?" He seemed to be asking himself the question.

To Sara's surprise and relief, it was Roman's mother who tenderly helped an unsteady Emma into the kitchen, answering the question Sara had wanted answered since Adam came back: Where was Emma?

Emma's dress was torn and muddy, her kapp was missing, and her wild hair almost hid her dirty face. Like a madwoman, Emma looked. Did madness run in the family?

As had been the case since they arrived, Adam directed his ire toward his mother. "Do you care to explain this foolishness?" he demanded, too harsh, too brutal, even for him.

Lena looked down at her hands. "It is men." She spoke barely above a whisper, then she raised her head and squared her fragile shoulders. "All men. My Emma is afraid of men."

"No!" Adam reared back as if he'd been struck, the same way he'd reacted when Sara said he was killing Abby, God forgive her. "That cannot be," he said. "I made sure. I made certain he never got near enough t—" Adam stopped, halted by his own words, and looked around, surprised by his audience. He wasn't pleased they heard what he said to his mother, but Sara wished he had finished his thought.

He wiped his brow with the sleeve of his shirt. "I fetched Roman when I saw that Emma was afraid of me. But she was afraid of him too, which made no sense."

And why, Sara wondered, would it make sense for her to be afraid of Adam and not of Roman?

Jordan, carrying his black leather bag, arrived to further splinter Sara's chaotic thoughts. "What are you doing here?" she asked. "I thought you were in Philadelphia."

"I saw the Coblentz carriage nearly run the girl down from the top of the hill." He shook his head, as though he didn't understand. "Who is she? She took a hard fall. I thought I should examine her to make certain she isn't hurt badly."

Adam's laugh revealed frustration, but it conveyed a thread of satisfaction as well. He crossed his arms and leaned against the Hoosier cabinet. "Emma will not let you near her. Sara will take care of her."

Jordan looked to Sara for answers, but she had none to give. Instead, she introduced Lena and Emma to Jordan, Roman and Mrs. Byler.

Emma said nothing; she kept her gaze on Hannah, sleeping in Lizzie's arms, as if the sight of the babe soothed her.

Roman and his mother said their goodbyes and left.

"Jordan is our local doctor, Mrs. Zuckerman." Sara handed Lena the plates to put on the table, giving them both something to do. "He wants to make certain Emma is well."

"Adam is right," Lena said. "Emma will not let him near her."

Thirty years, and his mother finally speaks up, Adam thought, and sides with him, no less. A day of miracles. Wonder fled, however, when he saw The *English* touch

Sara's hand. Adam uncrossed his arms and stood straight.

"Sara," The *English* said.

Her name on the doctor's lips scraped Adam's raw nerves. Sara belonged to him, damn it.

"Take Emma to undress and lie down, then I'll take a look at her," The *English* directed, ignoring their warnings, daring to order Sara in her own house.

Adam's fists relaxed as Sara looked to him, her husband, as should be, for direction. Which room should she put his sister in, she asked with a look, and should she do what The *English* wanted?

"Put her in the big room upstairs," Adam said, watching Sara's eyes widen in surprise before she nodded and took Emma's arm, urging her toward the stairs and up, her gentle voice sweet and coaxing, The blasted *English* right behind them.

After they were gone, Adam sent the girls into the best room to play, and he regarded the old woman who'd once been young, beautiful and dear . . . then dead to him since almost forever. "Why did you leave?" he asked, finally.

"Because I thought I had found you."

"No," he snapped. "Back then. Thirty years ago."

"Leave? I did not."

"You did! I saw you climb into that buggy and drive away!" She would never know how he had cried because she left him behind. She would never know that his tears, worse when he'd been told they were dead, were less because his mother and sister were beyond reach—his mother had always been—but more because they had been delivered, and he had not been delivered with them.

"I left to care for my sister who was ill, dying," said the woman who gave him his sorry life, then abandoned him to it. "He knew," she added, the word "he" carrying a meaning both understood. He, being her husband, Adam's father—Satan.

Adam shook his head, the pain in his chest like to fell him. Of course he knew, of course. Why had Adam never realized it? Because he was five years old when it happened, that's why.

"When we came back, after she died, you were gone," Lena said. "No one knew where."

So, Aunt Pris had died. No wonder she had not come for him. The woman he had hated for not taking him to raise had died and the woman he had hated for abandoning him had lived. Adam shook his head at fate. Did his mother know what happened to him; did she care? He went to the stove and saw the chicken cooling. "He said you died, you and Emma. Carriage accident."

Tired now, older even than when he first saw her standing here in his own kitchen, his mother nodded and wilted. "I never expected it, even from him."

"You should have," Adam said, setting a platter of chicken firmly on the table, shaming his red-faced mother into jumping up and finishing, while she motioned for him to sit.

But Adam could not; he could not stop moving. He had to walk—despite the pain in his leg—or explode. "You should have expected anything from him," he bit out. "Anything."

His mother nodded but said nothing, her gaze pleading as she approached him.

He raised his hand to stop her. "You left a five-year-old boy with that—"

"You were strong. I thought—"

"Go away," he ordered, closer to her, of a sudden, than he cared to be. "When she is better. . . ." He pointed toward the ceiling, to where his sister rested upstairs. "You go." He spoke the last words as though tasting something bitter.

"She will never be better, and there is nowhere for us to go. I sold everything to come here. We have nothing but our clothes and a wrong-colored buggy." Her attempt to lighten the mood failed. Badly.

Adam was more upset than he had remembered being since before his father's death. No, frustrated and . . . furious enough to . . . to smash something . . . someone, except the man responsible was already dead. This woman who bore him was a pawn, a puppet, and damn, he almost hated her for it.

Adam stepped close to his mother then, closer than he thought he could bear. He watched her eyes and spoke low, so only she could hear. "Whatever happens, old woman, you keep your mouth shut. You don't tell Sara anything about life back then, you hear me? You do and you will be out so fast, you will not have time to blink. I will send you back myself, come to that, whatever the cost."

She nodded her agreement, all the while keeping her eyes on his face.

"My's hungry, Datt. Pris too," Katie said, bright as an English button, wringing her purple skirt, standing like a waif at the entrance to the best room.

"Soon Katiebug. Go play with your sisters till I call." He turned back to his mother. "How did you find me?" Why not try sooner? he wanted to ask. Years and years sooner.

"Mercy Bachman, from our district, gave birth when she was here visiting kin. Your Sara delivered her baby girl."

His Sara. Adam shook his head, and sighed. One baby she delivers, and that brings his mother back. Where had Sara been twenty-five years ago?

"Adam, you must know I looked for you. I looked for years," she said. "I questioned anyone who'd been on a visit, on any trip, short or long."

This was his mother, Adam kept telling himself as he stared at her, her redeeming words floating in the air around him. His mother. Alive. Not dead. Gray of hair and lined of face, but alive and pleading with him to understand. He should be glad she wasn't dead, but it only made him feel thrown away. A piece of garbage. An ugly knot of gristle off an inferior cut of beef. Worthless.

Adam knew his gaze must be cold. He watched her as she poured out a jumble of words amounting to a plea for understanding. But understanding, forgiveness, would not come.

Niceties of feeling had been beaten out of him long ago.

Still, he supposed he should try. He would try.

He attempted to focus on her words.

"I used to save the egg money," she said. "Until I could afford to take a train, to a different town each time, to look for you, but you had vanished."

Into hell, Adam thought. The very fiery bowels of it, where gristle like him writhed and crisped and disappeared altogether.

Even in his numbed mind, he knew he could not remain there, pretending he cared what she had to say. Adam shook himself, refusing to wallow in the bone-deep pain crushing him. But Emma, his little Emma. . . . "What about her?" he shouted. "She is my sister, for God's sake, and she cannot even bear the sight of me!"

Upstairs, Sara washed the raw, bloody cuts and scrapes on Emma's hands and arms, the gash on her forehead the worst. She helped the girl undress and got her into one of her own nightgowns, since Emma's things had not yet been brought from the yellow buggy.

Emma answered none of Sara's questions, so Sara spoke in a continuous, soothing tone, the way Lena did. "My marriage makes us family," she said. "I have always wanted a big family."

Emma gave her a sweet smile and fingered the pleats on Sara's kapp. Sara took it off and gave it to her to look at.

"Doctor Jordan wants to look over those cuts," Sara said, but the girl's breathing changed and her gaze began to dart frantically about the room, a cornered animal seeking escape. When she saw none, she threw Sara's kapp against the far wall. Frustration? Refusal? Fear?

"Hush, hush now," Sara said, stroking Emma's rich brown curls. "You have hair just like Lizzie, and Baby Hannah, too, I think."

Emma smiled, calm once again.

Sara pulled down the quilt on the bed. "Lie down and rest for a while. I'll sit with you, shall I, till you sleep?" Sara brought the covers to Emma's shoulders. Sweet and trusting, the girl seemed—though not of men, of course. "That's a dear. Just close your eyes."

When Jordan entered the room, he seemed arrested by the sight of Emma in the bed. "My God, she looks like an angel."

Sara supposed he was right. Clean and sweet, hair brushed, curls fanned on the pillow, Emma no longer seemed a madwoman. But an angel? "She tossed my cap over there in the corner, when I said you wanted to examine her. Best do it now while she sleeps. The angel has a temper."

Jordan nodded. "Right." Then he noticed Sara's dresses hanging on the pegs, and he paused, caught by the sight.

Sara felt her face warm. He knew they were hers by the colors; Abby had favored black. And he knew, now, that Adam slept downstairs. "This is your room." His statement carried pity, as did his look, and Sara was too humiliated to respond.

After an uncomfortable minute, he sighed. "Your choice, Sara? If so, you had the right, under the circumstances."

Her choice. She looked at the floor. Yes, Jordan was like a brother, and they had been through many embarrassing lessons together, but to reveal that her husband did not want her, even to a friend as close as him, seemed. . . .

Jordan touched her cheek. "Not your choice, I think, and you do not know how to change the situation, do you?"

Sara shook her head. "How do I?"

Her friend's chuckle was low, soothing. "I may have needed to teach you to deliver babies, and even, academically, how they get to where they have to be delivered, but I do not think you need me to teach you how to make a man want you in his bed."

Adam's grip on Jordan's collar cut his words and the air through his windpipe.

Sara tried to pull them apart. "Adam," she whispered furiously. "Adam, let him go!"

"Where is your kapp?" her husband shouted, waking Emma, making her scream.

Adam cussed again—another new word, he used—and let the doctor go.

Jordan cussed him back, with a string of words that brought a glimmer of respect to her husband's look. Then Adam regarded Emma, ordering her, above her screams, to calm down, but his sister only scooted farther up the headboard, sobbing.

Jordan grabbed Adam by his shirt, stopping him, cutting

a little of his air, and glad of it, Sara thought. "Jordan. Adam. Stop," she ordered. "Go away, both of you. You're acting like children, and scaring Emma to death."

Jordan released his grip. "She's right. We *are* scaring her. But, Adam, you scare her worse than anybody. I can see that, even if you're too stubborn to admit it. Step aside now."

Adam did, taking Sara with him as far as the doorway. At first he clutched her arm firmly, but his grip eased, then he slipped his arm around her waist.

Deciding that was a fine place for it to be, Sara did not move away.

Jordan rubbed his throat, threw a piercing look at Adam and turned back to Emma. Before their eyes, almost unaware that Sara and Adam were watching, Jordan became the gentle doctor who dealt so well with a woman in labor. With flowery English words, he coaxed Emma to stop crying, to take a deep breath.

For a while, he spoke nonsense, about the valley, her pretty hair and yellow buggy, baby Hannah and her sisters. Speaking the same soft, coaxing way he calmed a wailing newborn, Jordan showed Emma everything in his black doctor's bag. He even explained what most of it was for.

After a while, Emma was so interested, she leaned closer. Jordan handed her the device he used to listen to his patients' hearts and had her listen to his. She was awestruck and refused to give the device back when he asked for it.

"Let me listen to yours, now," Jordan said, but Emma only shook her head. He coaxed her to sit on the edge of the bed. "Emma, sweet, give that to me and let me hear your heart the way you heard mine."

When Emma handed over the stethoscope, Sara felt Adam's arm around her stiffen.

Jordan listened to Emma's heart and gave her a delighted smile, like the one she'd given him, making her giggle.

"Sara," Jordan said, his voice still calm. "There is blood on her hem. I think her leg is bleeding. I want you to come and raise her nightgown."

When Sara knelt by Jordan, he kissed her cheek, which pulled Adam sharply back into the room, and stiffened Emma's demeanor.

Jordan smiled, though Sara could tell he was annoyed. "Emma needs to see that Sara is not afraid of me," he told Adam, obviously working to keep his voice calm.

"She is not," Adam said, more in accusation than answer.

Sara hugged Jordan, making him grin. "Laying it on thick," he whispered close to her cheek before he kissed her again. "For whose benefit?"

Sara winked in reply.

Jordan chuckled. "Raise her gown."

Jordan applied an ointment to Emma's bloody knees while he talked to her about stitching a quilt. "For now, I'll just put this salve on that gash on your forehead. But I might need to stitch it like a quilt tomorrow. We will watch and see."

Adam snorted.

Emma swallowed the drink Jordan fixed her, then he and Sara tucked her in. She drifted right off.

"That's it for now," Jordan said, turning to Adam. "She should not travel anytime soon."

"They are staying," Adam said. "For now." He went farther into the room and took Sara's dresses off the pegs. "Get the rest of your things," he told her as he left.

Jordan smiled at Sara's wistful sigh. "Want to come home with me?"

"Sara?" Adam called, from not too far distant, a note of warning in his voice. "Come."

Sara collected her few personal items and found her husband waiting for her in the hall. She expected to move in with Lizzie and Katie, and squeeze into their tiny bed, like three sausages in one skin, but Adam made for the stairs.

"Where are you going with my dresses?" she asked, following.

Sara was shocked to see him step into his own room and hang her dresses on the pegs beside his Sunday suit. Sara swallowed the lump in her throat. Tears came to her eyes. If marriage had a picture, this would be it.

For the first time since the upper room, her marriage seemed real.

Adam examined her expression but said nothing. He took her things from her hands and made room for them beside his. "This," he said, still furious, slapping his mattress, "this will be your bed from now on. Our bed." He stepped forward, grasped her arms and hauled her against him. "It will be me, not that fancy *English,* who will teach you whatever it is you think you need to know about a man's bed."

What? Oh my Lord, he had heard her and Jordan talking, but obviously not everything. Sara might explain, if she were not so delighted with the result. "You will teach me, Adam, what I need to know about the marriage bed?"

Though he paled, he examined her, head to toe, touching her lips in a kiss that began as a test of textures but deepened to passion, wonderful, but when she put her arms up around his neck, he cursed and stepped back.

Sara was frustrated, though he continued to hold her at arm's length, as though he were dizzy and in need of an anchor. After a minute of long, deep breaths, he frowned.

"Damn it, Sara, you do not need such a lesson."

Perhaps she needed no lessons, Sara thought, her mind awash with possibilities as she followed her rigid-backed husband into the kitchen, but one of them certainly did. She smiled, her heart aflutter. Yes, during the long nights ahead, while she and her husband shared a bed, one of them had some lessons coming.

This must be exactly how Eve felt in the Garden of Eden.

Chapter Nine

Sara followed Adam into the kitchen, her happiness coming in waves, more certain of her standing as a wife now than she had been since her wedding.

Her place as Adam's wife was only part of her joy. She had always dreamed of a big family. Spinster Sara, a wife, a mother, a daughter-in-law, a sister. However had she come to deserve such happiness?

In the kitchen, Adam's mother was telling her wide-eyed granddaughters a story while they ate, though it was Lena they gave their attention to, not their food. The story was about a rabbit who had begun its tiny life in a hole in Lena's garden.

Sunnybunny had refused to go out and discover the rest of the world, like his sisters and brothers had done. He had stayed, instead, to live off Lena's summer vegetables, for longer than Lena cared to admit. So Sunnybunny ended up becoming Emma's pet, because Lena could not find it in her heart to chase the small rabbit away.

Katie asked Adam to help her catch a rabbit of her own, taking his answering growl in stride and shrugging her shoulders. Then she charmed her *grossmommie* into giving her another slice of vanilla-peach kuchen.

Adam decided against sitting and went to the window. He watched the snow, hating the way he had responded to Katie. His mother would think he was like his father, which of course he was, but not for the same reason, damn it. And he refused to explain himself, especially when it was her story set Katie off in the first place. He scrubbed his face with his hands, granting that she had likely not intended to put such foolishness into Katie's head.

When he turned to make amends, whatever he tripped over squealed like a piglet.

"Sunnybunny!" Lena said, making for the lop-ear trembling behind the broom and picking it up to soothe it, Katie at her heels.

Adam bit down on a growl. He wanted to snarl or roar, the Lord above knew he did. Instead he looked at Sara and saw from her look that he was supposed to shrug his shoulders and live with a rodent sprinkling pebbles about the house.

"He is trained to go outdoors," his mother said, as if, like Sara, she could read him, which was not good. Not at all.

Sara gave his mother the kind of smile Adam would like turned on him once in a while. "Sunnybunny is as welcome in our home as you and Emma. And thank you for making supper and feeding the girls," she added.

Adam crossed his arms and kept his uncharitable thoughts to himself, relieved, he supposed, that everyone ignored him.

"*Kum, esse,*" said the woman who'd given him life, then left him with his father and took it away again. There she stood, offering beets and chow chow to tempt him. "Come, eat, my son. Good dinner."

Adam stiffened at her use of the rusty title, but he remained silent as he rubbed his thigh. Damn the leg. He wished it would just heal. He'd worked it badly today. Chores always aggravated it, but between chasing after Emma and going up and down the stairs so often, he could almost feel it festering.

Actually, his chest felt a lot like his leg right now. This new ache had begun earlier when he'd found his mother . . . back from the dead, so to speak. It was sharp then, keen enough to fell him. Adam shook his head. Now the pain in his chest was more general, but spreading, which made him rub below his ribcage.

He wished . . . he wished he were alone with Sara, so she could rub it for him. If only she would. He knew, from his experience with her tending him after his fall, that where Sara touched, comfort flowed . . . even when the new ache her touch set off had nothing to do with wounds and everything to do with—

Bad time to remember that, with Sara about to share his bed. Adam went to the table and sat, examining the food his mother was piling on his plate. How could a man be hungry, yet not hungry at all?

Adam picked up his fork, moved the food around on his plate and watched Sara delight over the company at table. Beautiful, his Sara, when she was happy.

Sara. His wife. He was going to be forced to share his bed with his wife. He almost laughed—a horrible feeling, that need to laugh, and unnecessary too. As if he would suffer for having his wife in his bed. His.

Sara, not Abby.

Everything changed so fast. Abby, his rock—his stable, practical, duty-bound Abby—was gone. And in her place was Scrapper Sara, happy, generous, passionate, a rock of another sort—stubborn, determined, steadfast . . . immovable.

While he carried a picture in his mind of Abby composed in gray and black, his image of Sara fairly bubbled with energy and bright color. While he supposed there was need for both in life, bright did seem more alive than drab, more light than dark.

Adam scrubbed his face again, more tired than he realized, for letting such foolish fancies into his head, and gave his attention to his . . . family.

His mother kissed Katie's offered lips. His dead mother. That was it, Adam gave over to the inevitable. Foolish or fancy, real or imagined, this was a night for the unbelievable.

His mother and his sister were alive, and here. He shook his head. Little Emma, asleep upstairs. Asleep and quiet, thanks be. Lord, but that girl could scream.

His mother's easy laugh flared Adam's anger. Odd for him to be so angry, when for years he had prayed for her return, picturing her as his young and beautiful mother, that tiny and treasured little girl by her side. The woman had aged badly, beyond her years, perhaps. Lines marred her perfect features, shadows darkened eyes that smiled rather easily, considering everything, though they remained troubled and sad, deep down. She had smiled more tonight than during the first five years of his life.

Emma the child had simply disappeared, that was all. The overwhelming sadness Adam had known at losing her returned. The knowledge that he badly wanted to weep grabbed him by the throat. He hated that, almost as much as his new and recurring need to laugh.

Adam slammed his hands on the table. "How long has she been afraid like that?" he shouted, furious all over again, especially with the woman who dared call herself mother.

"She has always been," his mother said, frightened, confused, as if he should know that.

"But of me? To be afraid of me, of all people." The faces of those in the room said that if he acted that way, they were not surprised Emma was afraid of him. He sighed, calmed. "She did not even speak to me."

"Speak?" The woman who claimed motherhood laughed, making him feel stupid, as if he should be used to that. The sudden knowledge that his mother had been directing her anger and frustration toward herself hit him hard; he knew self-contempt when he saw it.

"Why would your sister speak to you now, when she never did before?"

"Of course she did."

His mother's laugh proved his point. She was hurting. That above everything could soften him toward her, but he hardened himself against her.

"She never spoke to me," his mother said. "And I cannot remember her speaking to you, either." Her words were clipped, matter of fact. No sorrow there seemed to be in her over such a—The meaning of her words hit hard. Adam wasn't certain he understood. He stood and walked away. Better to leave than strike out. He turned back. "Are you saying that Emma never spoke? Ever?"

"Not to me."

"That's impossible," The *English* said, whipping Adam around, freeing him from the ugly place he'd been.

The doctor stood at the bottom of the stairs frowning, looking somewhere deep into that book-filled head of his. Interfering, annoying man. "You should be an Elder," Adam snapped. "Shoving your nose where it doesn't belong all the time."

Adam strode toward the doctor until they stood facing each other. "Why is it impossible, smart man?" he asked, fists clenched, happy for the challenge of the question, hoping for a greater challenge, for a reason to use his itching fists.

Sara scowled at him; then she turned a smile could

sweeten gooseberries toward The *English*.

Adam growled, but no one paid him any mind.

"Come, Jordan, sit and eat with us," Sara invited. "And tell us how Emma does."

The doctor ate the food he had provided, Adam thought, without so much as looking in his direction. "No lasting damage," The *English* said. "And she's sleeping well. But what you said about her never speaking, Mrs. Zuckerman, puzzles me. If she has a voice to scream, she has a voice to speak. She's stubborn, though, if she's chosen her whole life not to use it." He did look at Adam then. "She may have your stubborn, but at least she doesn't look like you."

Lizzie and Katie giggled.

"She does when she smiles," Sara said.

"Datt don't smile," Lizzie said.

"Datt goes 'grrrr,' " Pris said, exaggerating a ferocious snarl.

"Like Trixie when Ginger takes her pups," Katie added.

"Someone steal your pups?" the doctor asked him with a grin.

Sara's easy laugh made the ache in Adam's chest grow for some odd reason. "Your Aunt Emma has your Datt's temper too," she said to the children, which increased Jordan's laughter.

And why it should anger him that they all seemed happy, Adam did not know. He pondered the question until someone knocked at the door.

A stranger, Amish, but from a different community, with thinning hair, big teeth and frightened eyes, spoke so fast, Adam could barely understand him. But The *English* did. "Sara," he said as he threw on his greatcoat. "Come with me for this delivery. Mary Jakeman's bound to deliver breech again, twins, I think. You'll never get another chance like this."

Sara nodded before Adam could respond. "Lena, will you get the girls off to bed?"

Adam snapped out of his confusion. "Now wait a minute—"

"Of course. What else are *grossmommies* for, if not to hear prayers and kiss cheeks?"

Sara did some cheek-kissing of her own. But not his, never his. Adam didn't want her to go, but before he knew what to do about it, she was tying her bonnet.

Why this odd sense of loss? She was only going with The *English* to deliver a baby. Wait a minute. "Do not tell me you need Sara's help?" Adam shouted.

Sara took offense, no missing it.

"Sara is not the only one who still has things to learn," The *English* said, implying that Adam could learn a few things, himself. "This birth is a good chance for both of us."

Adam was surprised at that admission, and yet . . . what was wrong with him? "Go," he shouted. "Just go."

The look Sara threw him before she went out the door cut him to the bone. He knew she was angry at his gruff; he just wished he knew why that bothered him.

The house was silent after she left. Too silent. Everybody felt it. His mother bid him goodnight with a look of understanding—which he hated—before she shepherded the girls upstairs and he was left alone.

He went right to bed, early as it was, and lay there. Alone. It took him a while to realize that what he felt was not anger, but disappointment. He had expected, but dreaded, having Sara in the bed beside him, and now he was alone. He should be glad. Except that she was with The *English*. Again.

During the night, he tossed in a bed that seemed suddenly too big and drifted in and out of sleep. When he heard the kitchen clock chime two, he sat up and saw that Sara was still missing.

He put on his trousers and went up to see if she was in either of the girls' beds, hoping, yet dreading the thought of finding her there. For if she chose a different bed from his, the die would be cast and there would be no budging, for either of them. He did not want her in his bed, true, but he did not want her anywhere else either . . . except home, damn it!

Adam sat in the kitchen rocker and lay his head back. Where had they said they were going? North, yes, but what was the name of that farm?

The clock chimed; Adam's head fell forward and he sat up straight. Four o'clock. All night. They had been gone all night. His wife had not spent the night with him, but with the fancy English doctor.

Jakeman; that was the name, and he knew that farm.

Adam hitched his horses to his buggy and set out after his wife. Enough was enough.

A frosty snow-cap blanketed the earth, the sun still far from rising, as Adam rounded the bend. The farm he sought lay in the valley, its windows lit even at this hour. That, Adam thought, was a good sign.

He left the horses standing, climbed the steps, opened the door and stepped onto the porch. At the same time, the kitchen door creaked open, pulled by the draft from the porch door.

All was silent in a dark kitchen that smelled of baked bread and pickled beets, except for the sound of a man's snores. The man with the big teeth, the husband, slept and snorted sitting in a kitchen chair, his head in his arms on

133

the table. The *English* snored too, but it was the position in which he slept, and with whom, that chilled Adam's blood.

It looked as if Sara had fallen asleep sitting on the daybed, though now she slept leaning way over sideways. The doctor's head was in Sara's lap, her hand in his hair.

The *English* looked relaxed, comfortable—who wouldn't be?—too bloody damned comfortable. His Yankee tie was loose, his sleeves rolled up, his arms bare. Sara's kapp had fallen off and her hair, unpinned on one side, hung in a flow of soft curls that rested in the doctor's lap.

Adam must have made a sound that only Sara heard. She opened her eyes, disoriented and sleep-soft. Something in Adam stirred, something both emotional and physical at one and the same time, and it started him trembling.

When Sara saw him, she looked confused for a minute, and when she recognized him, there was no life in her awareness. But her gaze softened when it rested on the doctor, and the warmth in her regard struck Adam sharply. She stroked the man's cheek with a finger, whispered his name, smiled . . . and turned Adam to stone. She knew exactly how to awaken the man.

As if that were not enough, The *English* moaned and rubbed his face against Sara's lap. His feelings were surely as far from Adam's as heaven was from hell, yet he slept on.

Adam heard the roar that came from his throat and was surprised even as he lunged.

Both men woke with a vengeance and shot to their feet, teetering between grogginess and vigilance.

The husband cursed and made for the stairs.

The *English* made to protect Sara by stepping in front of her, his expression changing from outrage to red-faced comprehension.

The whole thing was a farce, but Adam's laugh became

another roar as he lifted the doctor off his feet and away from the object of his need.

Adam knew in that blink of time that he needed to touch Sara, to claim her, despite disguising urgency with outrage. This new wife of his had not slept beside her husband, but beside another, likely not for the first time, judging by their mutual ease in the situation.

Adam grasped Sara's arms. Touching her was pain, it was succor. "You will never—"

"Doctor Jordan," the husband shouted. "It's started again and it's—" The man's voice quivered and died.

Sara and The *English* ran.

Adam was alone again, abandoned in his foolishness. Hating the feeling, he took the stairs, determined to reassert his ire and claim his wife, but what he saw inside that bedroom stopped him cold.

Sara and the doctor worked furiously, but as perfectly together as gears in a thresher, to help Abby—no, it was another woman this time. This time a different husband cowered, tears streaming down his face.

Adam left, and fast, determined to outrun the fiend at his heels. Though he refused to acknowledge its presence, he knew with gut-slicing instinct that it followed too closely behind for him to slow, even for a minute.

Hours later, Adam heard Sara's buggy in the drive. Sitting on a hay bale in a dark corner of the barn, he removed his hands from his face and watched the woman who shattered but renewed his spirit make straight for him. Her eyes were wild, and challenge thrummed in her every step. Strong, unbreakable Sara, marching to meet him as a foe, while he, her foolish opponent, longed only for her return.

"She lives," Sara said, as she stopped, framed by the wide, open barn door behind her, her black cape billowing in the snapping wind. Sunshine blurred the edges of her form, giving her the look of an avenging angel. Dangerous. Beautiful.

"Mary and her new daughters live," Sara repeated, her voice rising with each word. "Because Jordan was there, Adam, and maybe because I was there too. You will not intrude on a birthing again, do you hear me? Never again." She stepped closer then, becoming no more than a woman, breathtaking in her righteousness. "Birthings are my private world, mine, yes, and the doctor's too, if need be, for however many days and nights necessary and in whatever place." She stood so close, now, Adam needed to look up to see her. "A place where you do not belong."

There were many such places, Adam thought, and one of them was beside this woman—at any time.

She walked away. He let her go.

The following night, Adam's wife slept silently beside him for the first time ever. He reveled in each breath she took and in each of her movements that rocked him.

They had not spoken the entire day.

With his mother, Sara shared every detail, sometimes whispering, sometimes crying, getting hugged and hugging back. And with his girls, she had laughed, even sung. But with him, she was more stone than sand, more foe than friend, more stranger than wife.

As was best.

If she had to go one more day not speaking to Adam, Sara thought she would scream and scare everyone. Despite her anger, she had so wanted to share the joy of that birthing with Adam. She wanted to tell him that she'd slept beside Jordan of necessity. She had almost wept that the first night she was to share Adam's bed, she had spent the night away from him, instead.

She and Jordan had needed rest to go on, so they'd be alert and ready when labor began again. No other room in the Jakeman house had a bed, yet every Amish kitchen had a daybed. It was used daily, for elderly parents, children with the sniffles, even for mothers who needed to rest as much as they needed to watch the roast on the fire or their children at play. Midwives, doctors, always used the daybed during long nights of illness or birth. That night had been no different.

Sleeping beside Jordan, Sara had felt relaxed, safe.

Sleeping beside Adam, she felt, if not quite safe, then freshly alive and teetering on the brink of . . . something . . . like a bud, swollen and ready to burst into bloom, frustrated, for only he could nurture her to flower. But in the days since that birthing, he had not nurtured, but seemed to forget her presence entirely.

Wilting, she was, and parched for Adam's look, his touch. If she were not so miserable, she might laugh at such foolishness.

That night, the third that they had gone to sleep without speaking, on far opposite sides of the bed, Sara was awakened from her own fitful sleep by Adam's thrashing. Trying to calm him, Sara was forced to grapple with him, until finally she held him down with the weight of her body, a hand to his brow.

Less at his brow did she feel real heat, than along her leg near his slow-healing thigh.

Even through his nightshirt, she felt the fire of infection. She looked back at his face in moonlight to see he'd awakened, fever visible in his eyes. He looked surprised to see her.

"You've got a fever," she said cupping his cheek, then

his forehead, with her palm. "You've let that leg fester without letting me tend it, haven't you?"

Adam grunted, trying to shift her off him she thought, but he only managed to dislodge her enough so that one of her legs fell between his.

She recognized the reaction in him instantly, warmed to it despite herself, and willed herself to move, but before she could make her lethargic body respond, Adam's hands were at her waist.

Whatever his intent, it changed. She felt it in his touch, in the altered beat of his heart. His hands slid upward to rest beneath her arms, his palms skimming the sides of her breasts, their pressure increasing. At the same time, Sara felt the heaviness of him, there, where she became more liquid as he became more erect.

Boldly, she fitted herself intimately against him, bringing a gasp, as much of appreciation as denial, from somewhere deep in her husband's throat.

Bent on seduction, she raised the hem of his nightshirt. But as she skimmed his thigh, she encountered the source of his fever and emitted a gasp of her own, for her hand came away wet and sticky with blood.

She scrambled aside to examine that thigh, and no mistaking what she saw. Following the direction of her look, Adam seemed as surprised by the sight.

Cursing, he pushed her away. "Blast it, Sara, can't a man get some rest? Took me long enough to get to sleep; now you have to go waking me up."

"Blast it, yourself," she snapped. "You've torn the wound open again and it's been getting worse for God knows how long." Efficient as the healer she was determined to become, Sara rose, lit a lamp and carried it around to his side of the bed. Even now, the sight of that angry wound was a shock. "Why didn't you tell me, *dummkopf?* Keep this up and we'll be having Jordan over to take the leg."

He looked at her sharply, to see if she was serious.

"I am not fooling, Adam. This is bad. If you go on like this, you will lose it for sure."

Adam sighed and lay back while Sara tended him. Just what he needed, to have her soft hands all over him. Well, it was what he needed, just not like this. "I am sorry," he finally said. "It started the other day when I went chasing after Emma."

Sara sighed. "I should have realized, I suppose, that would cause damage, but so much happened that night; then I went off on that delivery with Jordan. Later when you came running after me, I was so, so—"

Adam growled, agitated all over again thinking about it. "Damn it, Sara, I was worried sick when I saw you had not been home all night."

"You never said you were worried." Sara was thoughtful as she washed the wound. "You acted as though Jordan and I were . . . carrying on or—"

"Which is what I found!" Adam shouted, memory and pain combining to make him cross.

"What you were looking for, you mean. Do you honestly think that a wife who . . . who . . . wants . . . a man other than her husband, would carry on while—Adam, honestly, you can be so dumb; David Jakeman was right there."

Adam felt dumb. Sara had her faults—many of them— but he supposed she had a point. "I guess it's because you and The *English* have been friends for a long time." He shrugged. "I guess I don't understand such a friendship."

Sara touched his cheek with the back of her fingers. "I'd like for us to be friends, too."

"Well that's just plain foolish," he snapped. "And dumb too. You can't be my friend; you're my wife. Talk about a typical Sara-notion."

"Well, here is another Sara-notion," Sara said, bending to touch her lips to her surprised husband's. "There is not a man I'd rather befriend, no, nor one I'd rather kiss, or sleep beside, either, than you, Adam Zuckerman, husband or no." She gazed into his eyes for a long moment, wishing he would pull her down and make her his in every way, but he sat as if turned to stone.

"While you think about that," she said, "I'll get some medicine to clean the wound and a healing tea for you to drink."

Sara mixed valerian and golden seal in the peppermint tea she gave him to drink. And before she finished binding his thigh, he stopped answering her questions, because the herbs had done their work and he had fallen sound asleep.

It was near dawn, and almost time for milking, when she finished and made to lower the hem of his nightshirt, but to her surprise, she began to raise it, instead.

She hesitated for no more than a minute, shocked at her own boldness, but that did not stop her from wanting to look her fill.

Chapter Ten

All those weeks after his fall, Sara had tended her husband, wondering exactly what a man looked like . . . there. Oh she knew, strictly speaking, because Jordan had taught her everything a midwife should know. He'd even showed her pictures in his medical books that gave her the knowledge of how a man and woman created a child together. She knew that when a man hardened, he wanted to mate with a woman.

But her curiosity, now, was more specific, more personal. She could admit to herself, in the privacy of her own bedroom, she supposed, that she'd wanted to know about Adam, almost from the first, though she'd dared not even *consider* looking back then.

Now he was her husband, and a woman should know about her husband. Ever since the upper room, she had wanted to see him in the bright light of day, and though dawn was naught but a distant glow on the horizon, the room was lit well enough by the lamp.

Gazing at Adam—at as fine a set of man parts as she might have imagined—Sara covered her fast-beating heart, afraid he would catch her, wishing he would, so he might know how much she wanted to be his.

He was beautiful, as large and sturdy, strong and pleasing a man, here, as everywhere else. Their Maker had done some fine creating with Adam, she thought, not for the first time. Everything fit together so well, so neatly. In repose, he appeared imposing, aroused he must look grand as a stallion. When she stroked the sleeping length of him, Sara was surprised at its soft silkiness, even folded against itself as it was.

She cupped his testicles, feeling them contract at her touch, and stroked his length again, watching mesmerized as those folds seemed to disappear and he grew before her eyes.

Warmth stirred within her. She stroked him again, feeling wicked, sinful, though she knew that touching was not wrong between a wife and her husband. Could it be wrong, however, in the event the husband did not know? Because the wife surely felt as if she were stealing . . . something.

"Sara," her husband whispered on a ragged breath, warming her with his fevered gaze, and she wondered if he could hear the quickening beat of her heart. Even as she pulled her hand away, his denial reached her and he stopped her withdrawal.

"Do it again," he begged raggedly.

She did, and watched the way his eyes closed, almost in ecstasy. Then he opened them again and tightened her fingers around his length, watching her face, guiding her hand with his own.

"Sara," he whispered again, but his hand fell away, and he slept.

Prickles raced up Sara's spine, her legs, everywhere. She stopped but did not let him go. This was the closest she felt to Adam, the most intimacy they had shared. She loved the power; she feared it. She could lose something of herself in this way, if she allowed it—and, oh Lord, she wanted to allow it. She wanted to be consumed.

Inside her hand, Adam shrank, softened, Sara was disappointed to realize. With a heady rush of affection, she bent to kiss him just there, but her own shock stopped her. Good Lord, she thought, as she lowered his nightshirt and covered him. What had she been about to do?

Red-faced, Sara dressed, and by the time she was on her way upstairs to speak to Adam's mother, she had thrust the embarrassing episode from her mind and turned her thoughts to the tasks of running a farm. She knew that rest alone would allow Adam to heal, and with Lena to dress and feed the girls, Sara would be free to do the milking in Adam's place.

Sara had barely begun when Emma came tentatively into the barn, silent and wary, and sat beside her to milk the next cow in line.

Barn sounds—milk splashing and echoing in hollow wooden buckets, lowing cows and clucking, scurrying chickens—lulled Sara, as did the presence of the silent woman beside her.

"Do you remember Adam?" Sara asked. "From when you were small, before you went away?"

Emma turned her forehead against the cow's side, her cheek still against it, and regarded Sara with a world of happiness in her eyes. She nodded.

"You love him?"

Again the joyful look.

"Then why are you afraid of him?"

Indignation, confusion, flitted across Emma's features. She shook her head, denying the question and asking for an explanation at the same time.

"Then you are not afraid of him?"

Emma sighed and seemed pleased Sara understood.

"I am glad," Sara said. "Because he could use a sister, I think." Sara moved to the cow on the other side of her sister-in-law then, causing the girl to pivot in the opposite direction. "Emma. . . ." Sara began.

Emma's expectant look, her open and trusting countenance, all said, "What? I'll tell you whatever you want to know."

That emboldened Sara. "I have no family . . . of my own, that is, and I . . . I always wanted a sister."

Still Emma waited, as if she did not understand the direction of Sara's thoughts, which discomfited Sara, though she forged on. "Will you be *my* sister, too?"

An array of emotions flitted across Emma's face. Surprise, definitely, but not loathing, and yet no real answer lit her eyes, leaving Sara embarrassed by her request. She gazed away from her sister-in-law and toward the filling bucket. Why? Why had she dared such a question? Lord, she hoped Emma would not be annoyed by her foolishness.

In her head, Sara went over the words that led to this uncomfortable turn. She wished she had remained silent on the subject. Then she wondered if she might have phrased it differently . . . until a milk-stream pierced her cheek and dripped down her face.

With a gasp, she reared back . . . and fell off the milking stool, regarding her sister-in-law with amazement . . . only to receive another face-squirt.

Sara shrieked.

Emma emitted a gurgle, and an all-out chuckle, as Sara wiped her face; then she demonstrated her ability to direct the milk in any direction she chose, sending the barn cats another treat, shooting her milking partner once more.

Sara tried getting Emma back, but her misfire into her own face had the girl doubled over with laughter.

As frustrated as she was charmed, Sara retaliated in the

only way she could think of; she emptied her bucket over Emma's head.

With a screech, Emma stood.

Sara laughed so hard, she could barely breathe.

Then Emma was kneeling beside her, kapp soaked, ribbons dripping, and hugged her. Laughter fled as they gazed at each other, Sara in surprise and inquiry, Emma silent with purpose.

She touched Sara's heart with the tip of her fingers; then she touched her own. She placed Sara's fingers on her heart and then hers on Sara's. All the while she did that, she looked into Sara's eyes, begging her to understand.

"Sisters," Sara whispered, almost in awe, afraid if she said it too loud, it would not be so, and she wanted this sister very badly.

Emma nodded, eyes glistening, and hugged her.

Adam opened his bedroom door, appalled that he'd awakened late for milking, only to find Sara and his sister laughing as they came in from outside, arm-in-arm and soaking wet.

He stepped back into his room, so as not to frighten Emma, and observed them from the shadows. How happy and excited Emma could be if he were not present. While it pleased him that she was not all sadness and fear, it bothered him a great deal that he was no longer her protector but—to her mind—a threat to her safety.

Even their mother's scolding, because Emma was drenched, failed to dim his sister's smile.

He would have to ask Sara later how they both got so wet.

Emma did a funny thing then. She touched Sara's and his mother's hands to each other's hearts, making Sara laugh as she regarded his mother. "She is telling you that we've become sisters," Sara explained.

No, no, no, Emma was saying with her hands and her expression, despite the fact that she was saying nothing at all.

"Oh," Sara said, clearly embarrassed as she turned back to his mother. "I hope you do not mind, Mrs. Zuckerman, but I think . . . I think Emma is trying to say that—in the same way she and I are sisters—you and I . . . might be . . . mother and daughter."

Something lodged in Adam's throat—at Sara's words, at the need in her eyes—because he knew, he *knew,* how much having a mother would mean to her. And he made a promise right then, that if his mother gave Sara that one gift, the gift of a mother, he would bury his anger and resentment against her, no matter how difficult it would be.

But he needn't have worried. "A new daughter," his mother said with a joyful smile, opening her arms to Sara. "Welcome, *mein lieb.*"

There and then, Adam Zuckerman discovered that forgiveness held the same power to speed a heart and knot a stomach as did hate, though the one uplifted and the other did not.

Life fell into a reasonably comfortable routine after that. Adam was able to be polite to his mother, if not loving. To his sorrow, he could be neither to his sister, because she remained distressingly fearful of him, even though Sara had tried to tell him she was not. Eventually, even Sara had to admit she was wrong about that. As to where Sara's notion that Emma "said" she wasn't afraid of him had come from, Adam did not know.

His girls got so much attention from their grandmother, their aunt and Sara that they rarely sought him out now. Adam found that when they did, he didn't mind it as much as he used to. He wondered if his mother had taken upon herself the role of protecting his girls; she, of all people, would realize the necessity. If so, the unspoken arrangement contented him.

Sara had become a somewhat sought-after midwife, and Adam could hardly complain about her going off on a delivery, even though he wanted to, when his mother and sister were so good about caring for the girls. Still, he wished Sara would just stay home, where she was safe. With him.

Was she safe with him? Even he did not know the answer to that.

In the days that followed, he turned his attention to hard work—ignoring his aching thigh—and to making his farm thrive again. And if Sara sleeping beside him at night disturbed his rest, he decided that not having her there would disturb him more.

If only she would not keep crowding him in bed. If she would stay on her own side. But inevitably in the morning, he would find her tucked against his eager body. Most often, her nightgown had ridden up and her bare bottom nestled against him, like now, flesh to flesh, a torture of the most incredible sort.

Randy goat that he was, he throbbed eagerly. If he did not know better, he would think Sara was deliberately testing his ability to resist her. But that could not be. Leave it to him to blame her for his own weakness. If Sara was anything, she was innocent.

No, the fault was his. Even now as she slept blissfully on, unaware of danger, he had awakened to find a lush breast filling his hand, its nipple peaked and eager. As if reading his mind, Sara turned in his arms and thrust that rosy, ripe morsel of temptation into his face.

Well, damn; what else was a man to do?

Adam fit his lips there, lightly for a moment, and then more firmly, his body taking instant and hard notice. Even through her gown, suckling Sara felt incredible. Then he received a jolt. He could forget the gown coming between them, even here. The blessed thing fell open, practically to her waist, her other breast exposed and eager as well.

Adam fingered its pouting nipple, budded it, traced its dusky ring. Unable to wait, he tongued the bud to a perfect peak and suckled it, until Sara's moan shot lightning-bright and sharp to every fiber of his body.

His focus and their positions changed, to Adam's surprise, and before he knew what happened, Sara began to move against him, in the world's oldest and most perfect rhythm. Hard and needy parts of him now nestled perfectly against warm, moist parts of her.

Adam closed his eyes to savor the torture for a second, then a minute, a few more. . . .

Sara moved one of her legs, unconsciously opening to him, and Adam slid into her before he realized what he was about, a cry of exultation on his lips . . . until he reached her barrier.

Shocked, trembling, glistening with sweat, he froze, took a breath and turned his brain, rather than his nether parts, to working.

He tried to absorb his surroundings: his bedroom, his bed, a woman in his arms. Sara. His Sara. His wife . . . whose life lay in his hands.

A heartbeat from completion, Adam took a breath, swore, firmed his resolve and began to withdraw, but Sara cried out and surged against him, tearing that delicate barrier, impaling herself.

"No!" Adam shouted, pulling away and spilling his seed against her belly.

Time passed with only their harsh breaths to mark the seconds, but Adam knew that as soon as he could get air into his lungs, he was going to beat his wife.

She had done this on purpose. She had—

Sara was crying. She was sobbing against his neck, holding him so tight, he could feel her body shudder. His strong, unflappable wife was crying, and trembling. Well, he was trembling too, but. . . .

Adam felt as if he *had* beat her. He knew, as much as he knew his own worthlessness, that his wife was shaking with unsatisfied desire.

He, at least, had found relief, though much less satisfying than he knew it would be with Sara, especially after her determined seduction.

He forgave her. He hurt for her.

"Shh, *mein lieb,* shh." Adam rocked his wife in his arms. "Tell me, Sara. Tell me what you want."

She lifted her face from his neck to look at him. Embarrassment, he could see. And he believed he was right; she had set out to make him break his vow. Except, of course, she did not *know* he'd vowed not to get her with child. She was only a woman who wanted release, as he had been a man who wanted the same, but received it.

"I don't know what I want," she whispered in despair.

"But I know," Adam said, turning her on her back, pillowing her head with his arm. He knew then that God intended her for him, so ideally did she belong in his arms and his bed. "I can give you the release you seek, *mein lieb,* but no more than that." He cupped her breast and thumbed her nipple, bringing her hips off the bed. "Ah, you are far ahead of me, I see." Ach, Sara, such a bright pupil. "Though I suppose I should say I was ahead of you. Here, sweet, here; this is what you need."

Sara gasped with shock and elation when Adam touched her in that place that ached, there where she was wet with wanting. She raised her head, looking down to where his hand separated and stroked her.

However shocking the sight, Sara knew it was right with Adam. Her husband. Her love. She lay back and closed her eyes, feeling him stroke every slick inch of her, exactly where she ached for him.

Aware, somehow, of his gaze on her face, she opened her eyes.

Adam. This was her Adam gazing at her with . . . caring. Yes, he did care, and the realization transported Sara, his touch the sweeter because of it. When he lowered his head, she raised hers and their lips met for their first stirring kiss since their wedding day.

Like starving souls, they drew manna from each other's lips.

Sara closed her eyes and floated.

Adam encouraged her, in gentle German. She could barely understand him, but his tone, oh Lord, his tone was sweet and coaxing, and that aching spiral at her core tightened, almost beyond bearing, but she did not know what she was supposed to do. In near-panic, she looked to her anchor, and he smiled and kissed her again. "Let it happen," he whispered against her lips. "I want to see it happen."

See what happen? she wondered, but for the life of her, she could not speak the words to ask. She knew only that the threat and fear of shattering was not as great as the knife-sharp pleasure infusing her, raising her toward a summit never imagined.

"It is good," Adam said. "For a husband to raise his wife thus, and a pleasure beyond words to watch her embrace the journey. Soar, my butterfly. Kiss the sun, my Sara."

With his claim, Sara gave herself over to his touch, to pleasure, sweet and raw, hot and shivering, to an intimacy so stark and all-encompassing, she was transported to that place where butterflies kiss the sun.

She called her husband's name as she lost herself in the wonder of it.

Adam experienced, for the first time in his life, an emotion that frightened him—happiness, untainted and pure. Unworthy though he was, he accepted the gift of Sara's release with the greatest humility. And once he admitted to himself that he would seek this intimacy with her again, that he must or perish, he held his wife in his arms and fell into the best, most restful sleep he'd had in months.

Lena Zuckerman saw a difference in her son and daughter-in-law that morning, as they sat down to breakfast, though she could not imagine what caused it. Adam's limp seemed more pronounced, and as usual, he evaded her questions about his leg. Yet, despite that, an ease emerged in the way he moved today, in his response to little Katie's barrage of questions. Lena even noticed, in her son's usually pain-blanked eyes, a softening, barely acknowledged appreciation for life. Such an expression she thought never to see on such a hard and rugged countenance, neither his nor his father's.

It frightened her how much Adam resembled his father, even in personality. Yet it seemed possible that the wife he'd chosen—his second, Lizzie said—was strong enough to counter his hard edge, perhaps in time, even to dissolve it.

Though she knew nothing about Adam's first wife, Lena was glad he had chosen his second better than his father had chosen his first and only wife. Lena would be eternally sorry her children had suffered from her husband's poor choice of wife and from her own lack of strength.

And yet, she did not know what she could have done differently. If she had dared to speak against her husband to the Elders, and reveal the horrible truth, their high holy leaders would have brought her before the district as a liar. No one would have believed such accusations against the fine, upstanding, God-fearing Amos Zuckerman.

If she had been shunned, she would not have been there to turn Amos from punishment, not that she had succeeded as often as she would have wished.

Yes, Adam was like his father, yet he was not. And poor Emma, she could only see the physical resemblance between son and father, not the difference in spirit, though Adam was a hard man, harder than Lena would like.

Still, she'd been glad enough for it when he was young. Adam's strength had been what kept her sane through everything . . . until she'd lost him. She'd not been quite sane for a long time after that. Perhaps, she was not, even now.

Yes, Emma had always been afraid of men; she had reason to be. Lena feared Emma thought Adam was his father. No matter how often she explained that he was not, Emma refused to listen. Her daughter could shut out talk on any subject she chose, almost appearing deaf when she wanted to.

It was that ability of hers to seem totally deaf that made Lena wonder about what the doctor had said; that she must be able to speak. Lord, was the girl so good an actress that she could pretend such infirmity? Had the skill been refined as a necessity to her daughter's survival?

If so, what skills did Adam possess? What fears?

Lena didn't know she had been crying until Sara bent to kiss her brow. "Don't be sad, *Mutter*. You are home now."

★ ★ ★ ★ ★

Adam got an incredible amount of work accomplished that day. If he fixed the windmill's broken blades too, so it would pump more water into the trough, he would be able to attend the horse auction tomorrow in Sugarcreek. He needed to get Sara a younger carriage horse to replace tired Old Joe.

He realized two hours later that he had wreaked havoc with his leg climbing to the top of that windmill, but only because he'd already done three days' worth of work, and it was only four in the afternoon. He admitted he might have overdone it when he dropped one of the new blades for the second time and had to climb down the fifteen-foot-high windmill and back up again. But finally, when he went inside for supper, the job had been completed.

He had washed in the barn, thinking about the night to come. If he wanted to surprise Sara with the horse tomorrow, he supposed he needed a different excuse to go to the auction, but he'd think of something.

Right now, he could think of nothing but getting his wife into bed. How foolish of him not to realize, sooner, that they could satisfy each other, at least. This way, he could keep to his vow not to risk Sara's life in childbirth, the way he had risked and killed Abby.

An emotion, reminiscent of guilt, but more like sorrow, filled Adam. Had he ever anticipated a night with Abby? Beyond his wedding night that was?

Accepting his touch had always seemed a stalwart duty to Ab; he'd suspected that right off. There'd been no pleasure, ever, for her. Had there been, she would have expired of shame. Often, he'd thought it just as well, because he might have allowed himself to love her, if—

Adam raised his head and swore. He would not love Sara. No matter the shaft of overwhelming and frightening . . .

sensation . . . that filled him when he held her in his arms and brought her release. No matter that she made him feel—

Nothing. She made him feel nothing. He would not have it. He would not. He did not need Sara.

He entered the house to the sound of laughter. It was always so with Sara around, and yet it was Emma who laughed . . . until she saw him.

He swore and Emma rose to flee.

"Stay," he ordered in harsh frustration.

She backed away instead.

"Honestly, Adam, why do you frighten her that way?" The *English* snapped.

And what was he doing here? Again.

"Because it gives me great pleasure to see my sister run from me," Adam snapped back, swallowing his curse.

"Come," The *English* said to Emma, holding out a hand, making Adam chuckle, until he saw that his sister's stance changed. Her shoulders relaxed enough so they were no longer touching the wall she had backed up against. And she watched the doctor's face as though waiting for something, her fear replaced with . . . anticipation.

Adam swore again. Emma stiffened again, her fear back in place.

The *English* rose and dared to step toward the skittish girl. Stupid move. Foolish man. Now, he would see, Adam thought, how fast the girl could run, which she was poised to do.

Still, The *English* took one slow step after another.

Even Katie became quiet as a mouse while everyone watched the man approach her frightened doe of an aunt. "I'm not going to hurt you," The *English* promised. "I want you to trust me, Emma. Can you?" The man turned to Pris, the child gifted with a whine that could send a braying mule for cover. "Pris, come and show your Aunt Emma that you trust me?"

Adam was speechless. Blanket trailing behind, Pris walked right over and stopped before him, as if to await his next command. Then to Adam's horror, she not only raised her gaze to the doctor's face, she raised her arms as well.

At the extraordinary invitation, the medical man made so bold as to lift Pris in his arms, and she did not kick, screech or whine.

"See, Emma," The *English* said. "Even Pris trusts me. And she doesn't trust many. You must have seen that already."

Emma nodded, barely, but there was no mistaking the way she focused on The *English*. Adam clenched his fists, remembering a time when *he* had been Emma's rock.

The bold doctor kissed Pris's forehead and put her down with a pat to her bottom. "Thank you, Sweetheart."

Adam really disliked that man, and the closer Emma allowed him to get, while she stood as if waiting just for him, the more Adam's dislike grew.

"You trust me, then," The idiot *English* asked when he stood about a foot away from Emma. Again her nod, though, perhaps, less certain this time. And why Adam hoped so was beyond him. She should be able to trust somebody, shouldn't she?

The *English* extended his arm. "Take my hand, Emma. Show me that you trust me."

Emma looked around, examining each face, wary, uncertain. She gazed at their mother and received a watery smile, then at Sara who beamed, then at him. And before Adam could force a smile he did not feel, Emma scooted right into the doctor's arms. The surprised man closed them around her while she buried her face in his neck.

155

Chapter Eleven

His mother began to cry and his girls to cheer over the step Emma had taken in trusting the fancy-talking English doctor. Adam tried to be pleased too. Emma trusting any man was worthy of celebration, but he wanted her to trust him, and only him, like she used to. And Sara knew it, like she knew everything else. He caught the look of pity directed his way, and that was more than he could take.

He gave her as close to a smile as he could manage with the biggest crow in six counties stuck in his throat, and went to their room.

It wasn't long, thank God, before the house quieted and he heard her coming to bed.

Sara was as shaken by the fact that Emma accepted Jordan as a friend as she was by the way Adam reacted to it. She would have bet anything that Adam Zuckerman would never allow such deep emotions to show. She went directly to his side of their bed and saw that his eyes were closed. He didn't want to talk about it; she knew him well enough to know that, if not well enough to tell whether he slept or not.

She took her time preparing for bed, not because she was tired, but because she wanted to turn her husband's thoughts in the direction she had turned them this morning.

Imagine a wife deciding to seduce her own husband. How brilliant. How easy and fast had come success. She had only been trying for a few days, though it had not quite turned out as she planned. She wanted him to make her his by coming inside her and giving her his child. Though that had not happened, a degree of intimacy, previously missing, now existed between them, and for that Sara rejoiced.

Uplifted by the possibility of future seductions, Sara hummed as she washed, moving the soapy cloth down her neck, between and over her breasts. But her nipples were so tender after this morning, that she moaned involuntarily when she did. That was the exact moment she knew Adam watched.

Because of it, for him, she performed a slower, more thorough, and very intimate, washing. She could tell by his quickened breathing that her show affected him, and she saw one other blatant and unbridled reaction as well.

After her wash, she chose the nightgown that had been wrapped in tissue forever, it seemed. Sheer white with a daring row of white embroidered daisies at bodice and hem, the gown her own mother had worn on her own wedding night.

Sara lay on her side of the bed waiting for Adam to join her. During the long wait, she grew less impatient and more aware. He must feel so betrayed by his sister's acceptance of Jordan. "You're upset," she said.

Adam sighed. "Yes."

"Because Emma trusts Jordan when she is still frightened of you."

"Because the seducer in this bed is not where she belongs!"

Sara's heart fell. "You want me to . . . to. . . ." Sara swallowed, "go and sleep with the girls?" She warmed at the break in her voice.

"The innocence of the woman who used her lures on me

157

this morning, and several other mornings as well, I suspect, surprises me."

Sara rose on her elbow to regard her husband, uncertain as to whether she should admit her guilt. "You knew?"

"I should not say so, but not until this morning, and only after I disgraced myself."

"Then how can you call me innocent?"

"You are innocent, because you do not know your place."

Sara nodded, her eyes filling as she made to rise. "I am sorry."

"It is here, Sara." He smoothed the sheet beside him. "Your place is here beside me."

Sara sobbed and threw herself into his arms, and with his mouth and his hands, even his heart, if he but knew it, and perhaps even his soul, Adam made Sara forget her worry.

In return, she tried to make him forget his sadness.

"How do you think you disgraced yourself?" she asked when their lips parted in search of air for their lungs.

In answer, Adam showed her that sexual play could be slow, deliberate and methodical, and what rewards could be had by sustaining pleasure and not reaching it too soon.

He taught and she learned. He played her, and her body sang.

By the time dawn began to brighten the room, Sara thought they might have made up for all the nights of their marriage in the one just passed. Perhaps they had even made up for the nights after his fall from the loft, and for the yearning brought about by the baths.

Even though her husband did not enter her, in the procreating sense, they had shared more than a simple physical intimacy, almost as if—But love could not be. Despite her own overflowing heart, she must be satisfied with a sated body.

As Adam cradled and nuzzled her, she buried the love flowering inside her. Such was not to be had from such a man, especially as he had always loved another.

Adam stiffened in her embrace, as if he read her, and he sat up, on the edge of the bed, and scrubbed his face with his hands. "Do not," he said, keeping his back to her, "do not make of this something it is not." He stood and faced her. "If you do, then I am sorry for us both, because this will be finished."

That fast, and despite her happiness of a moment before, Sara felt as if she had been struck.

As Adam washed and dressed, his demeanor silent, hard-edged, he tried to hide the fact that his leg pained him. "I am going to Sugarcreek to the horse auction today," he announced. "I will be gone all day."

Sara swallowed the tears that hovered, angry for her weakness. "Let me take a look at your leg, before you go."

"It is fine."

"It is not fine. I can—"

"I know how my own damned leg feels," he snapped. "Leave me be. Sometimes you can be a real nag, Sara Zuckerman, and I cannot abide nags." With that, he was gone from the room, from the house . . . but not from Sara's aching heart. She wept. He had not said in weeks that he did not need her, but he had as good as said it then, with different words.

When her mother-in-law knocked on her door at seven, Sara said she wasn't feeling well, and Lena told her to rest; she'd see to the children.

She was a coward, Sara knew, but facing the day seemed impossible. Her husband did not love her, yet she had revealed something about herself that he disdained. She needed love.

She would never bear a child of his. What had she done to make it so? He was capable; that was abundantly apparent.

Then again, what did she know of such things as happened between a man and his wife? Oh yes, she remembered his words, though they had paled in cruelty beside her own. She supposed she was justly served for her malice, for what had passed between Adam and his first wife would never happen with her, and for that Sara mourned.

Jealousy was an ugly failing. Sara knew it, but she could not seem to escape it. Abby had been her friend, the mother of the children Sara loved. Baby Hannah, with her silk fingers and dimpled smile, would always be more hers than Abby's, and even while Sara rejoiced in every new and exciting event in Hannah's life, she mourned Abby's missing it.

Having Hannah had become a blessing beyond her ability to express, as were Katie, Pris and Lizzie. But Sara wanted babies of her own. Hers and Adam's. She wanted to feel his child quicken in her womb, to hold it in her arms. She wanted the love and intimacy with Adam that would create a child. And, God help her, she wanted to give him something Abby could not. A son.

Aware of her selfishness, but wallowing in self-pity, Sara cried herself to sleep.

Around nine, Sara heard a strange man's voice in the kitchen. A babe was on its way, and Sara remembered the one saving constant in her life, and she rose.

No matter what else happened, she needed to bring life into the world and to win over death. It was a vow she had made while she rocked a lifeless baby boy in her arms—the brother she never knew but missed dreadfully.

Because of that, Sara donned her wrap and went into the

kitchen in time to stop Lena from sending the stranger away. "No, Mother, wait. I feel better now." She nodded her greeting and introduced herself. "Tell me where you live and I will be along directly."

His name was Saul Petershein and he'd traveled a great distance to find her, all the way from Waynesburg, along the pike to Pennsylvania. The expected child was their first, he said, and his wife was frightened. She had no family in the area and needed a woman right now. He colored when he said it, so shy he was, and Sara's heart warmed—a husband, no more than a boy. "How old is your wife?" she asked.

"Sixteen tomorrow," he said proudly.

Shortly after he left, Sara set off, following the directions he gave her. A light sprinkle of snow began to fall, and by the time she arrived two hours later—to find that Susan Petershein's labor had barely begun—Sara suspected she might be making her way home in more than a simple snowstorm.

"The worst spring blizzard in sixty years," the old peddler Adam passed at four had said. And as afternoon turned to dusk, and he labored to keep his horses calm and working together amidst the icy white depths they trudged through, Adam knew the peddler was right. Many a buggy horse snapped a leg and got put down for traveling in snow this heavy.

Tawny slipped, even as he thought it, almost taking Titania down, and Adam cursed; then he sighed and nodded his thanks to the Deity when disaster was averted.

The consistent fall of thick white flakes created a blanket between him and the world around him, making it difficult to know whether he remained on the road or not. With the difficulty he was having maneuvering both buggy and team, they could be crossing a lopped cornfield and not know it until somebody's porch stopped them.

His beard had long since iced over, as the sweat pouring off his face froze, trickling down his whiskers. Fortunately, or unfortunately, however you looked at it, his beard was the only cold place on him. His thigh felt as though somebody had stabbed it with a hot poker, and the heat radiating from there served to keep the rest of him warm.

He hoped the horses' blankets kept them half so warm. So far, it had taken three times longer to get this near to home than to drive to Sugarcreek this morning.

At least the auction proved a success, despite the weather. He had bought Sara a fine chestnut filly, with a starred forehead and a proud gait. It even had a swift, sure foot, when it wasn't trying to plod though a blizzard. Lord, he'd hate to have it break a leg in this. Considering the danger, Adam stopped and went to untie it from the back of the buggy and bring it alongside, so he could hold the lead and keep an eye on it. Having to shoot Sara's gift before she received it would pretty much ruin the surprise.

For a while, Adam thought about stopping at the next farmhouse. But by the time he spotted one in the far distance, he knew he was no more than a mile or two from home, close enough that going on would not make a difference to him or the horses.

To give them a break, he had taken midday shelter with a Mennonite family who wiped them down, watered and fed them, and gave them a clean stall to rest in. Eliza Barkund fed Adam too, though he was less concerned about himself than his horses at the time. She had even given him a hot water bottle for his leg after she asked about his limp. He'd ended up apologizing and giving it back. The weight of it had hurt like the devil and he'd been too warm as it was.

Adam heard a dog barking, the first sound, other than the snuffling of his team, in miles. He stopped to listen, wishing he could tell the direction from which it came. Dogs usually meant people, and it would be good to know where help could be found. Full dark was falling fast. Good thing Sara was safe at home and not out in this. Her little one-horse, two-seater buggy would get bogged down and stuck for certain.

In all weather, Adam preferred this family-sized Germantown box-buggy; its sturdy build and weight worked especially well in snow. And its wide back seats were perfect for the girls to sleep, if they wanted. Not that he'd ever used it for the family before, not until he took them with him to the buggy factory. The day after that trip, he realized something dreadful. In trying so hard not to be like his father, he had failed his children in a different way.

Damn, he wished he had not remembered that now, though he supposed he could be wrong about failing them. He might be doing the right thing, keeping them away from him. He should talk it over with Sara.

Adam cursed. Sometimes he really disliked this notion that he could talk to Sara about anything. Well almost anything. He felt as if he had betrayed her, somehow, by not telling her why he wanted her to take the girls.

Why hadn't he? More to the point, why had he been able to tell Abby about a father who amounted to the devil, and his fear of being the same, when he could not bring himself to tell Sara?

Sara would understand as well as Abby. Not only would Sara understand, she would probably try to make the girls understand. As far as Sara was concerned, nothing was as important as keeping those girls happy. Ab had kept them clean, dressed and fed, but she was not a happy sort. He always thought Pris had Abby's disposition, except that Sara could, more often than not, make even Pris smile . . . well, she could make her forget to whine, anyway.

No, it wasn't that Sara would not understand; he simply did not want to admit to her what a weak, flawed and worthless man was Mad Adam Zuckerman. He shook his head. He wanted her to consider him strong, as strong as her. Stronger.

If only—

He heard that dog bark again. Nearer now. Adam turned in his seat, looked around. "Where in blazes?"

Close. As close as . . . someone weeping? A woman.

The dog barked louder, faster, frantic, right beside him. Where?

Something rose up in his path. *"Vat's Iss?"* An overturned wagon, large, heart-stopping.

Adam released Sara's horse and pulled his team up fast, but not fast enough.

Twelve hours after Sara arrived at the Petershein house, she delivered a fine healthy baby boy, a gift for his mother's sixteenth birthday. They named him Peter Petershein, which Sara tried, and failed, to discourage. She washed both mother and son and settled the babe in his mother's warm and eager arms to suckle. By then, it was nearly one in the morning, but despite the hour, Sara was more than ready to leave for home.

Saul offered her the use of their daybed for the night, so she could wait out the storm, but she felt uncomfortable about staying. Something compelled her to get home, worried her—not the children, she realized as she drove away.

Even if she and Adam were both held up by the weather, the girls would be fine with a doting grandmother and aunt to care for them. No, it wasn't them. It wasn't even Adam's harsh words, though if she let herself consider them, she might break down and cry, she was so tired, and her tears might freeze on her face.

It was something more. Something weighed heavy on her that she could neither name nor shake. She knew only that she must get home and fast. She felt sick with worry because she wasn't there already. *"Fescht, schtarrig,"* she urged her horse. "Move, can't you?" But instead of going faster, Old Joe went slower, and instead of letting up, the snow became heavier and accumulated more swiftly.

Sara had never realized the middle of the night could be this lonely, as if no one existed in the world but her, though she was glad she was wrong about that. It comforted her to know that Adam existed, that when she reached him, he would close his big, burly arms around her and warm her both inside and out.

She had never seen the world so dark and still. Desolate. Yet spread about her lay an awesome beauty. Like a pristine blanket, the snow glistened in reflected moonlight. Brilliant. An awesome power, it held as well, to trap the unprepared and unwary.

Sara stopped the buggy to climb down and look back to see if the Petershein farm was still in sight. When she hit the ground, she screeched, the shockingly cold snow reaching nearly to her knees.

She had best go back to the Petersheins and stay the night. Except that their farm had disappeared. She thought she had driven a straight path, but did not seem to be on the right road any longer, on any road, for that matter. She walked a few feet, lifted her cape so it wouldn't drag in the snow, and turned in a slow circle. Nothing for miles, except a white veil obscuring all but a far stand of trees. She must have taken a wrong turn. On her way there, she had never lost sight of a farm.

Perhaps farms surrounded her but the falling snow kept her from seeing them. Sara shivered. Glad she had accepted extra blankets from Saul, she plodded back to her buggy and threw another over Old Joe. She had a sick feeling that if she wasn't careful, she would spend the night there, in her buggy.

She tried to lead the horse in a turn, so they could follow their wheel tracks back to the Petersheins'. But when she finally got the horse to take a few steps, turning churned up the snow and the wheels got stuck. Then Joe's job got really difficult and the horse refused to take another step.

Sara shivered and pulled her cape tight. If she had brought the big buggy, she would be able to climb in the back and lie down. As it was, she had no choice but to sit there with the snow hitting her in the face. She'd been better off before this foolish half-turn; at least she had been protected from the snow driving into her face.

She looked at that far stand of trees and thought perhaps a house sat behind or within its shelter. It was worth a try and didn't seem too far to walk.

Sara climbed down again, and began her trek into the teeth of the wind. The snow felt somehow deeper, colder now. Her cape, dragging heavily behind her, became more hindrance than protection, so she unfastened it and let it fall, giving herself a freedom of movement. Lifting her skirts to keep them from bogging her down, Sara was able to move at a more satisfactory pace.

A long time passed before she reached the trees, and once she was there, the distance around them appeared to be much farther than she expected. She decided to cut through, but, up close, what had seemed a small grouping of trees resembled a forest.

Within its bower, the light of the moon became obscured, and Sara walked a dark path, frightened at first, except that she felt warmer than when she'd walked in the open amid the snow and wind.

When she saw the clearing up ahead, she thought it might be part of someone's yard and practically ran, until the ground cracked, shifted and fell from beneath her.

Adam's horses turned in time to escape disaster. His buggy did not.

He used his horses, along with Sara's new chestnut, to carry the farmer and his wife—injured before he arrived upon the scene of their accident—and their children back to their nearby farm. He refused the grateful family's offer of shelter for the rest of the night. The man's horse was suffering and needed to be put down, which they silently agreed not to do in front of the children, and Adam wanted to get home, for more than the obvious reasons. He could not define, even in his own mind, the obscure disquiet compelling him to continue on. He knew only that he must.

To keep his horses safe, he left them with the farmer and his family and went to put down the man's horse. Then he began the long walk home. It was hard going, but at least his leg no longer pained him. The deep snow soothed the ache in his thigh considerably. Funny, the Mennonite wife thought heat would help it, but cold actually did. Or it numbed it. Either way, it felt better than it had in days.

As Adam finally approached his farm, he saw lights on in the kitchen, the best room too. Sara must be worried he was so late. Knowing her, she would be pacing. He wasn't certain how he felt about that, except that maybe it was a good thing. He could use her soothing hand on his brow about now. In a few other places, too, her hand would be welcome.

The thought cheered him, until the kitchen door flew open, and his mother, Emma behind her, came running out. Emma stopped when she saw him. His mother stopped too, nearer though, near enough that Adam thought she might have wanted to throw her arms around him. For a minute he was disappointed.

"Where have you been?" she asked in a rush. "Where is your buggy? We've been worried sick." Not one breath did she take.

Adam looked at his sister. "You mean *you* have been worried," he told his mother, shaking his head with regret as he watched Emma back up a step for each he took toward the house.

"*Nein, nein,*" his mother said, waving him onward. "Emma worries about you too."

His sister froze in place when she heard that.

Adam hated to frighten her further, so he stopped, as well.

His mother scolded Emma and told her to move, distressing her, and Adam experienced, even now, his old need to protect her. He swore and took a wide berth around her, so she could do as she pleased with no fear of him. He was too damned tired to be stubborn about it. He needed to sit down and—

He stopped. His mother was so close behind, she walked into him. "Go, go inside," she said. "You'll catch your death."

He stood stock still. "Where is Sara?"

"I do not talk until you go inside, sit down and drink dandelion wine."

Adam wanted to swear, but he did as he was told, instead. And while he did, it occurred to him that, for all the woman hadn't mothered him for years, she sure took to it easy enough. She was treating him and his sister exactly the same as she used to. And for some foolish reason, it warmed him.

Sara was not in the kitchen, their room either. He went to the bottom of the enclosed stairway, looked up and knew he did not have the strength to climb halfway up. Besides, he knew she was up there.

He had hurt her this morning and she had decided she was sleeping with the girls. Well, let her get a bad night's sleep; then she'd come crawling back, where she belonged.

He went and sat in the kitchen rocker, which his mother placed before the fire. He lay his head back. He should tell her he was too hot to sit near a fire, but he was too tired to speak. A cup of something warm was placed in his hand. He opened his eyes to see her looking down on him with worry. Talk about a trip back in time. "Yes," he sighed. "Again, bruises."

She nodded, her eyes bleak. "Your buggy?"

He drank the wine. It tasted good and warmed his frozen parts. "Gone. Turned over. I'll tell you about it in the morning."

"And you, just bruises?"

"Snow's soft. Felt good."

His mother frowned and placed her palm against his cheek. "Ya, as I thought. You have fever. Burning up, you are."

"Sara will fix it." For all the hand on his brow belonged to the wrong woman, it soothed just the same, and he was too tired to fight it.

"Sara is not here."

His mother's words opened Adam's eyes.

"She never came back."

Chapter Twelve

That fast, every part of Adam, body and mind, surged with life as he shot to his feet. "Sara is not back from where?" The shout sent his sister skittering out into the snowy night.

"Get her back in here, damn it." Adam followed his mother outside to find Emma standing in the yard, a distance away, her arms around herself.

Worried she'd run farther, he could think of only one thing that would get her attention. "Sara may be hurt. Come inside so I can go and get Sara, instead of chasing you."

Emma hesitated but started toward the house, slowing when she got near. Then she raised her chin and walked a half-circle around him.

"Good girl," he said, loud enough for her to hear.

She faltered, but kept going.

"She trusts you will put Sara first," his mother said. "It's a beginning, son."

"Do not call me son." Adam wished he'd turned away before hurt dimmed his mother's eyes. Son was the boy who was cowed and belittled. Son is what the monster who sired him called him. Perhaps, someday, he would explain that to his mother, without hurt on either side. "Call me Adam. Come into the barn and tell me where Sara went while I hitch up your buggy."

Adam was ready to go in no time, his mother predicting he'd kill himself going off with such a fever, even as she

170

placed a jar of dandelion wine on the seat beside him. "For medicine."

All he could think about were the directions she gave him and the places along the way where Sara might stop for shelter. But panic soon became his companion. No one along the route had seen her, though they all said they'd pray for her. One foolish woman went so far as to urge a lantern and matches into his hand. "For guidance and warmth," she said. "Just for maybe."

His mother's buggy horse was a prime goer and the wheels on her buggy were wide, better in the snow than the one he'd lost earlier. Still, before long, the snow was so deep, he was forced to abandon the buggy and continue on foot. He left his mother's horse, the lantern and matches in a lean-to beside an empty shack where he abandoned his last real hope of finding Sara sheltered and warm.

Who was he fooling? He hoped to find Sara safe behind every tree.

How tired he had been standing at the bottom of the stairs just hours ago, too tired to raise his foot to the first tread, let alone ascend. Now, here he was trudging through the snow, strong as anything.

"For Sara," he said louder. She had come to mean so much to the children. What if he—they lost her? How could they go on, if—

"For the children," he cried. "Because she is the closest to good ever happened to them." And to me, he did not say, for he would not tempt fate with another opportunity to do damage in his name.

Sara mattered to his mother and sister too. Already, they loved her, and she, them.

For every one of them, he needed to find her, keep her safe. And for Sara herself, who had so much life to give.

He had seen the good she could do as a midwife, first-hand, though he'd not said so that day, nor the next, because he was still angry about the way he found her and The *English*.

He should have told her how well he thought she did, that he was proud of her, though pride was frowned upon by their people.

"For Sara," he said looking up. "And for the children she would bring into Your world, Lord." He regarded the black, starry sky, vast, the stairway to a place he often doubted existed. "For Sara. Please."

He said it, over and over, in a prayer-song that gave him strength and kept him moving. "For Sara." In time, he said it more loudly, more quickly. With the words, his pace became swifter and his heart brighter with hope . . . until he saw her buggy, abandoned, belly-deep in snow, her horse down. Dead, he saw when he got close.

Poor Old Joe.

An hour ago, he knew exactly how that horse must have felt before it fell. Not now, though. He wasn't weak or cold now. Right now, he felt almost as strong as Sara usually appeared.

He'd been right; her horse had been too old and weak to stand the cold. Damn, he should have replaced it sooner. If he put Sara in danger. . . .

Adam shook the thought away. Such thoughts could be defeating, dangerous: buckling-the-knees and giving-up dangerous. He must stay positive, so he could keep going, no matter what.

He walked around the buggy and saw, immediately, where the snow had been disturbed by someone trudging through it. Even though the later snowfall had smoothed it somewhat, the trail remained lumpy enough to follow, thank God.

Almost at once, he came upon a half-buried cape, and swore, hope dimming by vast degrees. Without protection from the elements, Sara would not have to go far to be in trouble. Stubborn woman. Foolish woman. Wandering off, getting herself lost.

Adam looked again at the heavens and doubted, as had often happened in his sorry life, the existence of anything beyond what could be seen and heard. Then, just in case, he whispered, "Please."

When he'd seen that old settler's shack earlier, he thought surely she was there, but no recent step had marred the thick dust on its raw-plank floor. He almost wished now that he'd started a fire in the old stone fireplace, "just for maybe," like the old woman said. Course he might have burned the place down, and that would help no one, Sara least of all.

Cursing, Adam grabbed the cape, shook as much snow off as possible and continued to follow the trail that must be hers.

Once he entered the stand of trees to which her tracks had led, he found it hard to locate any further sign of disturbance and wandered around for a bit before he picked up a trail again.

When he saw a clearing in the distance, he hoped for a homestead, a family and a welcoming fire, where Sara waited for him.

He hoped she'd know he would come for her, then wondered if he had ever given her any reason to believe in him.

"Best stick to the problems at hand," he said to keep the should-haves crowding his mind from driving him madder than usual.

If there were a house, and if Sara were inside, then soon her hand might graze his forehead, hers, finally. For the rest of tonight, they might share a daybed in a stranger's kitchen. If so—Lord, let it be so—he would not let her go all night.

He began to walk faster than he imagined possible, given the condition of his leg, so fast, he damned near stepped over the snow-covered lump in his path. But a sudden sense of awareness made him stoop down to investigate, which cost him mightily.

Rather than pressed leaves over hard earth, Adam felt, beneath his palm, a soft trace of warmth, barely a trace. Apprehension made his hands shake and his head and belly sick as he dug out and turned the form.

An iron fist shoved through his chest and gripped his heart.

Sara lay at the edge of a pond, the part of her still in the water surrounded by a thin veneer of ice. If he'd stepped over her, he would have broken through and been no use to her.

The iron fist squeezed hard. When Sara failed to respond to his call, it got a grip on his lungs as well. Her face, her lips, were as blue as her legs. The skirt of her dress had frozen to the ice. Adam ripped it and left it to the elements claiming it . . . but they could not have Sara.

Once she was free and in his arms, he could not discern the rise and fall of her chest. His shaking hands and escalating panic hampered his progress as he tried to wrap his greatcoat and her cape tight around her. As he carried her back toward his buggy, he sensed that she was no longer inside herself. It frightened Adam more than he could afford to acknowledge.

Despite his determination to hold steady and remain strong, something fierce and ugly tried to claw its heaving way up from a place so deep inside him, Adam had not known it existed. Though it pained him more than dying must, he feared letting it out . . . yet holding back was useless.

His howl, when it came, sounded inhuman, feral, even to him, but stopping was beyond him. Anyone in hearing distance would expire of fright or come running.

No one came and Sara never woke.

It was too late.

Adam Zuckerman, heart pounding, fever raging, sure now that he was as mad as everyone claimed, hugged his burden to his heart and raised his face to the stars.

"Just this once," he raged. "Could you not have listened, just once!" He pulled Sara's icy face into his neck and shouted as he walked. He made so many promises—to Sara, to God—he'd have a parcel of work to do fulfilling them all—if only he would be given the chance.

Impossible as it seemed, hope walked beside him. Pain too, but that had been with him for a long time. The pain, he ignored. But hope, now that was another story. Where had that come from?

He'd felt nothing like it since . . . since he was four, almost five years old, at a time when he believed his mother would be there forever. He remembered the hope, because it was probably the last time he experienced it . . . until now.

He'd found a missing calf in a snowstorm and wanted it to be alive. He was too young and stupid to accept death, he supposed. He'd wrapped it in a blanket and held it close to his body, to warm it while he carried it to the barn, the way he carried Sara now.

He entered the clearing, the woods behind him now, and made for Sara's buggy. He took the extra blankets from behind her seat and wrapped her again. He even took the blanket from her dead horse's back and threw it over his shoulder. If he could get her to that shack and start a fire, he'd lay it out to dry. Sara might need it later.

He thought of that calf again. He'd brought it to its lowing mother and right away she'd begun to wash it. He remembered how happy he was, because she would have ignored it, if it was dead. It was too weak to nurse so he'd gone into the house to warm some milk, which he practically poured down the hungry mite's throat.

The calf had opened its eyes. It had even begun to move a bit on its own, until his father had come out of nowhere and gave it a kick. He laughed at his "weakling son's" tears over a dead animal and tossed the calf on the heap behind the barn, like so much garbage. "No use wasting energy on a lost cause," the bastard had said.

Adam remembered when his mother found him crying. Her hand on his brow had felt as good tonight as all those years ago. She offered hope when she placed that jar of warm dandelion wine beside him "for medicine."

He stopped. Damn, he'd left the wine in the buggy and that was farther away than the shack. He looked to the heavens and started walking again. He would get Sara to the shack, warm her, then fetch the wine.

One thing he'd learned since that day with the calf; there were no lost causes. Oddly enough, it was the woman in his arms who taught him to believe that again, and not so very long ago.

If they made it to the shack . . . no, when they made it, after he got a fire started, he'd get Sara out of her wet clothes and wrap her in blankets. He'd leave her by the fire while he went for the wine. Then he'd pour it down her throat, by God.

After what seemed like hours, during which Adam feared

he'd lost his way, he was surprised to see, through the veil of snow surrounding them, that foolish yellow buggy, like a beacon lighting his way, for the shack stood somewhere between them and the buggy, not as far away as he thought.

Hating to let Sara go, even for a minute, he lay her down on the floor of the shack, before the cold hearth, but not without rubbing her limbs through the blankets, hoping, hoping to revive her by rubbing some warmth into her.

She failed to stir. She barely breathed . . . if at all.

Wiping his eyes, he got up and set to work on the fire. Broken furniture lay scattered about. Even the sound of him breaking it up failed to rouse Sara. A rotting old wagon in the lean-to had crumbled when he kicked it aside to make room for his mother's horse. He went and fetched the wood from that.

Given dry kindling, the fire started right away. Adam lit the lantern and brought it close to examine Sara. White face, blue lips. He buried the sob that rose in him and set to work. "I will not give up on you, Sara. No more than you gave up on me. I will not."

He hated that he could not strip her until the room warmed, so he wrapped her with another blanket. Though he hated as much to leave her, he needed to fetch the wine.

He was back in no time, but felt as if he'd been gone forever. Immediately, he tilted Sara's head back and brought the wine to her lips, but she failed to sip any on her own, so he poured a bit into her mouth, massaging her throat to help her swallow. When the first bit had slipped down, he tried again, convulsively swallowing himself, so badly did he want her to do so. He even tried issuing an order, but Sara failed to respond.

This was no time to panic, he told himself. Nevertheless, panic rushed him. And heat. So much heat, he could hardly bear it. Just the same, he brought Sara nearer the blaze to unwrap her. As fast as he could, he removed her shoes and peeled off her stockings; then he practically ripped the rest of her clothes off. He massaged her bare arms and legs in turn, covering the rest as he did. Then he put his head to her chest to see if he could hear or feel her breathing, but he could not.

The only sign of life had been her passive swallowing of the wine, and even then. . . .

Adam shook his head, denying negativity.

When he had her wrapped tight again, he held her in his arms, her face in his hot neck, and told her . . . everything—about his father, himself, about wanting to do murder when he was no older than five. He told of his shame and his fears, then and now. He told her how he had once protected his sister and how and why he protected his girls. He told her why he chose Scrapper Sara to care for them, even why he hadn't told her before—because he was ashamed of not being as strong as her.

When he looked at her face again, he thought maybe her lips were less blue, more pink. That made him try more dandelion wine.

It was difficult to hold her and feed her the liquid, but he couldn't bear to let go, as if releasing her, physically, meant letting her go . . . forever. He stubbornly held on, but nearly dropped her and ended up pouring too much into her mouth. When he made to massage her throat, a noise startled him.

A gasp.

Grating.

Horrid.

Wonderful.

Dreadful.

Like someone drowning.

He sat her up fast, frightened he'd kill her trying to cure her. Her gasps gained strength but were drawn out and painfully repeated.

Jagged torture.

He pounded her back, rubbed it, slapped it again.

He swore in German. At himself. At God.

At his mother for giving him the foolish wine.

Like a madwoman, Sara began to struggle free of his hold. When her arms cleared the binding blankets, she swung them to throw off the rest and rose on her knees. Like an avenging angel she appeared, hair wild and free. The roaring blaze behind her limning her in light, she tilted her head back and struggled to pull air into her lungs.

Adam watched, helpless, immobile, mesmerized by the brightest star in God's universe, her life hanging in the balance.

Her grating, lung-pulling gasps stretched on long enough to kill him, enough to prove air was being forced into her lungs.

She stood, hands pressed to her back, head back, and dragged in one deep wheezing draught after another, painful to hear and see, yet infinitely more painful to experience, he had no doubt. But blessed as well, because Sara was alive. She was alive.

She paced before the fire and away again, gasping, sobbing, tears coursing down her cheeks. Adam's cheeks, too, were wet. He wiped his eyes with the back of a trembling hand.

She was going to catch her death, fire burning her on one side, air freezing her on the other. "Sara. Sara," he shouted to catch her attention. "You have to wrap up."

She regarded him without recognition for a minute, taking in the shack. Him again. "The water," he thought she tried to say, but her voice was too raw to be certain.

Adam stood, and only then did he realize how badly his whole body was shaking. He picked up the blankets and wrapped them around her from behind, holding them closed, allowing the feel of her, alive and breathing in his arms, to soothe him. "You have to keep warm," he said, his words little more than a rasp and nearly as ragged as hers had been.

But she heard and turned in his arms. When she saw his face, she reached up, touched his cheek and examined the fingertip that came away wet, her look akin to awe. She croaked his name and rested her head on his chest.

He held her so tight, he was afraid he'd hurt her. Her bare feet on that cold floor, the wind whistling between the planks, was all he could think about, yet he held her and held her. She sought comfort from him, and he could not let her down. Not again. "I thought I had lost you," he said into her hair. "My Sara, my very own scrapper, I was so scared."

Then he was the one being consoled and crooned to, or so she tried with barely a voice. And when she chided him for taking so long to find her, scratchy throat and all, Adam finally believed he still held within his grasp the most wonderful gift God had ever given him—his wife. Right then he promised the Deity—He who had favored him with a response to his plea, for the first time he could remember—that he would see that no harm came to her.

When Sara went limp in his arms, Adam's panic flared anew and he lowered her to the floor, wrapping her neat and tight again, but chills shook her nonetheless. A horrible shaking. As frightening as it appeared, Adam supposed it meant she was coming 'round. Cold was better than numb. Wasn't it?

The blazing fire could not seem to warm her, yet Adam was sweating so fiercely, he discarded his wet clothes with great relief. It occurred to him suddenly that Sara could use some of his heat as much as he could stand some of her ice.

Removing his pants was difficult, because blood, sticky with infection, matted the fabric to his wound. No wonder he had fever, he thought, when he saw the festering thing. No wonder he was limping. A wonder he could walk at all, he thought at almost the same moment the blasted leg gave way. Falling to his knees sent a shaft of pain so fierce up his thigh, Adam feared for a minute he might black out. After a bit, the dizziness passed, but he needed to work fast. His leg had taken enough abuse for one day; even he knew that.

He grabbed the corner of the wet blanket he'd dragged off Sara's horse and lay it on the ground for him to lie on; then he unwrapped Sara to settle her on her side at the edge of the warm, dry blankets.

Heaven blessed him with relief from the sharp edge of pain when he finally lay down. It also beset him with a new, incredible and downright frightening sense of . . . destiny . . . when he took Sara into his arms, skin to skin, for the first time ever.

Pulling those layers of dry blankets over himself to keep them over her became a trial by fire, but a small price to pay for Sara's life. A very small price. Besides, he had learned tonight that he would do anything to keep Sara safe. Anything.

Even walk through the fire of hell.

Sara woke, basking in the heat surrounding her. When she opened her eyes, she discovered herself in a place she could not name. Dark. Dismal.

Awareness came in slow beats.

It took a minute for her eyes to adjust to the darkness, but finally she discerned a small room, splintered shutters closed against a cold that, nevertheless, whistled in. Board floors, scattered debris. But no scurrying creatures that she could see . . . or hear. Sara swallowed with relief, surprised at first that her throat hurt.

Warmth from more than the fire surrounded her. Adam's face rested between her breasts; his beard tickled her belly. One of his hands cupped her bare bottom. She smiled, appreciating the feel and significance of having it there.

She was safe.

She had been lost, might have drowned, but Adam must have found her when she wasn't looking. She remembered leaving the Petershein farm and getting lost. She remembered . . . the pond, covered, like a trap, by a pristine and inviting blanket of snow, a circle of bright welcome amid a darkened wood.

A shiver prickled her spine. She'd tried and tried to climb out, but couldn't gain purchase. And then she'd seen the branch, like a reaching hand, but not reaching far enough.

After a very long time, it seemed, she'd almost given up. Except that something—stubbornness, Adam might say, though it was more like faith that he would come—kept her trying. Finally she had caught that branch and tried to pull herself out, but it was no use, so she simply clung to it . . . and waited.

She was so tired, she'd feared if she let sleep come, she would let go of the branch and slide back into the water. For a long time, she fought to keep sleep at bay.

She remembered, as her eyes closed, thinking perhaps she was going, finally, to join Mom, Datt and her brother.

How many years had she wished for just such a gift? But for the first time since the day she lost them, she wanted to stay. She had more to do, people to care for.

Then Mom was standing there, like it was yesterday: bright smile, forest green dress, black apron and kapp, stirring spoon in hand. A rush of love had filled Sara, a need to follow, and yet. . . .

"Mom, no," she surprised herself by saying. "I love and miss you all and I want to be with you. I do. But I . . . I have things to do. People to care for and love." She meant the girls, of course.

Her mother nodded, smiled. "Your Adam needs you. He does and for certain, more than we do right now, *liebchen*."

It had been years since she'd seen or heard Mom so clearly, so when she was gone suddenly, Sara expected a renewal of the grief that had been her companion forever, but joy, rather than pain, filled her.

She knew, then, that Adam had come for her. She no longer felt alone or afraid, but protected, and she found herself struggling to pull air into her lungs.

Adam had come.

Where they were now, Sara did not know, but it was cozy, if drafty and dilapidated. Turning her awareness to the man beside her, Sara realized with a start that he burned with fever. A high one, she feared, but a heat she'd likely needed as much as he might have needed the cold that seemed to permeate her. She must have sought his warmth almost as easily as his embrace.

Sara freed an arm and finger-combed her husband's unruly hair at his nape. Lord she liked his face against her breast. "My love," she whispered.

At the sound of her own words, Sara's hand stopped moving, as nearly did her heart. Did she? Did she love Mad Adam Zuckerman? And if she did, was she foolish enough to think he could love her in return?

No. She sighed. No, she wasn't that foolish. And, yes, God help her, she loved him. This was the time to admit it, now when it must have pained him mightily to come for her, or no time would be right.

"Adam," she called softly, surprised at the scratch in her voice. "Adam, how do you feel?"

He raised his head a bit, purring like a score of barn cats after fresh milk. "Nice," he said. "You feel nice."

Sara smiled. "No, how do you feel?"

He rubbed his face between her breasts. "Nice," he said again before taking her nipple into his mouth.

The liquid sensation only he could incite moved from her breasts to her core, where it radiated outward in thrumming spirals, warming her the more.

"Spinster Sara," Adam said, tasting, laving, teasing the nubbin with fascination. "Fire and ice, hard and soft, strong and gentle. You make me ache. You yell and I ache. You insult and I ache. You are my best dream, sweet Sara, awake or asleep."

Sara might soar with joy if worry did not fill her. In his right mind, Adam would not say such things. She had never known anyone to burn so with fever. He did not know what he was saying. "Adam, you are burning up."

"I know," he said running his hands over her bottom, bringing his face to hers, and pulling her against his arousal.

With a worried chuckle, she pulled away, so she could examine his eyes. Glassy, they were, and unfocused. She put her cheek to his forehead, his heat all but scalding her. "You're burning up!"

"It's the fire," he said. "In my blood. For you."

"Delirious," she said. "I knew it. We've got to get you out of these blankets and away from the fire." Unwrapping him was easy, getting his hands off her body was not. Worse, because she wanted them there.

When they were both free of the blankets and Sara was about to help him away from the hearth, Adam lay her back down again in a move she did not expect. Fever or not, bad leg or not, he was strong. And determined.

Then he was there, somehow, covering her, devouring her, branding her, it seemed, with his hands and his mouth.

"Adam," she said, placing her palms on his face to raise his head and reclaim his attention, before all conscious thought was lost. "Adam, we have to move you from the fire. It is too hot. You are too hot."

He smiled then, lazy, self-assured, despite the fever in his eyes.

"Adam, the fire—"

"Did you know?" he said, serious, alert, suddenly. "That butterflies need to raise their body temperatures to fly." His smile became earnest, boyish. "I want to make you fly, my Sara."

Sara stopped focusing beyond the wonder of his hands on her body, of his lips . . . everywhere. Were it not for the fact that she was, indeed, well on her way to flight, she might very well blush. Never had such pressure built inside her, not even that time in their bed. This was hotter, higher. Softer, harder. Wider, narrower. Inside and out.

Her world dissolved, yet it expanded. They were alone in the universe, she and her love, alone and rising, climbing toward, toward. . . .

Adam moved above her and slipped inside her before Sara knew his intent. Shock was quickly replaced by a joy

185

that consumed her. With inborn instinct, Sara Zuckerman arched to pull her husband deeper inside her body, to envelop and welcome him.

As she did, he threw his head back and called her name, then he stilled for one tense, silent moment, wherein neither so much as breathed. Then he came for her and took her mouth, and kissed her in the way of lovers.

With a certainty as old as time and as far back as the first Adam, Sara knew that this Adam, her very own Madman, was the mate God intended for her, in life and through eternity.

As if that knowledge were not enough, he raised his head, his eyes bright and clear as glass. "You are the first and only home I have ever known, Sara Zuckerman. You are my own perfect butterfly."

Chapter Thirteen

Tears filled Sara's eyes, joy overflowed her heart, and as her love began to move inside of her, bringing her and himself to a higher plane than she imagined existed, that incredible spiral inside her coiled hotter and tighter.

Adam whispered; he shouted. He moaned; he begged. He beseeched and thanked her . . . and the Deity. He rode her hard and he raised her up, till he brought her so high, she thought she might expire. Then he lowered her again, setting her softly to rest, only to raise her up once more.

Sara caught and matched his rhythm as Adam began to speak words of love, though the word "love" itself was never used. When he told her she'd touched his soul, Sara allowed her deepest secret, that she loved him, to burst from her lips.

Adam shouted in exaltation, though his response, if any, died on the lips he pressed to hers. She didn't care. This was Adam. Her Adam. And he was taking her, loving her in the way God intended them to love. And she was grateful and happy and soaring gloriously.

The stars rushed them, coming fast and furious, sparkling, despite a climb that had been slow and intense, and beyond-belief wonderful.

They arrived in a blinding flash, touched wonder and encompassed it for one long, thrumming beat, then they floated toward earth once more.

★ ★ ★ ★ ★

Sara had been gone for twenty-four hours. Jordan shook his head with worry and urged his carriage horses faster.

Roman told him that Lena had left Emma with the children and driven to his house, the next farm over, at midmorning, a whole bloody day after Sara had left for a birthing. Lena, Roman said, had been no longer able to sit still and wait, even though that's what Adam had ordered her to do the evening before, as he set off to find Sara himself.

Roman listened to Lena's tale, sent her back to Adam's house and set out immediately to get Jordan. Jordan cursed. His life among the Amish could bear a great deal of improvement. He was merely a man, an English man, who some of the Amish foolishly believed could fix anything, while most were certain he could fix nothing.

When he arrived at the Zuckerman house, Jordan listened to Lena tell him about Sara and Adam, and Jordan told her she had done the right thing by going to Roman, though Jordan did not think she believed him.

Adam's sister, beautiful, ethereal like a fairy princess with invisible wings, waited as if for him to speak directly to her. But not one intelligent word came to mind, which went to show how foolish he was, where she was concerned. "Good morning, Emma," he said, damning himself for an idiot, and stepping near enough to smell springtime and touch stardust. He took her hand, inordinately pleased that she seemed to want his touch as much as he wanted to touch her. "I'll bring Sara home; don't you worry."

Lord, and didn't she nod as if she believed him. Really believed him. Considering the number of women who put their trust in his skill every day, he wondered why this woman's humbled him beyond understanding.

Uncomfortable with the odd sensation and the undefined reason for it, Jordan turned back to Roman, who had just come inside. "Hope you brought your biggest buggy, Roman, so there'll be room in the back, in case. . . ."

Roman gave an affirmative nod to Jordan's unfinished sentence, deepening the worry on Lena's face.

"Lena, can you come with us?" Jordan asked. "Having a woman there for Sara would be—"

Emma tugged hard on his arm and pulled him around to face her. No doubt about it; she wanted him to pay attention as she pointed to herself, panic and some deeper need in her eyes.

"You want to come instead of your mother?"

Emma nodded, the movement of her head almost comical in its determination and speed. Charming brat. "Adam will be there, too; aren't you afraid of Adam?"

She shook her head as if that was absurd. No wonder Sara got that impression. Emma's answer made Jordan wonder if she thought Adam was someone else. "The man who lives here, Sara's husband," he said, watching her look turn haunted. "He will be with Sara. That Adam is your brother."

That certainly gave Emma pause, but stubbornness rose to negate worry. She nodded once, decisively, and went for her cape and bonnet. Then she went to the wide-eyed silent children and kissed each head in turn: Lizzie, Katie, Pris, then she snuggled her face into the baby's belly, a laugh gurgling in them both at the same time. The nagging puzzle of the silent, seductive girl arrested Jordan once more. Why her inability, or should he say her refusal, to talk?

Though Emma's look proclaimed her worry over her missing brother and sister-in-law, she all but danced out the door, her step was so light.

Jordan took Lena's fretting hands to still them. "I guess it's settled." He shrugged. "Emma is coming with us." That made Lena smile as he intended, but the smile faded quickly.

"They will be fine. I promise," Jordan said. "Freshen their bed and warm some bricks. Heat some water too, in case . . . they need to bathe."

For surgery, he thought. In case either of them was badly hurt. If they had found shelter, that was. If they had not . . . no surgery would be necessary. Jordan chased the thought away with optimism and hope, a leaf he had, some time ago, taken from Sara's book of life.

Outside, he found Emma on the driver's seat of Roman's family buggy. Like a queen, she sat, head high and stubbornly set, as if to say, "Enough talk. I am ready."

Jordan got in the back and Roman climbed up to drive, but Emma screeched when she saw him and shoved him with all her might.

Off the seat and into the snow Roman flew, and on his duff he landed, up to his neck in snow.

Jordan laughed and jumped down to help him up. "Sorry old man. I'll just take the reins, then, shall I?" Jordan wasn't sure why he thought Emma would allow it, but it had to do with the look she'd bestowed upon him in the house.

After a few miles, it began to rain, and Jordan became aware of Emma watching him. Worry, he saw in her look, and a need to be reassured. Lord, he'd never seen a woman who could say so much while saying nothing.

"Sara will be fine," he said, knowing which of the Zuckermans she was concerned about. "She will."

He could see she hadn't decided whether to believe his groundless reassurance or not, so he sighed and turned back to the road. Smart girl.

The rain did much to melt the snow, high as it had been, except for where it had drifted. That was the thing about spring blizzards. They could be lions one minute, lambs the next.

Jordan held the reins one-handed as he felt for his medical bag on the seat between them, just to reassure himself that everything he needed was there. He had just encountered it, when he felt Emma slip her hand into his.

From her look, he saw that she had decided to place her faith in him. Heady stuff that, blind faith. Jordan wasn't certain he was up to it. If she knew him better, she wouldn't even consider it.

When they found Lena's yellow buggy, missing its horse, the tightness in Jordan's gut got worse. That the horse was gone might be cause for hope, however, and he said so.

Roman grunted noncommittally, but Emma beamed.

They found the lean-to sheltering Lena's horse less than a quarter mile away. The chimney of the hovel beside it emitted a thin spiral of smoke. Roman was down and running before Jordan could stop the buggy.

When Jordan stepped inside the crude cabin and saw the entwined couple, Roman frozen in shock beside them, Jordan thought they were both dead for sure and had to bite back a cry of denial.

Up close, thank God, he saw that they were both breathing—barely—and he was able to reassure Roman, and Emma standing behind him, her hand to her throat, her face white.

Before Jordan could unwrap the embracing couple, he asked Emma to go and feed her mother's horse, to which suggestion she nodded and complied. Then he told Roman to go and make sure she was all right.

As Jordan had suspected, Adam and Sara were both naked beneath their layers of blankets. Their clothes must have been sodden. One of them had been very smart; problem was, he could not tell who had saved whom. They were both very ill.

One of Sara's lungs was full of fluid, though her fever was nowhere near as dangerously high as Adam's. The man's thigh was so infected, Jordan fully expected to have to take the leg. The next few days would tell.

He covered Sara with blankets again after listening to her lungs. Emma could dress her while he and Roman carried Adam out.

He poured brandy on Adam's wound, wringing a scream from his throat, and put his stiff, dry shirt back on him. There would be no getting pants over that thigh, so Jordan removed his greatcoat and wrapped Adam in that, before he wrapped him in a dry blanket.

"Roman, Emma," Jordan shouted. "Come and help me."

Roman came. "Emma has been standing still as stone ever since she heard Adam yell."

Jordan swore and went out to her, and she relaxed visibly when she saw him. "Adam is sick, sleeping, Emma. No reason to be afraid, but Sara needs you."

Just like that, Emma ran inside. "Get Sara dressed for me, will you," Jordan asked, following her in, "after Roman and I take your brother out to the buggy?"

Emma nodded, stepped forward, saw Adam and stepped back. She did not bend to her task until he and Roman moved Adam from Sara's side.

Jordan went back in twice to check on Emma before she finally finished dressing and re-wrapping Sara. The third time, he found the girl kneeling beside her unconscious sister-in-law, stroking her cheek, crooning reassuringly, in her own throaty way.

Emma sat in the back with Sara's head in her lap on the ride home, and she watched Adam as though she would defend Sara against him.

Witnessing that, a compelling need was born in Jordan, to see inside the silent girl's head. Who did she think Adam's face belonged to and why could she not equate it with the brother she'd obviously loved? Why was she afraid of men, but not afraid of him, a stranger?

The doctor in him, the man who had failed once so badly, wanted very much to find the medical reason for her inability to speak. And if there were none, then, damn it, he wanted to hear her . . . say his name. Jordan swore and urged the horses faster. He'd found a haven in their hilly little Ohio town, where so many people needed him that he could forget he was lost too.

This visit, Sara enjoyed her time with her Mom and Pop and her brother, Noah. Rocking Noah, Sara told her parents how much she had missed them and how badly she wanted to stay.

But her Pop was wise, Sara realized later, because he asked her about her husband and children.

For her parents, Sara described Lizzie, her thirty-year-old five-year-old, everyone's little mother.

She told them about her middle child's impish bent, how she had taken right off to dogging her Aunt Emma like a pup following the scent of a bone. Katie had even taken to speaking for Emma, turning her aunt's looks into jokes and silly rhymes. Sara told her parents the way Emma's eyes twinkled as she went along with the silliness Katie invented in her name. Like the day Katie told them at breakfast that she and Emma planned to build a bed for Sunnybunny.

Hadn't Emma gone right out to the barn for wood and nails? And hadn't she bundled Katie up warm and taken her down to the summer kitchen to build the thing? They'd even whitewashed it and topped it off with a mattress and quilt they'd stitched over several evenings.

Sara told her parents about Pris, the pretty one, who whined less these days, but had barely learned to smile. "Pris looks at you when you talk now, mostly. And her whine, when she uses it, lasts far less time than it used to. But still," Sara said, "my Pris needs something more than she's getting and I just don't know what it is."

Sara shook her head as she pulled Noah close—the brother she'd always missed. "Then there's the baby. Hannah was a gift, given us with her mother's last breath. She will have a special purpose in life, our Hannah."

"Well," her Pop said. "You can't stay with us then, can you? Learning what Pris needs, and Hannah's purpose, and seeing they're met, must be what you're called by God to do right now."

Mom nodded. "And your Adam, Sara. So big and bright in your heart he is, we do not need your words to know him. But he hides in a dark, cold place. And, *liebchen,* he has been there so long, he does not know how to get out."

Sara sighed. "I know, Mom. Lord, I know. But I cannot seem to—"

Her mother touched her hand, a peaceful touch. "No one else can bring him home. Only you. Else he will be lost forever."

Sara wept then. She wept for Adam and for the knowledge that she must leave her parents to get back to him. "I have to go," she said. "For Adam and for our girls."

Her father and mother kissed her cheek and hugged her

in turn, and when she kissed little Noah, she wept. "I cannot leave you again," she told her mother. "I cannot."

Her mother held and rocked her as if she were a little girl. "There are babies, my Sara, who will not see God's great world if you do not go back for them."

Sara sobbed, torn, because the people she loved existed on two different planes. And she wanted badly to help babies be born. "I do have to be a midwife," she said clutching her mother tighter. "I have to help those babies."

Her mother smiled. "One of them, a special one," she whispered, for Sara's ears alone, "is with you now, growing beneath your heart." She kissed her stunned daughter's cheek.

It was warm and bright where her family stood waving her off and dark in the direction she headed, yet fear did not fill her, only hope, for her family waited.

Sara looked back one last time, the distance between her and her parents seeming to grow before her eyes, a greater span than she could bear. But before she could call out to them, or change her mind, their light dimmed and the dark world ahead beckoned.

The air grew thinner as her visit with her parents became no more than a wistful dream. Then Sara struggled for every breath as she searched for Adam and the girls. The thought of finding them brought a greater joy than finding her parents after so long.

A time for everything under God's heaven, Mom had said.

Light tickled her eyelids, air filled her lungs and Sara realized that the darkness would disappear if only she could open her eyes. She tried and tried, but her lids were too heavy.

Some time later, when she finally succeeded, she saw that the light here was brighter, more beautiful than the light surrounding her parents had been. She was in her own bed, hers and Adam's, the sun slanting into the room as it often did of a noon. Heavens, so late abed.

She was not alone; though Adam was not beside her, the girls were—Lizzie and Katie on one side, Pris on her other, all of them sound asleep.

Sara tried to pull them close, but her arms were too heavy. Still, the world was good. Life was good. These were her babies.

A need to see baby Hannah, to hold her smallest in her arms, filled Sara, and then she remembered what her mother had said. *One of them is with you now.* Joy surged within her. That night in the old shack, had they made a baby? Adam's fever had blazed, and though he spoke of what was happening at the time, she wasn't certain he had been fully aware of it. She blushed now just thinking of the things he had said.

Then panic rushed her, tearing joy from her heart, bringing strength to her limbs. She coughed as she moved Pris so she could sit up. She had to find Adam.

"Adam," she called, her scratchy throat and voice reminding her of that night. "Adam," she tried again as she stood.

Then her room was filled with people. Jordan catching her in his arms. Had she fallen? Lena clucking like a mother hen over the girls in her bed. "Not to bother Sara, did I not tell you?" Emma, herding them into the kitchen.

Sara looked beyond Jordan as he laid her back down. Where was Adam? Why wasn't he here? "Adam?" she asked, in no more than a whisper, her heart setting up a new and terrible beat. "Adam," she said again, hearing the panic in her voice as she pushed against Jordan's restraining arms, but it was no use.

She had to rest a minute, but after she did, she hit Jordan as he tried to listen to her chest. "Where is Adam?" she shouted.

But Adam did not come and Jordan only shook his head as he sat beside her and took her hands, the way Adam should be doing. Sara choked back a sob as Jordan regarded her. "His fever is serious, Sara, though not as high as it was."

Prickles of relief ran through her, strong enough to make her lose her breath and begin again to cough. It took a minute before she could speak. "I have to go to him," she said, glad she'd found her voice, feeble as it sounded, but still annoyed that Jordan tried to keep her from rising. Weaker than she expected, she had no choice but to lie back down. "Where is he?"

"On the daybed in the kitchen. The fever made him wild for a while, delirious actually. You needed rest and quiet to heal and he needed constant care."

"I need no rest. It is Adam who—"

"Pneumonia, sweetheart. Took a swim, did you? In a blizzard?"

"Oh, that. How did you know?"

Jordan chuckled. "Leave it to you to toss pneumonia off. And I know because in his ranting, Adam has been furious with you for going to a birthing in a blizzard, for getting lost and falling in a pond. There are some things he very much liked about your time in that shack, however. Those rantings interested Emma very much and made Lena chase her and the girls from the room."

Sara warmed and knew color stained her cheeks, but

Jordan was too much a friend to mention it, thank God.

"You've been very sick."

"For how long?"

"Four days."

"Adam still has fever after four days? That's too long, isn't it?"

"His leg is bad, Sara. I don't know yet. . . ." Jordan took a breath. "Don't know if I can save it."

Sara used the word Adam had when he'd fallen from her bed. Instead of looking shocked, Jordan nodded his head. "I know."

"I need to take care of him." Tears filled Sara's eyes, because she had no strength to rise, never mind nurse her own husband.

"Lena and Emma are helping me do that. If you want to help, the best thing you can do for him is rest and get well."

Sara looked toward the window then back at her friend, her worry near to bursting, for Adam, for. . . . "Jordan, is pneumonia bad for a baby?"

"You know it is; you've seen me treat lots of babies with—" He noticed her smoothing her flat stomach, soothing the child she wasn't even certain existed.

"That's not what I mean," she said. "I mean, if the mother has pneumonia—"

Jordan was a smart man, a good man, Sara thought. His eyes softened in understanding. "Is there a baby, love?"

Sara nodded, knowing he'd think her mad if she admitted the child was conceived only four days before and that her dead mother had told her so. "I think," she said. "I'm almost certain."

Jordan smiled. "Only one of your lungs was filled with fluid. There was always enough oxygen for the little one. What does old Adam think?"

"Old" Adam would strike "The *English*" for that remark, Sara thought, but fear replaced everything in her mind. "He cannot know. Don't tell him, Jordan, please."

The doctor rubbed his face with one hand and sighed. "I'm not going to ask why or how he can't know, but don't you think he'll figure it out sooner or later?"

Sara sighed, too, and closed her eyes. When she opened them, worry remained with her. "Later would be better," she said. "Keep my secret?"

Jordan rose and bent to kiss her brow. "Sleep, little mother. Your secret is safe with me."

Little mother. Sara smiled as she drifted off.

Two days later, the first time she saw Adam after their night at the shack, the deep angles and planes chiseled into a face grown lean shocked her.

He looked at her, for all the world as if he did not know her; worse, as if he disliked her. And despite the fact that Jordan had reassured her that Adam was no longer delirious, Sara almost wished he were. Otherwise, Spinster Sara and Mad Adam Zuckerman were back to the relationship, or lack thereof, that they had shared on the night she arrived to deliver Hannah.

"Come to give me one of your blasted baths, Sara Zuckerman?" His words were a challenge, yes, but they were also heartening, despite the hard edge to his look.

"So you remember who I am, and that we're married, do you?"

"Our mistakes live with us forever."

Sara's reaching hand stopped midway to his brow and began to shake with pain from the knife-thrust of his words. She pulled back and turned away to hide a hurt bad enough to double her over, if she allowed it. When she looked back at her angry husband, she saw regret lining his features, though as usual he tried to mask it.

"You believe our marriage was a mistake?" she could not help asking.

He growled, that old harsh sound that used to frighten her, but now only confused her. "No," he said, almost grudgingly. "The girls need you."

Only the girls. Not him. His beautiful words in the shack played through her mind. She had been his hearth and home, his bright butterfly.

Sara summoned all her strength not to break down and weep. "You must be sorry, then, that we rushed into a wedding. Once your mother and Emma came, you would not have needed to marry me."

Adam scoffed outright. "The Elders gave us no choice and you know it."

"The Elders were not with us in the shack," she said, tired of skirting the real issue. His true regret, Sara was certain, was that they had made love . . . not that he would call it that.

Adam's look turned to insult, pure unadulterated fury, anger so blazing Sara stepped back. "Know this, Sara Zuckerman," he shouted, causing himself to lose his breath, though he recovered it and his ire fast enough. "Had I known for certain that saving you would cost me this foolish leg, I would have done it." He looked down at the leg and then back at her, hurt taking ire's place in his eyes. "I would have done it had my life been the cost."

Confusion made Sara dizzy. She sat and gazed at the hands in her lap, identified them as her own, and realized how blessed and yet cursed was this love expanding her heart. When she looked at Adam, finally, he was watching her, a desperate need sitting so near the surface, she could weep.

They'd stepped so near to a communion of spirits that night; they had become one in the physical sense. Adam had been as near to revealing his hidden self, as he was even now, after thinking she'd lost faith in him. But his memory of their loving, of the most beautiful experience in her life— maybe even in his—seemed to have disappeared.

"I never doubted you, Adam. You misunderstood my question. I knew you would save me. Even when I was the most frightened, I knew you would do everything humanly possible to get to me. I was so sure of it, I allowed myself to sleep while I waited."

Adam's face paled. "Asleep, were you? And there I was, thinking you'd—" He swallowed, shaking his head.

She had difficulty swallowing herself, until some unspoken tautness between them urged her forward. She rose from the chair and sat on the edge of the daybed to lay her head on his chest. After a minute, Adam covered it with his big, often clumsy hand. But his touch was soft as a dove's feather as he held her against his fast-beating heart.

Hope renewed Sara. He might have forgotten, or turned away the memory of their physical intimacy, yes. They had stepped back, yes, but not so far back that the care growing between them was lost. Not that far back, praise be.

They could begin again, pick up the pieces of their marriage and return to the way they'd been, almost friends, maybe more. Except that if Adam knew her body with his hands again, he would learn, with time and without doubt, about their night in the shack. The babe she could not help but believe grew in her womb would soon give away its secrets.

Perhaps she should try to discover where and why existed that dark place inside Adam that her mother spoke of. He worked so hard to keep himself from her in so many ways. If she only knew why, perhaps she could confront and challenge whatever caused his determination to remain an emotional mile away.

And if he was determined simply to have no more children, how would he react to the knowledge that another was on its way to them, even now?

Sara shivered, and Adam pulled her close, as if he sensed her need to be held just then, or as if he needed the contact as much.

Jordan came every day to check Adam's leg, and refused to let him get up, no matter how much he threatened—and Adam threatened loud, and often, to break The *English* in half, if he didn't let him get up.

"I'll tie you down, if I have to," Jordan shouted back, on the fifth day after Sara was up and about again. "And I'll get Roman to come and sit on you to keep you there. He would do it," Jordan added. "You know it as well as I do. And he'd take all the credit for saving your leg on top of everything. It'd give him something to crow about for years."

Jordan and Sara laughed. Adam did not.

Sara saw that Emma smiled at their laughter, leaning against the outside door, clear across the kitchen. The girl mostly avoided the kitchen now that Adam was awake and grousing, but not when Jordan came to visit. Being lovesick herself, the malady was easy for Sara to identify in someone else. She wondered if Jordan realized that Emma had come to adore him.

Poor Emma. To love outside the Amish faith was *ferbudden*. No good would come of it, Sara knew, especially if Adam discovered it. He already disliked Jordan enough without such a threat.

Sara shook her head at the impossibility of it all and went looking for Lena.

She found her mother-in-law outside with the girls. They were giving her a tour of the yard.

"We'll make gardens together, ya," Lena promised them as Sara approached. "In the springtime."

The girls loved the idea and began suggesting flowers to plant: nettle, lupine, foxtail, bleeding hearts. Laughing at the odd assortment, surprised by their knowledge of such unusual flowers, Sara sent them into the barn to get Roman for lunch. Their poor beleaguered neighbor was back doing Adam's chores, not that Adam appreciated it. He might never forgive Roman for suggesting their marriage, she often thought.

Sara disregarded the twinge the realization brought and watched Lena watch the children, love shining in her eyes, and she took her mother-in-law's arm with a squeeze to lead her to the house. "Tell me, Lena, has Emma been baptized in the Amish faith yet?"

Lena shook her head. "*Nein.* The Elders thought her silence meant she was too childlike to know her mind. But she understands enough to choose Baptism. Why do you ask? Do you think she is ready?"

"No," Sara said quickly. "Far from it," she added. "I just wondered."

With Jordan's infinite capacity for patience where Emma was concerned, it just might be that her sister-in-law's fondness was returned. In which case, with Emma not baptized, there would be one less . . . horror . . . among many, to deal with, if the worst happened, if they discovered love and declared their intent to marry.

Only a baptized member of the Amish Church could be shunned for marrying outside the faith. While a family might be saddened by a non-baptized member's choice of a non-Amish spouse, communication and visits between them would not have to stop.

For Jordan and Emma there remained hope.

For Adam and Sara, who knew?

While the light frosts turned into the morning dew of spring, Sara's hope wavered from one day to the next.

Buds not damaged by the late blizzard blossomed, while lambs kicked up a frolic in the meadow and cows dropped calves on the hillsides.

Amid all these signs of new life, Sara Zuckerman became more and more certain that she carried her husband's child.

Chapter Fourteen

While Adam was still stuck in the daybed, the Zuckermans welcomed unexpected company. Jonah and Susan Lutz, little Annie and littler David came to thank Adam for saving their lives the night of the blizzard and to return his horses.

It was the Lutz market wagon that had turned over in the worst spring blizzard Ohio had ever seen, pinning Jonah beneath it. Annie hadn't the strength to move it; neither could she find a way to bring her children to safety.

After Adam's buggy collided with their wagon, he freed Jonah and put the family on Titania and Tawny to take them to their farm. He'd set Jonah's leg and put down their horse before walking home.

Sara was shocked to learn what he had gone through that night. At how many miles he had walked on that leg. It was a good thing Lena didn't know how bad it had been when he got home, or she would never have let him go out again.

Sara might have died that night. "Five people you saved that night," Sara said, drawing everyone's attention, then needing to explain what had happened and how Adam saved her too.

In the telling, Sara realized Adam had really saved six people, because their little one would not have been conceived if he hadn't come for her. She wondered if the day would come when he would be pleased to know it.

It was good to have new friends. Sara saw right away that she and Susan could become so. They found humor in the same odd situations. Their children played well together for the length of their visit, almost making Sara believe hers was a typical, happy family.

In May, Sara felt well enough to deliver several babies while Adam remained sentenced to the daybed in the kitchen, demanding all the while that she stay home.

Her telling him, once again, that he could stop her when he could stand up and do so, made him roar Emma out the door, but eventually he calmed and Emma returned.

Adam feared she would get lost again; Sara understood that. She even understood the reason for his orders, despite the fact that she could not obey them. She went on her way, delivering babies where she was needed, but now she took Emma along for company.

She delivered more babies after Adam had been allowed the short trek back to their bed, when he was still too weak to stop her.

After he rejoined her in their bedroom, however, he spent another two weeks growling like a bear.

At the end of June, Jordan pronounced Adam's leg healed, once and for all. "But the limp will be a lasting reminder of your stupidity," Jordan added.

Adam was out of bed in a shot. After he sent the doctor packing, he went to the barn to throw Roman Byler off the property as well.

Jordan took her husband's bluster in good stride and Sara laughed at his mock-hasty retreat. Then she laughed again as Roman ran toward his buggy, Adam shaking his fist from the barn.

"He loves you like a brother," Sara called to Roman as he scrambled into his vehicle.

Roman spat off the side of the buggy. "Ya, a blood

brother, one whose blood he wants to spill." And he was off.

Adam came up beside her and raised his arm toward Roman in a last gesture of threat as their neighbor cleared the drive.

"He loves you like a brother," Sara told her husband.

"Bah, you'd think—"

Adam's skeptical response was halted by the brightly colored Yankee peddler's cart entering the drive. "You the midwife?" the grizzled driver asked.

When Sara responded in the affirmative, the man passed her a note, nodded goodbye and turned his cart around.

"It's from Hetty Yoder," Sara told Adam. "She is in labor. I have to go."

"She is being shunned, Sara. You cannot go. It is against the ordnung. You will be shunned, too, if you go."

"Her baby should die, maybe her too, because she thumbed her nose at a bishop or something?" Sara shook her head and went to the barn to hitch her buggy. "What horse should I use?" she shouted, hands on hips, as Adam entered. "You will want yours for farm work and your mother has taken hers to market."

Adam nodded toward a far stall, where Sara saw the new filly Jonah Lutz had brought with Adam's horses. She looked from the filly to Adam and back.

"I bought her for you at the auction on the day of the blizzard," he said. "I only told my mother I bought her to breed, so I could surprise you. I didn't think Old Joe was in very good shape."

"You were certainly right about that. Poor Old Joe. Wait a minute; you were angry with me, yet you almost got yourself killed to buy me a new horse . . . as a surprise?"

"I was angry with myself," Adam said, "for being angry with you."

Sara about wilted with relief, almost enough to change her mind about going to Hetty Yoder's, just to please him. But two lives were in jeopardy and she could not afford to falter. She reached for the harness. "Thank you, Adam. She is beautiful."

Adam took the harness from her hand and returned it to its peg.

Sara took it down again. "I told you, I am going, no matter what you s—"

"If you speak to Hetty and are shunned, your heart will break, because you will lose the companionship of the people you care about, including the mother and sister you have just found."

Sara let go the halter and fisted her hands, feeling bested, but only for a minute. "Fine then, I will not speak to her. I will speak to her husband. Surely he—"

"Her husband has been dead for a year, Sara." He raised a speaking brow. "And she is with child. That is why she is being shunned."

Sara released an aggravated breath. "Fine then. Emma will come with me. She has not been baptized, so she can speak to Hetty without fear of being shunned for it."

"Emma?"

"Your sister communicates fine. You have simply not seen her do it. And she likes to help me with deliveries."

"But you—"

"Nowhere, nowhere, I tell you, in our ordnung, does it say that I cannot take a child from its shunned mother's body."

His wife's plain speaking startled Adam, but he recovered quickly, despite the embarrassment warming his face. Sara had managed, however, to disarm him enough to make him give in. "Fine," he said, hiding a grudging admiration. "We will take the big buggy. It will be safer."

"We?"

"I will take you, in case of bad weather."

"Bad weather? It's nearly summer. Besides, Emma will be frightened if—"

"Better get your bag," he said. "Or I will leave without you."

Sara chuckled. "But Emma," she said, placing her hand over his, to make him listen.

He regarded their hands for a bit, sighed and wove their fingers together. "I will be as gentle as a lamb and silent as a stone. For Emma."

Sara outright laughed. "As if you could."

Adam's eyes might just have twinkled then, Sara thought. "Emma may hesitate when she sees me," he said. "But she will climb into the buggy just the same, if only to protect you from me. She is stronger than we both believe, our Emma."

And for once, Sara saw, when Emma came outside, Adam was right.

As they drove home, Adam was pleased to be right, but he was also shocked at the way Emma had related to the laboring woman. She did communicate, did their Emma, in ways most people might have ignored, coming as they did from a speaking world.

And when Sara had placed that wailing baby in Emma's arms, just as he entered the room in response to her call, his sister's smile was so wide, directed even for a beat at him, that Adam knew he would not have missed that delivery for anything.

No, nor any other either, he decided. Because he was

never going to let Sara go traveling without him again. Besides, he had to face facts; his Sara was a born midwife.

Several days later, the Bishop did not agree with Adam's assessment. In fact their white-bearded Elder roared his disapproval, not once, but half-a-dozen times at least, as he paced their best room.

Sara sat in a rocker, head bowed, deceptively docile. Adam knew better. But then she raised her eyes to his and silently begged his help. Damn.

Rather than flash her the I-told-you-so look he'd kept at the ready, Adam was forced to let it go. "Bishop Weaver, you mistake the matter," he said. "Sara never once spoke to Hetty. Neither did she sit at table with her or take food from her hand."

"She broke the ordnung. Hetty Yoder is being shunned."

"Nowhere in our rule of life does it say that a midwife cannot take a birthing babe from its shunned mother's body," Adam said, and Roman began to cough. He coughed so hard, he had to step into the kitchen for a drink of water.

The harried bishop blustered, but after several impotent buts, words failed him entirely.

Adam was about to continue when he caught his wife's warm look of gratitude, and a melt took place somewhere deep inside him, bringing with it a warmth he refused to consider. Whatever it was called, it straightened his spine and stood him taller. "My Sara will tend every mother and child that comes within her power to tend, and, frankly, I would have it no different. If you wish to bring Sara before the church district for saving the lives of our women and children, that is your choice. I will say the same before everyone. So, too, I suspect, would the women who might not be in attendance, but for Sara."

★ ★ ★ ★ ★

Adam turned over in bed yet again. Tired as he was, he could not sleep, probably because Sara was driving him crazy staying on her own side of their bed, which she had been doing since he moved back into it, despite her gratitude to him for averting her excommunication.

Last night, he had tried to coax her into his arms, but she wouldn't budge. Even sound asleep, she was stubborn, though he'd been certain she was pretending. Now she slept beside him, but apart. He listened to her soft breaths and inhaled her vanilla scent, but touching the woman was useless.

Adam was troubled, not because of his sexual frustration, but because he sensed as much banked yearning in her as himself.

Had he done something to turn her from intimacy? Had he frightened her in the shack, the day of that terrifying blizzard? The way he'd left that morning, perhaps . . . in what might have seemed to her to be anger?

But he had been gruff previous to then, and that had never stopped her from welcoming him in their bed.

He feared what might have happened in the shack. He kept having a wild dream that made him pulse with need, a fantasy that haunted him, especially in his delirium, so vivid, he did not even need to be asleep to have it.

In it, Sara was like a . . . a pagan goddess, God help him, all bright, blinding light, her head thrown back, her soft hair flowing down her naked body. Too beautiful to be real, too incredible to be his. And yet Adam was certain that was how she looked, except that he had never seen her naked. He had touched her, yes, but to envision every perfect curve, the way her proud breasts lifted away from her body, their pouting tips outlined by the fire behind her, became an ecstasy all its own.

And the way she had fit herself over him, like a glove made of the softest leather, tight, supple, milking him— Adam groaned and changed position again. How was it that he had wished for so long that she would stay away from him, and now that she did, she drove him madder than the world claimed him?

"Adam?" Sara said, sitting up, as if he'd brought her to life with the depth of his need.

He tried to pull her down against him then, to settle his need where he wanted, to be taken inside her—though he would not breach her—but she pushed him away.

"The door," she said, rising. "Someone is knocking at the door." She donned her robe, but Adam rose behind her and placed a staying hand on her arm. "This is the middle of the night. Wait. I will see." He lit the lamp and took it as he left their room.

The man at the door needed a bath; Adam did not need the lamp to know that much. The stench of sweat and liquor hovered about him like a pall. It was a scent he had worn himself, those months after Abby and before Sara. That kind of pain could cause a man to fall, and far. Perhaps this man had fallen as well, and with good reason. Adam swallowed his judgment and his frustration at the intrusion. "Can I help you?"

The staggering man entered and passed him for Sara standing in the shadow of their bedroom door. Adam closed his eyes, his need sliding away with his hope. Another birthing, at midnight no less. . . .

They were on their way in no time. "Never will you say no; I know that now," Adam told Sara, perched on the buggy seat beside him. "Because if ever there was a man deserved that answer, Butch Redding is the man."

"His wife does not deserve such bad treatment, however. The child she has been nurturing in her womb does not deserve to die."

"Sara," Adam said, regarding her, sudden concern prickling his nape. "You will not save every one of them. You cannot. If you think to do so, you will fall hard when you fail, harder than I did from the loft, and you will not mend as easily. I understand that much, if little else, about you."

Sara waved away his caution. "I know what to do. Don't worry about any of them."

"About you, I worry," he said, but she did not hear, or she did not choose to.

After a quiet minute, she flashed him a smile, likely calculated to ease his concern. "Imagine if I had refused to respond to Mad Adam Zuckerman's call."

Imagine where his girls would be now, he thought. Where he would be. "Hell," he said; he would be in hell. His girls too, without Sara.

"Cuss all you want," she said, misunderstanding him. "Just go faster so you keep up with him."

Leave it to her to be in a hurry, even now, given the prospect of a midnight delivery with a drunken husband underfoot. Sometimes Sara was like the horses his people had taken to buying for their buggies, always eager to go, always ready to run. When Sara could not do what she wanted, she was like a racehorse at the starting gate, forced to a stop, heart racing the way its eager legs wanted to do, unable to move forward until the gate opened.

He wondered what would happen if nobody ever opened the gate. Would racing hearts give out and die? He feared she might die of it too, his Sara, of not being able to give all of herself to her work, to their children, to anyone who needed her. She would die, as certainly, if she failed, he thought.

It occurred to him, then, that he had been trying to stop her from giving all of herself to him. Was that why she had turned from him—physically, at least? He needed to think more about it, though now was not the time. Butch Redding needed to be caught up with.

"It will not be pleasant, with him," Adam said. "But I will be beside you, no matter what happens. You will be safe," he promised.

Sara turned to him then. He did not see or hear movement, but he sensed her eyes on him, and something more. He took the reins in one hand and reached for her.

It was there, her hand, reaching too. She laced their fingers together, raised them to her lips and kissed his knuckles. *"Danke,"* she said.

That was all.

It was enough.

It was everything. Adam blinked to clear his vision. In their bed, he had yearned for . . . everything. Now he had it. And it wasn't even what he thought it would be.

It was better.

The man's house was as bad as him: smelly, unkempt, dirty. Barefooted children in a cold, barely heated kitchen were dressed in threadbare clothes that needed washing as much as them. Why were they not in bed at this hour?

He saw Sara hesitate when she saw them. Damned if he didn't see her swell with the need to help them, too, but a woman's scream brought her to her purpose and she ran.

Adam sat at the table even as the man upended a bottle of whiskey against his lips. Greedy, slovenly. A shaft of pain hit Adam to see the way the children watched their father.

His girls might have watched him that way at one time, except that he had waited until Sara had taken them away to drown his worthless self in drink.

Like these children feared their father, Adam had always thought he wanted his children to fear him. He had been stupid to think they should. It might be enough that he reined in his temper with the same force he used on an unruly beast. He was more manageable surely than an animal, though his father had not been.

One of the smaller boys asked to go to the outhouse.

Ignored by his father, he began to cry. Again, he made his need known.

Butch Redding swore and took another drink. "Shut up," he shouted.

Adam rose and extended his hand. "I'll take you."

It took the boy a while to extend his own, and by then it was too late, because he was standing in a puddle on the floor.

The child cowered before his drunk father lunged. "Son of a bitch!" The man's hand shot out like a snake and sent the boy clear across the kitchen.

Adam saw red. The boy's bloody face blurred to the blood-smeared face of the little girl Adam once tried to protect. Emma.

The drunk flew through the kitchen as fast as his son had done, but Adam had aimed him in a different direction. He landed in the trash. And with a roar, the bastard was up and charging, but Adam met him halfway, and the brute hit the wall a second time.

More blood. More fury.

Sara screamed as Adam toppled the heartless bastard, smashing his fist into that hideous face, the one he wanted to hit, and hit, and hit, until it broke and breathed no more.

Sara screamed his name; she shouted for him to stop, but he had to keep the man from hurting—

Adam received a sharp blow from behind, despite the fact that his adversary lay before him, a blow that rattled him to his bones. Then the room shifted, tilted, and he fell.

When he opened his eyes and rose, Adam shook his head, and saw that blood covered the man's face, that he was unconscious but still breathing.

Sara threw a broken chair to the floor.

Adam was pretty sure, by the feel of his head, that she had used it on him. He looked around while she tended the small boy with the bloody face, and realized where he was and what he had nearly done.

Murder.

He went outside to the pump to fill a bucket and came back to throw water over the man. When the bully came to, Adam bent down and grabbed him by his collar, just enough to lift his big ugly face from the floor. "You touch another of your children and I will kill you. You hear me?"

Sara grasped Adam's shoulder. "It is not our way," she said, her brow furrowed, her gentle fingers stroking the stubborn head she had just finished cracking with a chair.

"It is the way I was raised," he said, nodding at the cowering children. "Just like them."

At Sara's look of shocked revulsion, he went outside to wash and wait in the buggy.

He was on his knees beside the pump, staring at the blood on his hands, craving delivery from the hell of his memories, when Sara came and knelt beside him. She kissed his cheek. "I love you."

"Do not."

She stood with a sigh. "I cannot help myself."

"I do not need you or your lo—" He grasped her skirts as

216

she made to turn away and buried his face in them. She held him there, stroking his hair, giving his unclean self an absolution he did not deserve.

It was all the deliverance he craved. Adam wept.

When he quieted, she smoothed his brow. "You did it because he struck the child."

"Evil struck," he said. "In more ways than you know."

"It could strike again this night. I need help, Adam. Your help."

He washed his face again and followed her inside. The man on the floor was snoring.

"The children?" Adam asked.

"I cleaned them up a bit and put them to bed before I went outside," Sara said. "They were exhausted."

He followed her up the rickety stairs and found his fury at the man building again with the squalor about him. But he swallowed his ire when he met the woman. She had been battered, more often than not, it was easy to see.

Adam read kinship in those eyes.

He walked her when she could barely stand. He sat behind her in her bed and held her up when she needed to push. After a long and difficult labor, she delivered a big, strong baby boy.

They had a chance to talk then, while Sara washed the babe. Adam told her right off that he'd beat her husband and left him on the kitchen floor. "You will take your children and leave," he said, bringing Sara's quiet protest, but neither he, nor the woman with the bruised face, paid her any mind.

"I would," the woman said, looking at the baby Sara washed. "If I knew where to go."

"I will come for you in a week and take you away for good. He won't follow. And he won't hurt you or the children between now and then, either; I'll see to it," Adam said.

"I believe you," the woman said. "My name is Jenny."

"I am Adam," he replied. "You've met my wife."

"Are you two finished?" Sara snapped, uncomfortable with what Adam was taking upon himself and with the bond that had formed before her eyes, however invisible it remained.

Adam looked free of pain for the first time since they arrived, and Jenny looked . . . relieved. Sara was actually sorry to spoil the moment for them both, but. . . . "The afterbirth is not coming," she said. "You are bleeding more than you should, Jenny."

Panic, Sara saw flare in Adam's eyes. "What can I do?" he asked.

"Jenny, I want you to kneel on the bed, and Adam I want you to massage her stomach while she does. We need to get the contractions started again." Sara wished desperately that Jordan were here. "I'll prepare some raspberry leaf infusion."

This was the first time Sara had seen her husband red with embarrassment, but he did exactly as she showed him, apologizing to Jenny all the while.

The woman laughed at his embarrassment. "Any man who defends one of my kids against Butch can keep me from bleeding to death."

Her words silenced him.

Sara took over for Adam after she made Jenny swallow the strong infusion. "The contractions have started again," Sara said. "I can feel them."

"Ya, me too," Jenny said, almost collapsing on the bed when Sara allowed it. The placenta came in two pieces, but it came, nevertheless. Sara fit it together to make certain it was all there and none was left inside; then she elevated Jenny's legs.

It was late the next night when Sara and Adam finally set off for home, almost twenty-four hours after they'd arrived. The children had been bathed, fed, and the house cleaned. They worked together to accomplish it.

After Jenny and her new son fell asleep, Adam took Jenny's husband to the barn to have a "talk" with him. Despite the fact that Adam returned a long hour later, Butch Redding had not surfaced again, though Adam assured Sara he had not laid another hand on the man.

Both tired, both silent, they drove toward home.

Disturbed by more than the beating he had given and endured, Adam shuddered. He had seen a child struck down. Picturing it chilled him even now. Worse, it brought on that rage that made him mad—good word for him—mad enough to kill.

He knew now, once and for all, that he was like his father, violent and dangerous to those around him. He should go away and free his family from his clutches, except that he had a responsibility to care for them.

Not that he'd been very good about caring for them. Until recently, it had been a matter of ritual, like putting one foot in front of the other. Now his care of them had become connected to an emotion he could not name, one that frightened him witless. Somehow, he knew Sara was responsible for this change, yet he could not decide if he was sorry about it or not. Disconnected was easier.

Not that he'd done a good job of disconnecting from Abby. He'd killed her anyway. Tonight he'd learned how, and probably why, that happened. If he had called Sara at the beginning of Abby's labor, Ab might have lived. If he had not gotten her pregnant, she certainly would be alive.

He had a lot to answer for.

"Jenny is grateful that you're going to take her away from that man," Sara said, breaking his silent hell. "You are probably saving her life. The children's too. But Butch will hate you enough to kill you afterward."

"Small price," Adam said. It should be higher; he deserved to suffer. The man should try, he thought. "I'd like to see him try."

"I would not. What happened, really?"

"He hit the boy. I hit him."

Sara put her hand on his arm. "It was more than that. You know what I mean."

"Leave it be."

"Adam, I—"

"You did a good job tonight. You learned a lot from The *English*."

"Adam, please—"

"That's what happened to Abby, isn't it? There was no afterbirth that night either."

Sara sighed.

"So if I had called you when her labor began. . . ."

She touched him again, and God help him, he craved the contact. He grasped her hand and brought it to his heart as if that alone could heal him.

"Do not blame yourself, Adam. We don't know if—"

"Who better to blame than me? You did. 'With so many babies so close, you're killing her.'"

"Oh, Adam. I never meant it that way."

Adam stopped the buggy and regarded his beautiful, full-of-life Sara; if her candle were snuffed, he would die himself. "What other way is there to put it? I will not do that to you, Sara. I will never expose you to the danger of childbirth; I will not get you with child. I will not kill you, too."

Sara went into her husband's arms and wept. She'd poisoned the man she loved with unfounded guilt. How could she take back those hasty, horrible words, so prophetically spoken? How young she had been that night, how harsh and careless. How very much she had grown since, yet it was almost too late.

Her stubbornness, her thoughtless judgment, had hurt Adam in a way from which he might never recover. "Foolish, foolish Sara Lapp," she could practically hear her Maker saying. She could even see Him shaking his head, looking down at her from heaven.

She'd crippled her marriage before it had a chance to begin. She'd broken her husband's spirit.

"Don't cry, my Sara. Don't cry," Adam said. "We have babes aplenty. And they need you for kissing tears and singing silly songs. They need you for making dresses in *ferbudden* colors, and they especially need you for laughing with."

Sara sat back and wiped her eyes. "The dress colors I use are not forbidden; they're the right colors, just . . . better, livelier. And, Adam, the girls need you, too, especially for laughing with."

Adam shook his head. "You don't understand."

"But I want to. Oh, Adam, I want so badly to understand. I want to be a real wife to you. I can handle whatever you have to tell me. I can handle anything that comes along, even more babies."

"No," he shouted. "Never that. And you will not coax me into it, either. You will be happy with what we have, or we have nothing. Else I will sleep in the barn, Sara. I mean it."

Sara was speechless. She was frightened.

"What we have now together is good," he said. "It is enough. It has to be."

It was good, she thought. They had come a long way since their marriage.

But the ground they had gained would surely be lost, and soon, because when Adam discovered she carried his child, he would never forgive her.

Chapter Fifteen

Adam set off in their big, new family-sized buggy to pick up Jenny Redding and her seven children to take them to the Amish settlement in LaGrange, Indiana, where he was brought up. His mother had written to friends, who'd responded that they would welcome Jenny and her family and help find a place for them to live.

Sara only hoped that Butch Redding would not pick a fight with Adam when he went for Jenny, because Sara would not be there to stop her husband this time.

"He is a good man, my Adam," Lena said as they stood side by side at the edge of the drive to watch Adam's buggy disappear over Mulberry Hill.

Sara nodded, but not before her mother-in-law saw the tears in her eyes. Sara could not speak for the lump in her throat, though Adam had promised her, repeatedly and with conviction, that he would not allow Butch to provoke him.

Sara swallowed. "I know I am being foolish, but I am going to miss him."

Lena placed an arm around her shoulder and squeezed. "He will be back, our Adam. He cannot stand the separation any more than you. I thought his eyes, maybe, seemed bright too."

Her mother-in-law walked her back to the house. "At least you have an excuse for tears," Lena said. "What is his, I wonder? Or is he the one with the sickness of morning in this family?"

It was meant as a joke, but Sara was too caught by Lena's perception to laugh. "You know? About the baby?"

"Of course. Did you think to keep it a secret, even from the people in the house?"

Panic filled Sara, but then she realized that Adam would never be able to hide such knowledge, so he did not suspect. Yet.

Lena stopped walking to regard her. "Adam doesn't know?"

Sara shook her head. "It wonders me that you know things I don't tell you, like the fact that I am expecting."

"Mothers are like that. Now, you tell me why your own husband does not know of this. You have been wrong to keep it from him."

It was the first time Sara had been chastised by this new mother of hers and it hurt not a little bit. "Oh, Lena, it is so complicated and such a long story."

"Adam will be gone five weeks at least. Plenty time for a long story, I think. And you will feel better for the telling."

It was so complicated that just trying to sort it out made Sara tired. But then everything made her tired these days. When they got inside, she sat at the table, looked at Lena and felt as if she were going to cry again. She did not even know where to begin.

Lena clucked like a mother hen whose chick has gone missing, urged her from her chair and accompanied her back to her room to lie down. Then this new mother of hers sat at the edge of her bed and took her hand. "Start from the day you see Adam first time, ya? Good beginning?"

Sara smiled. "The first time I saw him, he was big and angry and . . . big."

"And handsome, my Adam."

Sara smiled. "Very handsome. But he never smiled.

Sometimes I felt as if he were watching me, especially after I had been laughing—"

"It is the bright butterflies Adam likes best."

"Your family likes butterflies a lot," Sara said, intrigued by the subject. Adam had called her his perfect butterfly.

"We do. Go on."

"But why butterflies?"

"They are bright and beautiful, one of God's most perfect creations, I think. They are a symbol for me, of God, of his healing power, even of light and sunshine. I passed my love for them to Adam when he was small. He held on to it, I guess, if you have heard him mention butterflies."

"His horses are named for them. Titania and Tawny."

"I did not realize. Such knowledge warms a mother's heart. Now tell me about the first time you saw him."

"It was right after the districts had been re-divided and I became part of this one. I knew no one, but already the Bishop was annoyed with me, because I had made known to him my plan to become a midwife. We were at a barn-raising, discussing the subject 'heatedly.' Bishop Weaver shouted that I should stick to women's work, so of course, I needed to prove to him that I could do anything a man could."

"Oh *liebchen,* what did you do?"

"I went to the stack of planks and followed the example of those who were bringing them to the men nailing them to the lower outside wall of the barn."

"And you handed one to Adam?"

"I didn't know who he was yet, but I saw him waiting for one, so I made for him, carrying the plank over my shoulder, as I'd seen the others do. But when I had just about reached him, I saw Bishop Weaver coming toward me with an angry stride, and it made me nervous. My grip on the plank faltered, and it tilted, down in the front, up in the back, and slipped toward Adam so fast, it hit him . . . hard . . . in a bad spot . . . between his legs."

Lena screeched and slapped her hand to her mouth.

Sara feared for a minute that her mother-in-law would chastise her again, but instead her eyes twinkled and she began to laugh. Sara was so relieved and so enchanted by Lena's merriment, that Sara saw, for the first time, the humor in that long-ago encounter, and she began to laugh as well.

Lena wiped away her tears. "What did my Adam do?"

"He set his jaw hard and made a face like this," Sara's tense face made Lena laugh again. "Then he bent over, very carefully, picked up the board and nailed it to the studs."

"And the Bishop—"

"Told me I was needed to watch the children."

"And after that?"

"Adam made me mad with his constant watching, not as if he thought I would hurt him again, but as if he were annoyed with me for being happy, so I did what I thought would bewilder him—you know, keep him guessing. I walked right up and served him first, that day, and most every time after, at fellowship meals, barn-raisings, whatever frolics we had in the district. I did it, you know, to show him I was not afraid of him, even if he wished me to be."

"My Adam would need a wife to give as good as she got. Do you think he wanted you not to be afraid?"

"I just know that he made me so uncomfortable, being rude that way, that I had this need to be nice to show him up."

"And annoy him a bit," Lena said on a laugh. "But he still married Abby instead?"

"Oh, he was already married to Ab when the district was re-divided. We became instant friends, his first wife and me. Abby was my only friend until Mercy, but Mercy lives in Indiana."

"*Liebchen?* I would think friends of yours would be plenty, with your easy laugh and happy disposition. Why none?"

"I was a woman who belonged nowhere and to no one. An Amishwoman who wanted to deliver babies, which was *ferbudden.*" Sara made to lower her voice like a man. "A woman should not take on so, an unmarried one, especially." She laughed. "This I heard often. But I am a rebel, a scrapper; I know it and everybody else in Walnut Creek does too. Sometimes, even now, Adam calls me Scrapper Sara, but it's better than Spinster Sara, which is what he used to call me."

"You might not have been happy to be a spinster, but you are pleased to be a scrapper, I think. Glad to break rules, like with your dresses of the rainbow colors for my grandbabies. Pride and stubbornness are both a weakness and a strength for you, my daughter. For Adam too. That's why you belong together."

That Lena thought she and Adam belonged together warmed Sara. She closed her eyes, her new mother's hand stroking her wrist, soothing her as no mother had done for some time. "Adam's first wife laughed at how I used to make the Elders mad," Sara said, opening her eyes again. "She told me she used to tell Adam whenever I had done so and he would get as mad as the Elders did. Madder. Ab seemed to think it was funny, the way I could make Adam mad, and the way I tried to annoy him by being nice, serving him and all, and joking with him. She did not believe me when I said he scared me."

"Tell me how it happened that you went from being my son's first wife's friend to his second wife. When did his first wife die?"

Sara's heart plummeted. "Last fall." She related the circumstances of Abby's death. "Adam always disliked his children. Everybody knew it. Not that he liked the adults. But with children, especially his own, his dislike seemed to go deeper. He stayed apart from them, frowned when they came near. The girls seemed nearly as afraid of him, back when Abby was alive, as Emma is now."

Distraught, Lena stood and went to the window, looking as if she might weep. After a minute, she turned back to Sara, disbelief in her look. "Adam hurt his girls? He closed their little fingers in doors and such?"

"Of course not! Why would you say such a thing? Oh no." Stricken, Sara sat up. "Please, do not say that his fath—"

Lena's hand sliced through the air, cutting off Sara's words, as if doing so could change the fact of them, and that's when Sara knew it was so, and she too wanted to weep.

They stared at each other as the color returned to her mother-in-law's face, but Lena shook her head, refusing further discussion. On the previous subject, however, she felt no such compunction. "Tell me more about you and Adam and his children," Lena said.

Sara decided she owed her mother-in-law the truth. "Adam gave them to me after Abby died. He said I should take them home to raise them. Just like that."

"So you said you would marry him instead?"

"I would never have suggested such a thing. The Elders decreed we must marry or be shunned."

Lena shook her head again, but seemed willing to let her

confusion pass for the moment. "You think Adam does not like his children, even though he never hurt them?"

"He wants no more." Tears of shame coursed down Sara's cheeks as she told Adam's mother how she had been so selfish and unfeeling as to accuse him of killing his wife when Abby was already dead. "And now he won't touch me, because he doesn't want to kill me—God help us both—by getting me with child. Oh, Lena, this will destroy him. What have I done?"

Lena let go of Sara's hand as if it burned her suddenly. "So this is not my son's babe you carry?"

Sara laughed at the accusation and the look on her mother-in-law's face, but her laughter became a wellspring of tears that could not be held back. Rolling away from the woman whose love was for Adam first, as should be, Sara let herself cry. She could use a mother of her own, right now, though. Then she felt Lena's hand rubbing her back, soothing her, a mother's soft voice trying to calm her, calling her *liebchen.*

Sara turned to face her. "Thank you." She rubbed the tiny mound of her child. "This babe beneath my heart is your grandchild. Adam was delirious in that shack we sheltered in and doesn't know he broke his vow. I only learned of the vow recently, or else . . . No," Sara shook her head in firm denial. "No. I would not have tried to stop him, had I known. Oh, Lena, I love him so much, it hurts."

"Love usually does, *liebchen,* but it is worth the price, though I have never known such a love as you and Adam share. Be grateful for the gift."

If only there were love on her husband's part, Sara thought.

Lena's eyes twinkled again and Sara saw where Emma got her spirit. "So you became my son's bride in truth on that snowy night, and the *dummkopf* doesn't even know it."

Sara actually giggled. She felt so much better, she hugged her mother-in law. "I needed to laugh just then. Thank you."

Weeks into Adam's absence, Katie came running into the room where Lena was showing Sara how to make a baby quilt. "The butterflies, they come." She grabbed her grandmother's hand. "Come *Grossmommie;* my take you. Sara too."

"Butterflies?" Lena looked as if her heart took to beating double as Katie dragged them into the yard.

Lena took Sara's hand in a grasp that hurt when she saw the children around the large stone-lined ring of plants. "Is that . . . is it—"

"A butterfly garden," Lizzie said. "Datt planted it special the day I was born, Mommie said." Lizzie looked at Sara with suddenly wide and regretful eyes. "Our first Mommie, I mean."

Sara kissed Lizzie's kapped head. "I know, Sweetheart."

"Did your Mommie tell you why your Datt planted such a garden?" Lena asked, almost begging for an answer, but Lizzie shook her head.

"I will tell you then." Eyes bright, Lena knelt in the grass and took the three girls into the circle of her arms. "When your Datt was a very little boy—small as you, Pris—I planted a butterfly garden for him, because your Datt was a sad little boy, and I . . . I was not strong enough to make him smile. I wasn't even strong enough to tell him I loved him, so I planted a butterfly garden to show him that I did. Butterflies are a sign of God's healing, and he needed lots of healing back then, your Datt." She looked up at Sara. "I think he still does, but I believe that he has found the one who can heal him, except that he does not know it yet."

Sara's heart filled with hope at her mother-in-law's words, and she knelt beside them in the grass. "Tell me about this butterfly garden your Datt planted," she asked Lizzie. "Did he ever tell you anything about it?"

Katie knelt at the edge of the well-tended ring, her curls breaking free of her kapp, her beautiful little face lit from within. "Datt says this one will bring the pretty blue butterfly over there."

"The Azure butterfly," Lizzie said, kneeling beside her younger sister. "And this is a juneberry for the Banded Purple butterflies. And that heart-shaped plant is a bleeding heart, my favorite because of all the little hearts hanging from it."

The bleeding heart . . . a beautiful and sad flower, Sara thought, its name alone a reminder of the girls and their father, with hearts in need of healing.

"The butterflies go away in the winter," Katie said sadly. "But they come back to our garden every year."

"Butterfly bush," Pris said, shaking a fragrant bush with spiked lavender flowers and making Sara and Lena laugh.

"She's right," Lizzie said. "That's what it's called. Painted Ladies come for that flower."

"Yes," Sara said. "But will butterflies come?"

Lena thought her grandchildren's giggles somehow charmed even the butterflies flitting about them.

"We'll have to bring Hannah out here and teach her about the butterfly garden too," Sara said. "I need to learn too."

"You can learn later," Lena said, taking her arm again. "We need to talk." She turned to her oldest granddaughter. "Teach Pris for a while, then come inside for lunch. Your Mommie and I have something to discuss."

Inside the house, to Sara's surprise, Lena's joy disappeared. Rather than begin the discussion she spoke about, she became pensive and quiet.

Sara sensed the need to be quiet also, so she brewed some peppermint tea and poured it before she spoke. "I have been meaning to ask you, Lena, why Adam thought you were dead. I've asked him, but he doesn't answer."

Lena sighed and took her hand. "Let me tell you first that Adam does not dislike his children. He loves them. He just doesn't know it."

"I would like to believe that, Lena, but—"

"There is proof. We just saw it."

"I don't understand."

"I planted him a butterfly garden to show him my love, knowing that the garden and the butterflies would say it for me every spring."

"Lena, why didn't you just tell Adam you loved him?"

"Because I could not, not without causing him harm."

"That makes no sense—"

"Shh. Listen. I believe Adam planted his butterfly garden for the same reason I planted mine, to tell his children he loved them. His father, the man I foolishly married, was not a good man, *liebchen,* not like our Adam is. Amos demanded perfection, even from a child. And for a child who stammered and had a frail body, like Adam, he had no patience. Worse than that, he was cruel. He told Adam he was unfit for farming, that he was worthless. Amos would get so mad with Adam's stuttering, he hurt the child in his determination to force him to stop the bad habit.

"Adam got whipped, Sara. He got his fingers crushed in doors, his toes crushed under the very rocker his father sat in."

Sara was too shaken by such cruelty to speak.

"He got locked in the smokehouse, the outhouse, overnight, summer or winter. He has scars on his body, and sometimes, I fear, deeper."

Sara rose to hide her shock and disgust, not only at Adam's father, but at his mother as well. But she could not hold her feelings back. "How could you allow such cruelty? How could you let your husband hurt your own son?"

"Adam was always strong, strong enough to endure—"

"You just said he was frail."

"Of body, he was, back then, but not of mind. He was stronger than Emma, at least."

Sara caught her breath. "Her father is why she fears men? Because of beatings?" As if that were nothing, Sara thought, and yet, anything worse was impossible to imagine, let alone voice.

"Because of beatings, only. Amos was cruel, but he was not . . . sick—"

"Oh, but he was, Lena. He was."

Lena paled to the color of flour paste and a forlorn sob escaped her. "He beat her, only, and never badly, not like he beat Adam. Adam saw to that. But Adam looks now like Amos did then and I think that's why Emma is afraid of him. When Adam is angry, it is his father's temper for certain that he struggles with, yet it is not so bad as my husband's was."

"Couldn't you have gone to the Elders and told them what your husband did?"

"They would never have believed that the pious Amos Zuckerman could harm his children. I feared being shunned for lying or disrespect to my husband. I could not take the chance. If I was right and I had been shunned, Amos would have had control over the children and my protection would have been removed from Emma. Adam was strong enough to bear his father's anger. But even you can see that Amos would have broken Emma." Lena sobbed again. "Maybe even killed her."

As much sorrow for Lena as for her son and daughter rose up in Sara, and she embraced her mother-in-law. "You have lived in hell, I think, but you are safe now with us. Emma too."

Lena stepped back and raised her chin. "You would have been proud to see how little Adam turned his father's fury away from his smaller sister and pulled it toward himself. He proved he was strong in the way he drew his father's anger and allowed himself to be beaten so Emma was not."

If it were possible, Sara fell more deeply in love with her big, bad, mad husband, though he was no longer any of those things to her. He was a good man who had suffered in his life and was suffering still. Now, only his heart she saw as big, and the "mad" she had taken into her own heart for what he had suffered. "Tell me about the butterfly garden," Sara said, sitting, patting the chair beside her at the table.

"I was afraid if I interfered between Adam and his father, Adam would have clung to me, making Amos see him as weaker still, and more in need of a strong hand. I told Adam the butterflies brought sunshine and healing, because I didn't know how else to tell him that all things ugly pass and God's beauty reigns in the end."

"Adam was only five when you left him with your husband. What made you do such a thing, leave him, I mean?"

Lena sighed. Her hands shook. "My sister was ill, dying alone. I went to care for her, despite Amos warning me not to. Adam tells me his father said I took Emma and left for good. It made my son hate me, and with cause. Within the week, Amos told him we died in a carriage accident and he brought Adam here to Ohio."

Lena's face looked suddenly ravaged, old, her look begging forgiveness, understanding. "All these years I looked for my son, and now I have found him, only to find, as well, the horror I wrought with my own weakness."

Sara took Lena's hand and squeezed it. "I understand, in a way, why you could not tell Adam you loved him, why you planted a butterfly garden for him. But why can't Adam just tell his girls he loves them, if, as you say, he does? Why does he need a butterfly garden?"

Sara went to gaze out the window. Three beautiful little girls were chasing the butterflies their father had all but provided. Then she envisioned that same man giving them away. "Why, for heaven's sakes was he willing to give those beautiful babies to me, if he loved them?"

"I don't know," Lena said, the words a cry of torment. "I wish to God I did."

While Adam was gone, Sara and Lena spent time every day with the girls in the butterfly garden. One morning the "rat-a-tat" of a woodpecker caught their attention. Lena took the girls to the tree and they saw the bird fly up to a nest in its upper branches. Lena told them the mother woodpecker likely expected little ones soon and maybe they would be able to show her babies to their Datt when he returned.

Sara learned all she could about the plants that brought butterflies. Some were feeder plants for the caterpillars to eat. Some were bright and showy to attract particular species.

The first time Sara actually saw scores of butterflies, all at once, she and the children sat right down in the grass to watch. They were beautiful—the butterflies, that is. Her children were beautiful too, their eyes aglow, rapt and eager to watch and study the bright creatures, as if storing new bits of knowledge to share with their father later.

He was a good man, their father. Sara knew it, even if Adam did not. He had put his own well-being in jeopardy to save a family in a blizzard. He had put even his horses' safety before his own, leaving them with that family, making it necessary for him to walk for miles on his bad leg. Then, without a second thought, he had walked even farther that same night, sick as he was, to save her life as well.

As to why he had hit that father for abusing his son, there was no question in her mind that he did it for the child, to save him, and his sisters and brothers, from further beatings. Now he was taking them and their mother to safety.

From the good and generous boy, who had taken abuse onto his own shoulders in his sister's place, had come a good and generous man. A loving man.

His sister loved him, the memory of him as a boy, that was. Now, either she feared that Adam was like their abusive father, or she thought he *was* their abusive father. If the first case were true, eventually she would learn that Adam was gruff but gentle, loud but kind. If the latter were true, Sara didn't know if they could ever make her understand.

Pris's giggles brought Sara back to the half-circle she and the girls made around the butterfly garden. It didn't take her long to notice, following Pris's pointing finger, that Hannah, sitting in her lap, had a butterfly perched on her kapp.

"What kind of butterfly is it?" Sara softly asked so as not to frighten the winged beauty.

"A Monawk," Pris said.

"Right, a Monarch," Lizzie said. "That's good, Pris."

"A bright orange butterfly that thinks Hannah is a big white flower," Sara said.

Katie doubled over with laughter.

Pris lay in the grass and folded her hands on her chest. "My's a flower too."

"My too. Lizzie too." Excited, Katie lay down beside her sister, and Lizzie shrugged and reclined as well.

Sara was chuckling at the three of them, side by side in the grass, when she looked up to see Adam standing there watching them. Watching her. Lord and didn't the sight of him pound her heart and weaken her knees? Seven long weeks he had been gone.

Handsome, Lena had called him. Ya, he was that. And big too, especially of heart. And the dearest man Sara had ever known. She was so happy to see him, she swallowed so she wouldn't weep for missing him. She also kept herself from jumping up to throw herself in his arms. Somehow, she didn't think he'd want that . . . then again, from the look in his eyes, she might be wrong.

Maybe, like her, he yearned for a few things he didn't dare reveal, even to himself, which possibility she would ponder at another time.

"I have been learning about butterfly gardens," Sara said. "The girls have been teaching me. And look here at the baby." Sara pointed to the tiny little kapped head where the Monarch sat, wings spread wide, sunning itself. "This butterfly thinks Hannah is a pretty white flower."

The girls, solemn, unsmiling, had all sat up to watch their Datt, the look in their eyes much like his right now, as if they wanted things they could not name and were afraid to breathe, they wanted them so badly.

"Look, Datt," Katie said, pointing to the huge old oak not too far distant. "There is a woodpecker in those branches, building a nest. I think she will have some little peckers soon."

Adam's eyes actually twinkled.

"Come," Sara said on a chuckle, extending her hand to him. "Come and sit by me and teach your wife and your daughters more about butterflies."

Adam came and sat so close, his shoulder brushed hers, and she knew it was not an accidental touch, but one born of yearning.

To tell him she understood and shared his need, Sara nudged him back and ended up staying that way, shoulders touching. When he turned to face her, silent, wide-eyed, as if he didn't believe her response, Sara made so bold as to kiss his cheek. "I missed you."

Adam looked down at his hands. Sara regarded them as well. Beefy, big-knuckled hands, trembling like a leaf in a breeze, hands that would never hurt a child.

To prove it, Sara placed the baby in them. "Hannah missed you too."

Startled, Adam grasped his tiny daughter as if she were made of spun glass, panic a near thing.

Sara refused to give into her inclination and take Hannah back. "Don't worry; she won't break."

"My missed you too, Datt," Katie said, from right beside him. She bent to kiss his cheek too. Then she sat on his leg, put her arm around his neck and her head on his shoulder.

Hannah, still in his lap, batted Katie's kapp-strings, making the both of them giggle.

Adam's chest rose and fell at a quick pace for a minute, and again, Sara fought an urge to rescue him.

Lizzie stood slowly and came over too, but she stopped and stood before him, watching, her look much as it had been the morning Abby died, when Adam filled the stairway entrance. His look, however, bore not so much severity as yearning. And Sara realized that Lizzie's fear was not of him, but of not being wanted or loved by him, a fear he should understand well. Sara intended to speak to him about it, as soon as she could figure out a way to approach the subject without scaring him.

At the notion that she could frighten Mad Adam Zuckerman, Sara giggled and Adam looked at her, eyes wide . . . beseeching. He was either afraid she'd lost her mind or silently crying for help.

In the event he didn't know what to do, Sara leaned near enough to brush his earlobe with her lips, and he leaned too, inviting the touch. "You can fit another daughter under that big, long arm of yours," she whispered. "Extend it and invite Lizzie in."

Adam swallowed a protest before he hesitated, then extended his arm. "Come Lizziebelle," he said, his voice riddled with gravel.

His oldest daughter's grin was instant and brilliant, changing her face from plain to wondrous beautiful. It made Adam swallow thrice more as Lizzie snuggled in.

Sara was sorry that his oldest daughter was not as bold as her sister. Lizzie didn't kiss him.

Pris, her pout hovering but not quite present, came forward finally, but to Sara she came and stood, even more awkwardly than Lizzie had.

"I have an empty lap," Sara said. "Just waiting for my Pretty Pris."

Fear filled Pris's sad, dark eyes then, and her old whine began, faltered and died. Lowering her head, Pris turned and walked away.

Sara's heart splintered; her mind raced. "My heart aches, Pris," she said, "for wanting to hold you so much."

Pris stopped. She took a breath so deep that, even from behind, Sara could see her whole body take air in and release it. Still facing away, the sullen child took a back-step in Sara's direction, speeding her heart.

Pris raised her head, looking far into the distance.

Behind her, her family waited in silence.

Not removing her gaze from Pris, Sara reached, and Adam's hand was there.

Just when frustration made Sara want to scream, Pris stepped lively back, tripped on Sara's crossed legs and fell into her lap.

Her sisters laughed as Pris turned into Sara's victorious embrace. Had Pris feared she was not welcome? Sara hugged her again. She would be sure Pris became well acquainted with her lap from now on. "Thank you, darling. My heart feels better now. Happy. How about yours?"

Pris's untried smile wobbled, but for a first effort, it was magnificent. Sara grinned at Adam, and Pris reached for baby Hannah's hand.

In the way her husband had stared at her when he arrived, as if he had forgotten what she looked like, he now gazed at the children in the circle of their arms with like wonder.

Sara laced her fingers with his and rested their clasped hands on his thigh. A family—connected by something less tangible than blood, but infinitely more binding. Love.

"Welcome home, Datt," Sara said, leaning into him. "You want to tell this little family of ours why butterflies need the sun to soar?"

Chapter Sixteen

Adam's voice faltered during his butterfly lesson, the marvel of his homecoming filling him with some kind of new hope. This was not so different from other butterfly lessons, he told himself, except that he was not standing a distance away, the girls looking solemnly up at him.

Except that his youngest slept in his arms.

Except that Katiebug's wayward curls tickled his neck and Lizziebelle's small hand patted his back.

His heart beat altogether too fast and he didn't know if happiness or something else made it pound so. To his surprise, he no longer feared his girls. At this moment, he didn't even fear hurting them—likely the first time since Lizzie was born—which should scare the wits out of him, truth to tell, though it did not.

Something more was at work here, Adam believed, than the usual, and if he were to give it a name, that name must be Sara. It was her. . . .

Adam faltered, searching for the right word. Magic was the only explanation that came to mind, and in a way it fit, for his wife did, indeed, enchant him, but magic was not an acceptable notion for his people. Love was not an acceptable notion for him, but he supposed it existed, between Sara and the girls, at least, which was fine, as long as he did not get tangled in it.

Whatever Scrapper Sara had wrought, it hovered all around them, almost as if. . . .

241

And then Adam knew.

Sara was their very own butterfly, bright and shimmering. With joy, beauty and color, she enticed them. While in her sphere, they became infused with her warmth and light, and their hearts also took wing.

About Sara, they gathered . . . almost like a normal family.

Adam cleared his throat and tried to continue but found that he could say no more. Blessed, he felt, grateful, and sure such wonderment could never last.

And so it could not, for here came his mother. "Supper time," she said, beaming down at them, the look in her eyes bright as he remembered it had been a hundred or more years ago.

So many wonders could never last.

The children stood for *Grossmommie* Lena as she gathered them up to bring to the house to wash, and Adam surprised himself by refusing to give up the baby. "She sleeps," he said. "We'll wake her if we move her."

Lena nodded and she and the older girls grabbed hands. Still sitting beside Sara, Adam watched his mother run with his children toward the house. Sara turned to him and he thought he saw in her eyes a look that said she had missed him as much as he had missed her, even though the words, when she'd spoken them, seemed impossible to believe.

He wanted her alone. He wanted her lips against his. He wanted so much more. He wanted . . . everything he could not have.

He rose awkwardly with Hannah in his arms and was glad when Sara helped him, not because he needed help, but because he had been starving for her touch.

They walked silently together, until he slowed. "Come," he said, veering toward the barn, wanting Sara to follow, which she did. He led her straight to the tack room and elbowed the door shut after she stepped inside, then he advanced on her until her back went up against the wall.

Sara could barely breathe for the hammering in her breast. Adam was home. He was home and they were alone. And he was going to kiss her. She read intent, lust, perhaps even caring, in his eyes. So eager she was to answer that she ordered her arms to remain at her side, else he would feel the evidence of their child. Their babe had done a lot of growing in the last seven weeks and he was now an undeniable form, nestled silent and unmoving beneath her heart.

Fortunately, little Hannah rested between them, even now, as Adam leaned in for a kiss.

A husband. Children. Another growing inside her. Happiness. Yet it took her husband's lips against hers, like a gentle flutter of butterfly wings, for Sara to know perfect joy.

When he pulled back, gazed into her eyes and swooped for her lips again, joy became desire, swift and pulsing. And Sara moaned and answered with as much desperation as his kiss demanded, and she reached for him, despite herself.

When, some minutes later, Adam pulled away and rested his forehead against hers, his breath coming in gasps, Sara did not need to be body-to-body to know how much he desired her.

Months ago, she would have crowed with delight to find her husband eagerly seeking her out, locking them in a room together away from everyone else.

But not now. Not with the secret of their child between them. She couldn't keep her pregnancy from him forever, she knew. But Adam had come so far with the girls, she could not break the tenuous bond that had formed any sooner than was absolutely necessary.

Somehow, she knew that when he realized there was to be another child, progress would falter between him and the ones he already had. As if that were not enough, all would be lost between the two of them, as well, because he would never forgive her for what he would think was an attempt on her part to make him break his vow. This she accepted. She had given him just cause to suspect her of seduction. But between him and his girls the bond must remain intact, however tenuous, for they could not bear to lose him again.

As she could not bear to be the cause of such a loss. Yet how could she keep from it?

Sara touched the whiskers on Adam's upper lip, to turn her thoughts and his. "You need to shave. Another night's growth and you will break the ordnung."

He scoffed. "They have rules for hair above the lips and none for men like. . . ."

Sara ached to ease the pain she saw furrowing his brow. "Let's go inside. You will have time to shave before supper so as not to scandalize your mother with your whiskers."

"If my mother knew what I want to do before supper, it would kill her." Adam's kiss was rough and possessive and it cut off her laugh. Sara loved it. She let her tongue play with his, felt herself opening, flowering under the onslaught of his need and her own.

Lena called to them from somewhere nearby.

Adam pulled from the kiss and swore beneath his breath.

Sara surprised them both with her giggle. "We'll be there in a minute, *Mutter*," she called, winning her husband's gratitude.

"I missed you too," he said, kissing her cheek, trailing that kiss to her ear and below. "Weeks I spent with Jenny, and all I could think about was coming home to my Sara."

"If I thought you'd feel any different, I would not have let you go," Sara said, her bold assertion a perfect balance to the melt taking place in her heart. *My Sara,* he'd said.

One of her husband's eyebrows rose at her daring, then he grinned, shrugged and followed her from the tack room.

Later that night, Sara washed quickly so she could change into her nightgown while Adam was still out bedding down the stock. Roman had fled like a field mouse before a barn cat the instant he spotted Adam. He'd not wanted to be thrown out again, her mother-in-law guessed. So Adam had more work to do than usual after supper, which was just as well.

Reaching for her gown on the bed, Sara stopped mid-move, when she felt something . . . different. And wasn't "a flutter of butterfly wings" the perfect way to describe it. Wonder and awe filled her as she smoothed the mound of her bare belly. Her child had just—it happened again. A flutter, yes. Movement, slight, but oh so grand. Her child saying, "Hello, I am here."

Sara's eyes filled as she stroked the swell and waited for another sign from the very precious and tiny life growing inside her.

Adam stopped as he beheld her. So intense was his Sara's concentration that she had not heard him come in or shut the door. He devoured the sight of her, naked, perfect, in the soft light of the oil lamp. Like a fall of water after a spring rain, her hair cascaded down her back, all turns and swells and soft as new wool. Her breasts, proud and uptilted, were as perfect as her long legs, even her fingers, as they stroked—

Adam reeled as his world tilted and fell from beneath him.

He had never seen a pregnant woman naked, but he

knew, without doubt, that he beheld one now. His insides lurched. Panic grabbed him by the throat. Sara was going to die. She was going to leave him. He would lose her in childbed and there was nothing he could do to stop it. He knew it as well as he knew he'd killed Abby and he cried out for knowing it.

Sara turned at the sound of agony that tore from him, her face glowing. "He moved," she whispered.

Adam swallowed his sob. What had he done? Why had he—

Sobriety could be painful. Reality could cripple.

Adam approached his wife, mesmerized by the evidence of her condition. When he blinked and looked again, it was still there.

Sara's eyes widened and she began to tremble. She grabbed her nightgown and held it before her, as if she could cover the evidence of her condition and deny the moment just passed. Fear, clear, undeniable, engulfed her.

The *English*. "The *English!*" Adam shouted in fury. "Did you know you carried his child when we married? Did you think to keep from being shunned by passing that man's bast—"

The sting of her slap came fast; Adam hadn't caught her leap from fear to fury. A spitting cat, she became now, attacking and shoving him with both hands.

Unprepared, unresisting, he stumbled but caught his balance.

"You stupid, stupid man. You are the worst of fools. You refuse love from your children when they beg to give it, and now you turn me away. I understood your fear because of Abby. My judgment on the night she died was unforgivable. I will be sorry for the words I spoke until the end of my days, as should be. I knew what this would do to you. I have worried myself sick over it. And this is how you repay my concern?"

"Hush," he said as her voice rose. "My mother will hear you."

"Your mother is right. You *are* a *dummkopf*. Too stupid to see the bounty you have been given. Go away. Go sleep in the barn like you once threatened. Just go." Sara marched to their bedroom door to open it and point his way out, as if *she* bore the wounds from this sickening revelation.

The sound of their door slamming behind him woke Adam to his surroundings. As the buzzing in his head lessened, his vision became clearer. He regarded the homey kitchen, the wide eyes of his mother and sister, and he cursed.

Emma disappeared into the enclosed stairway. His mother rose from the rocker and approached him. The fury in her eyes matched Sara's. "What did you do?" she asked.

"What did *I* do?" he shouted with affront, despite the fact that he felt as if he *had* done something wrong, except he did not know what, damn it. "Did you know?" he whispered furiously. "About the babe?"

"What if I did?" his mother responded in the same hushed tone.

"You know my wife carries the English doctor's brat and this does not bother you?" His whisper had risen and he lowered it again. "But why should it? Your husband beat your children and that didn't bother you."

His mother's slap stung worse than Sara's. Shock rendered him speechless. This woman had once seemed to fear her own shadow. "Why did you never turn on my father this way? Why were you so weak then when you are so strong now?" He'd questioned her honestly, in a normal tone, with

247

neither anger nor accusation. He simply bore a strong need to know the answer.

But in his mother's eyes, he read aversion, contempt. "You use nothing more than harsh words and severe looks upon your wife and children, where your father used brute force on his, but yours is still abuse."

Inside Adam, rage churned and boiled, but he resolutely held himself in check.

"I'd bet my life you didn't raise a fist to Sara just now," his mother said. "But I am certain you wounded her with words, in the same way you injure your girls with the lack of them." She shook her head. "You are just like your father."

The tempest within Adam gained a strength and momentum he fought hard to control. Releasing it would only wreak havoc and prove the horrible accusation correct.

Sara touched his arm, checking the storm with the simple act, calming its fury. "No, mother, you're wrong," she said, cleansing his soul as well. "Adam is not like his father, but he is so changed by your husband's brutality that he beat another father who mistreated his child."

Condemnation.

Acceptance of proof came hard to Adam. Like his father had done before him, he'd brutalized another. His vision turned again to a brilliant red. Hot. Burning. To spare his family the inferno, he quit the house at a determined pace, and before he knew what he was about, he crossed his northernmost field at an all-out run.

An hour, maybe two, later, when he'd covered so many miles he didn't know in which county he stood, Adam stopped running. And there in the middle of a barren wood, Mad Adam Zuckerman allowed his demons to catch up with him.

* * * * *

Lena had forced Sara to drink a cup of rosemary tea, tucked her into bed and sat with her until she thought she slept. When her mother-in-law left, Sara rolled closer to Adam's side, took his pillow into her arms, buried her face in it and wept.

Her marriage was over, if it had ever really begun.

She had thought she could climb the mountains that loving Adam set in her path, but the knowledge that he didn't trust her rose up before her now, a peak too large to scale.

She believed she could have spent her life loving him, in spite of the fact that he could not love her in return. Now she wasn't certain.

She spent a fitful night in and out of sleep, sometimes glad Adam was not beside her, at others weeping because he was not, mourning her marriage as lost. And despite everything, she yearned for his return.

Sometime during the night, however, she had lost the heart to continue the battle. Only he could make things right between them now.

Except nothing could ever be.

Sleep might shortly have claimed her—she was that tired when she heard their bedroom door open. "Go away," she said. "Whoever you are." Her words were instinctive, self-protective. But even as she lauded her strength in uttering them, she prayed, if the intruder were Adam, that he ignore them.

"Who else would it be, but me," he said.

Glad she lay with her back to him, Sara didn't move. She barely even breathed while she hoped fervently that the evidence of her tears had disappeared.

His weight dipping their mattress, as he slid into their

bed behind her, soared her heart and gave her hope. His arm came around her, one big hand cupping the slight mound of their child. Sara closed her eyes at the gentle claim, or so she wished, but held herself in check, not moving a muscle.

"What, no more slaps?" he said against the ear he nuzzled. "Maybe I need a few more."

"Too tired," she said. "Go away. I need sleep to keep Jordan's baby healthy."

"Always a smart mouth. I used to think that's why you weren't married. But what do you know, you're married anyway, smart mouth and all . . . to me."

"We all have our crosses to bear."

"Your cross is bigger than most, I think. About six and a half feet tall and wide as a barn door, with the word *dummkopf* written clear as day across his brow." He nibbled her neck. "But Lord he loves that mouth, sass and all."

Sara turned in his arms to push him away. She didn't want him to be nice. It confused her. It made her forget how sad she was, how mad. It almost made her forget that he couldn't love her.

She shoved him hard. He blinked in surprise.

She all-out slugged him. He let her. He didn't fight back.

She hit him harder, much harder. He laughed.

That stopped her. The laugh was real. Deep and easy. Of all the times for him to laugh, finally. Damned if she wasn't entertaining him. That made her madder, which made her fight the more.

With another laugh, Adam captured her hands and placed them around his neck, then he pulled her close and cupped her bottom, his mouth coming for hers with grave intent. "It's mine," he whispered against her lips.

His kiss made Sara dizzy, but she would not give in to

the enticement of it. "Yes," she whispered when she had breath enough to speak. "My mouth is yours."

Adam growled and took that very mouth again. When he came up for air, he gave her a gentle look. "The babe is mine." He kissed her with care then, as if to show he meant what he said. "I thought our coming together was a dream, a perfect dream of you, of us." He spoke with such a timbre in his voice as to shiver her in his arms, then he clutched her tighter as a result of it. "It happened at the shack, didn't it?" His breath tickled her neck.

Sara nodded; she couldn't speak, because Adam's lips were doing wonderful things to her ear, her throat, lower. His hands worked the same enchantment everywhere else.

"You are so beautiful in that dream," he whispered. "I really, really like that dream. The only thing about it that confused me was that I could dream it wide awake, while I lay beside you at night, while I worked in the barn, during Sunday service, even."

Sara giggled.

"I couldn't let it go," he said. "Through all those weeks away, I dreamed that dream over and over while I ached to come home to you. And when I arrived today and saw you with the children by the butterfly garden, I realized you are the best and smartest dream I ever had." He put her away from him and rose to light the lantern.

Sara felt bereft.

He sat on the side of their bed facing her. "I have to keep from touching you while I try to explain what happened—" He slapped his chest with his fist. "In here, tonight, when I saw that you were. . . ." He swallowed and made to reach for her, stopped and gave her a sheepish grin.

"I swear to God, I saw. . . ." He cleared his throat at the catch in his voice. "I saw you in your casket and felt the blow to my marrow, the pain worse than anything I have ever known." He wiped a tear from her cheek with his thumb. "It hadn't even happened . . . your death . . . and I could not bear knowing it would come. Worse, was the knowledge I was the cause. Then, I didn't remember that I could be."

Sara rose to kneel on her haunches to face him. She took his hands, glad he allowed it, and waited for him to continue.

"Blaming The *English* changed that dreadful torment to fury," he said. "With furor I am familiar and more comfortable." He shook his head, with dissatisfaction, almost as if he had not yet found the correct words. "I don't want to think you're going to die, Sara. I need to believe you can survive this birth. To face another day of living, I need to believe it. I will believe it. Many women do. Many of them have . . . because of you."

He stopped her from reaching for him by grasping her shoulders and holding her an arm's length away. "Do not think this is love. I cannot love you, or anyone, especially not the children." He bent his elbows, bringing her a fraction closer. "I guess I can hold them sometimes, though, as I did today. Maybe I was wrong, always turning them away, and I will try to be more open to them. But I won't let love happen and you must be glad for that. You must."

Sara thought he might like to shake the sense of his words into her, except that they made no sense.

"Promise you will be satisfied and not expect anything more from me?" he asked.

It would be difficult to spend life without his love, but Sara believed it would be a worse burden, one she could not bear, to spend life without him.

There would be time enough later to make sense of his

plea, or to change it, if that were even possible. "Do you know what I think," she said, sliding his suspenders off his shoulders and down the arms he'd let fall to his sides.

He tried to pull them back up. "What do you think? Stop that."

Despite his lack of cooperation, she began to unbutton his shirt. "I think that if the horse has already escaped the barn, there is no longer any point to shutting the barn doors."

"What?"

"You're thinking about horses and barns, aren't you, Adam?"

"Well no, I was thinking about. . . ." He cupped her breasts to illustrate.

Sara sighed, pleasure blossoming inside her. "I was thinking about what it would feel like to have my husband deep inside of me."

"Now, Sara, you know, we—"

"Cannot? Why? Afraid you'll get me with child?"

Sara heard as much pain in his groan as desire and placed her palms against either side of his face. "I will be the healthiest new mother you ever saw. I will rise from childbed and bake Christmas cookies. I will shovel snow alongside you and I won't lie down until I chop enough wood to—"

"Shut up and kiss me, you sassy thing."

He ravaged her mouth—there was no other way to describe it. And she loved it. Loved him.

Sara learned that night what it was like to become a wife in truth. She learned that the real difference between hard and soft rested in the tip of her fingers. She gained a wife's knowledge of her husband in countless ways. In taste and texture. In length and breadth. In the speed of his heart and the rise and fall of his chest. In the whisper of his ragged breath in her ear, the splendor of him collapsed atop her.

She discovered her power as a wife.

She found joy in the feel of his sweat-slick back beneath her palms, exhilaration in riding and controlling him. She experienced the surge to be had with speed and the heights to be gained with a slow ascent. She took to licking and nipping, to taking and giving. They suckled, they petted, they laved and loved.

Sara gave Adam her body and threw in her soul. He gave her his body and retained his soul, but she decided attaining that prize would be worth the seeking. If loving Adam was part of the work she was called upon to do, then call her a willing laborer.

They found new meaning in the word paradise, not once, but twice, and when dawn bathed their entwined limbs with shafts of light, they were driven to reach the firmament again.

After a silent breakfast of speaking glances, Lena and Emma went off in the carriage with four little girls and a picnic basket. Sara waved them off, wondering what had gotten into her mother-in-law. She hoped Lena hadn't heard them last night or this morning. Then again, if her wonderful new mother had decided to give her and Adam time alone together, who was she to argue? Getting Adam back into bed was all Sara could think about once Lena suggested it.

But dresses needed ironing and socks needed mending. And now that Adam knew about the baby, she supposed she should go through the baby clothes. After four children, she was certain a few new things were needed.

She'd just about decided to deny herself the sight and company of her husband, so they could both get some work done, when she saw him come from the barn to wash his hands at the pump.

As if he realized she was watching, he stood to gaze at her across the yard, his eyes piercing, and her breasts filled and budded as if he stroked them.

That gleaming regard drew her closer and closer, until she could see the twinkle in eyes, as gray, but no longer as distant as the horizon. She could even see the dimple formed by his newfound smile.

So easy, that grin, considering its novelty, like his laugh last night. She wanted to hear it again. "Don't look at me as if you could devour me, Adam Zuckerman," she said, clasping her hands behind her, playful of a sudden. "You know how shy I am."

There. The laugh. Light, carefree. "I don't look at you as if I could devour you, wife." He advanced in such a deliberate way as to make her retreat. "I look at you in this way because I have already done so."

Sara squealed and scooted into the barn, her husband at her heels. She laughed when he just missed her and landed in a pile of hay. His delicious threat, as he rose spitting straw, made her scramble up the loft ladder.

Once there, Sara turned in a circle. She had nowhere to go, except to jump out the hay doors, but even with the haystack below, she would not take a chance with the baby.

Adam topped the ladder and a shiver of anticipation ran through her. "I give up," she shouted, making him laugh. "You win."

He stepped into the loft and fell to his knees, drawing her down with him.

"I didn't know you could laugh," she said stroking the hair from his brow.

He shook his head. "Neither did I."

"I want more."

"So do I."

"I mean laughter. From you."

"This first," he said pulling her across his lap. "I want you first. Laughter later."

Their coming together was not hot and rushed like the first time last night. Nor was it slow and slick, skin to skin, like the second. Not even a lazy burn like at dawn. This was a heated mating, a marking of territory, as much for her as for him. In the barn, in the hay, skirts pushed up, Sara aching to pull her husband in. Adam, impressive and throbbing, jutting proudly from the broadfall flap of his trousers.

A mattress of hay beneath her, Adam above her, gilded and warmed by sunbeams with dancing motes of strawdust, Sara watched Adam watch her. Her brawny husband, paradoxically tender with touch and words, the truth of which she could see in his expression and hear in his voice. Caring. Concern. Adam, her lover and mate, whose eyes darkened and glazed as he filled and left her, over and over, each thrust more pleasure-rising than the last.

The sound that grew from deep in his throat, the sight and taste of him, his warmth beneath her hands, added to her joy, life-giving, vibrant, as he carried her up and into a world new and brilliant with shattering promise.

Thrumming with her own release, Sara basked in Adam's unrestrained shout as he slid into her one last deep time. To her surprise, he carried her with him, up and over one last exhilarating peak, while he filled her with his seed.

Peace, Sara knew, there in that unlikely place, like none she had ever known, a vast contentment, acknowledged in the light of day. Real. Her marriage. Her love.

She knew too that the essence of this moment would live

forever in her mind as the mingled scents of hay and desire. She would never forget the sound of his slowing breath against her neck, the nipping kisses he pressed to her cooling skin. She would remember the weight of his hand against her, there, where she'd taken his seed.

Sara smiled and closed her eyes, drifted as on a cloud above the earth.

When she opened them again, the sunbeam had shifted and she heard, somewhere below, Roman calling her sleeping husband's name.

Chapter Seventeen

Her husband came awake with a start and jumped up so fast, he hit his head on a loft beam.

"That you, Adam?" Roman called.

Adam looked at Sara, at their bedraggled states, and grinned.

Sara grinned back and giggled. Wide-eyed, she slapped her hand to her mouth. When they heard Roman at the loft ladder, she scrambled to right herself as Adam hurried to put himself away and button his broadfalls.

Roman crowned the top of the ladder and jumped when he saw her. "God a'mighty, Sara, you were so quiet after I called, I thought it was rats—Oh, Adam, you here t—"

Roman summed up the situation in a blink, then he was the one grinning.

Adam was not.

Sara giggled again; she couldn't seem to stop.

"What the devil do you want?" Adam snapped. "Sara, stop laughing."

Roman looked from one to the other.

"Sara, stop. . . ." Adam's voice broke and a rolling rumble of laughter escaped him; then Sara and her husband fell over each other laughing like fools.

Roman just stood at the top of the ladder watching, shaking his head, until he could not help but laugh with them. "Congratulations Sara," he said when they caught their breaths. "Knew you'd bring the stubborn fool back to life."

That got Adam's back up. "What do you mean by that? Did you come here to snoop on me and my wife in a priv—"

"Hush," Sara said. "If he didn't suspect anything before, he certainly does now."

Adam glared. Sara shrugged.

"If he didn't suspect anything before," Roman said with a wink, "he would have to be deaf and dumb. And I am neither. But I didn't come to snoop, just to say the rest of your family is having dinner with us, supper too. Won't be home for hours yet." He wiggled his brows, tipped his bedraggled straw hat and disappeared down the ladder.

Their gossipy neighbor whistled his way out the door.

Neither Adam nor Sara spoke until his buggy had cleared the drive.

"Nosy man."

"Nice man. We're going to be alone for the rest of the day."

"Good. We have things to do." Adam climbed down the ladder.

Sara was taken aback but tried not to show her disappointment. She felt foolish for suggesting . . . anything. What was the matter with her?

She went down, not wanting Adam to see she was embarrassed. When she reached the bottom, he took her hand and headed for the house.

"Where are we going?"

"Chores," he said. "Long overdue."

Sara stopped, pulling him up short. "My chores are in the house, Adam Zuckerman; yours are back there, in the barn."

"Inside," he said. "It's bath time. Let's go."

She stopped again and this time he stopped with her. "Remember the baths you used to give me?"

All Sara could think about was how embarrassing and . . . and she became warm just thinking about it. "What about them?"

"I told you. It's bath time." Adam wiggled his brows the way Roman had done. "And this time, we're going to get it right."

What started out to be a sponge bath became a tub bath, but Adam was just too big for Sara to fit in the blasted thing with him, which made him curse to high heaven, or low hell, however you looked at it.

But once she knelt by the tub and began to sponge him off the way she used to—except she didn't stop at his belly this time—then Adam stopped fussing and began to enjoy the experience.

He did, at least, until the sound of a carriage pulling into the yard and a crying baby got his attention. And then when somebody began knocking on the door, he started cursing again.

But Sara was laughing so hard at the way he pouted, that she could tell he had a difficult time staying mad, even though the poor frustrated man looked as if he might need help getting all of him back into his broadfalls.

"I'll just go and see who it is," she said, trying to get serious, "and then you can come out when you're . . . ready." She slipped into a giggle again before she opened the bedroom door, then she squared her shoulders, went out and shut it behind her.

She heard him curse once more before she opened the kitchen door to find Mercy and Enos Bachman standing on the steps, little Saramay wailing in her father's arms.

Before the kitchen door closed, Mercy and Sara were in each other's arms.

Sara was delighted to see the woman who had become a

friend in one heart-binding afternoon. "How wonderful you look. All blossomed out again, I see."

Mercy stepped back and gave Sara a considering look. Had she pinned something wrong or left something showing?

"You're blossoming too. I am so happy for you."

"I am happy for me too, almost as happy as you are, I think."

Sara took her namesake from her father. "You look tired from your journey, Enos," she said, patting the fussing baby's back. "Will you stay and have supper with us?"

Enos nodded. "Got to feed the horses."

"My husband will be . . . ah, here he is. Adam, here is Enos and Mercy Bachman. I delivered this little darling for them last winter, remember, when you were laid up?"

Adam nodded at Mercy and shook her husband's hand.

"They're staying for supper," Sara said. "Take Enos out to feed his horses."

Adam gave her a bland but speaking look, and Sara couldn't help her smile. "Mercy and I will begin cooking right now, so take your time."

Adam led Enos out.

"He doesn't say much, your husband," Sara said, though hers had been silent as a post beam too. "I thought, when you delivered, that he didn't talk because he was worried, but he's the same now. Or is he shy around strangers?"

"Enos is tired. He's had a hard life and I worry about him still working so hard at his age. He should have grown sons helping with the farm, but he's still doing it by himself."

"Since he is a good deal older than you, and you didn't marry him to care for his motherless children, did you fall in love with him?"

"Sara Zuckerman," Mercy said, opening her dress for her daughter to nurse. "Don't tell me you are a romantic? Not many of those among our people."

"No, nor many midwives either. So I guess I'm different all around. A scrapper and a rebel, Adam says."

"Special," Mercy corrected. "And in love with your husband, I think."

Sara smiled and nodded. "But don't tell him I said so. Hearing it scares him silly. When is your baby due?"

"Late November."

"Mine is due a month later. They will play together, our children."

Mercy regarded Sara's middle with some surprise. "But you're so small."

"No, you're so big."

"Am I?" That troubled Mercy.

Sara knelt before her. "What's wrong?"

"Twins, then, maybe. I've lost two sets, remember?"

"Ach, yes. I almost forgot about that. You're staying till the baby is born, right? My mother-in-law told me you were coming."

"Everything we own is in our wagon. We're staying for good."

That frightened Sara. "Not because of . . . I mean I'm only. . . ."

"Don't be afraid, Sara. I would never blame you if something went wrong; you should know that."

Sara bit her lip. "I know, but I would blame me. It does frighten me, your history and all. Promise me, the minute you get settled, that you'll let Doctor Marks take a look at you. He'll know if you're carrying more than one baby. And Mercy, if you are, please think about letting Jordan deliver them."

Her friend's obvious disappointment bothered Sara. "I'd be there too. But the doctor has so much more knowledge of this than I do. He was my teacher."

That made the difference with Mercy. "All right," she said, grudgingly. "Both of you, if it's twins. But just you, if it's not."

"Good. You're staying with May and Cal Sussman like the last time, right?"

Mercy nodded. "Until we find our own place."

"Close by, please, so we can visit every day?"

Mercy grinned and Sara laughed. "Good. Now give me back that baby girl so we can get reacquainted."

As the nights grew colder and the days shorter, Sara Zuckerman grew big with child, and the bigger she got, the more Adam worried.

He had never . . . needed . . . anyone before, and he hated to think that he might now. He had never been so . . . captivated. This overwhelming "necessity" to make lo—

"No damn it!" Longing, friendship, he felt for Sara. He liked—all right, he liked her a great deal more than he'd ever liked anyone in his life. So what? Whatever such overpowering liking meant, whatever the act such liking inspired might be called—he could not bring himself to use any of the cruder words—Adam wanted it with Sara. Again and again. And damn it, his plight wasn't even that simple. This fascination was more than lust, more than a need for sexual satisfaction.

He wanted Sara—Sara, not just any woman, but his Sara—to enjoy their . . . encounters . . . as much as he wanted to enjoy them himself. More. Probably because it was such a new and unexpected experience to bed a woman who liked the physical side of marriage as much as he did.

Even bedding her sounded sordid. Damn it; if he could just identify this fascination, he knew he could deal with it.

He'd tried to tell himself that all of this was normal. Sometimes he believed it. Other times he feared he was as mad as everybody thought.

After weeks of worrying the dilemma, Adam thought he might have discovered what ailed him and why this unexpected preoccupation with his wife. He was afraid that buried so deep he didn't realize it existed, lived the notion that if he could get enough of Sara, it wouldn't kill him if . . . he lost her in childbirth.

Adam rubbed his tight chest and coughed to dislodge the bramble in his throat. All right, so the very notion all but killed him. God help him, he almost hated the child she carried as much as he hated himself for putting it there, though he could never let Sara know how he felt.

More than once, he had come upon her, natural mother that she was, crooning to the child she called Noah. Never in anyone else's hearing had she named it, yet he'd heard her do it twice when she was alone. Already she loved the child so much, it was a wonder she could stand the wait until she held it in her arms. If she ever held it.

It, him, her. A girl named Noah. Adam almost smiled, but, damn it, what did a name matter, if after the child was born, it had no mother?

Adam groaned and kicked a fence-post. Had a man ever been so haunted? He needed to talk to somebody. Somebody who would not make jokes, so that left Roman out. But who would see the sense in his fears. A woman would, but it had to be a man, a man who would understand, but what kind of man could?

A doctor. "Shit." The fence-post came down with his kick.

Adam sighed. Perhaps if he did talk to the doctor, the man would tell him Sara faced no danger, that she did not have to die. God knew, he would not believe it, if anybody else told him so.

Bloody hell. He needed to talk to that bloody damned *English*.

He must be in real trouble if he were actually considering talking to that gold-buttoned fancy man about anything. Adam kicked the downed post one last time before stalking off.

Jordan was surprised the day Adam Zuckerman showed up at his surgery door. The Amishman greatly disliked him; Jordan knew that much. "Is Sara all right? It's not the baby, is it? She's not due for two more months."

"Sara's fine. Far as I know, the baby's fine. Kicks all the time, always letting us know she's there."

Jordan thought he detected a bit of jealousy. Perhaps the child intruded at the wrong times. The doctor coughed. "Sit, Adam. What can I do for you?"

The big muscular farmer was clearly out of his depth and uncomfortable in his surroundings. Appearing trapped, as if he were tied to the chair, he turned his hat in his hands while regarding a white enamel pan of lancing instruments on the near shelf of a glass-fronted cabinet.

"Feel free to stand, or even pace," Jordan said, "if it will make you more comfortable."

Adam took up his suggestion with apparent relief. He placed his hat on the surgery table and ran his hand through his hair. "You know that my first wife died in childbirth."

Jordan nodded, concerned about where this was going.

"I don't want to lose Sara that way," he said, his plea so clear and heartfelt, Jordan believed a true miracle stood before him. Mad Adam Zuckerman loved his wife.

He only wondered if Mad Adam knew it. "I see."

"I don't care what you see. I want you to promise me—and I don't want her to know about this—that when her time comes, you will save her."

"Your wife was here yesterday making the same plea for Mercy Bachman. What do you all think, that I am God? Believe me, you are wrong. I am only a man, a doctor, human, flawed. Badly flawed."

"I know that," Adam said.

Chagrined, Jordan shook his head. "I can't promise you anything, Adam, any more than I could promise Sara that I would save Mercy's twins."

Jordan put his hand on the Amishman's arm when he paled. "I can only promise that if you call me the minute Sara goes into labor, that I will do everything I can for her and your child."

Adam sat as if he were too weak to stand. He rubbed his face with a shaking hand. His expression, when he looked up, held panic, desperation. "But if it comes to a choice," he said, his voice pain-graveled but determined.

Jordan stiffened. "Between her and the babe?"

Adam looked suddenly more ravaged than he had after months of drunkenness. "If it comes to a choice, no matter what Sara says, save her first."

"I have taken an oath, Adam, to save every life I can, but sometimes that means choosing to save one more likely to survive . . . over one less likely."

For weeks after his visit to the doctor, Adam's obsession with Sara got worse.

His mother seemed to understand their need to be alone and cooperated whenever she could. Once, she kept the girls for two days while Adam took Sara with him to Sugarcreek. From there, they took the Wheeling and Lake Erie train to Zanesville, where they rented a room in a hotel and spent nearly an entire day in bed.

It was awful, Sara had said with a grin, how they could be . . . indecent . . . in the middle of the day, while somebody else cooked the meals, brought the food to their room and cleaned the dishes after. She would never be able to show her face in this district again.

Adam personally thought he might go to hell for spending money in such a way, but he wasn't certain who enjoyed the experience more, him or Sara.

In the fall, he took to seeking her out after chores, just to sit out on the hill overlooking the rolling pastures and talk. Twice, they came together in the woods. Once, she seduced him on a quilt by the stream.

Right there, in the light of day, beneath God's blue heaven and two feet from Zeb Troyer's dry stone wall, his wife pushed him onto his back and unbuttoned his broadfalls to release him into her hand.

Adam gasped, he moaned, he cried out. He begged for more, and more, until she mounted him, shocking him to his soul, but not so much that he would stop her from riding him. In fact, the events of that afternoon became his second best daydream ever, right after their night in the shack.

Even big with his child, Sara was beautiful. Her cinnamon hair shone when she let it down for him to run his hands through. Her cheeks glowed, her green eyes sparkled like the emeralds they'd seen in that Zanesville jewelry shop window.

Sara actually seemed to thrive on his sexual attention. How amazing to have such a wife.

As the nights grew crisp, they took to walking through the meadow after supper, while they planned next year's crop. Often the girls came along, gamboling around them like a frisky litter of newborn pups. It was then, when they'd speak of the year to come, that worry intruded into Adam's new world.

He began to pray again, in earnest, a practice he had all but abandoned after Abby died. Sometimes he even thought God might hear and answer. But as Sara's time drew near and hope became more and more difficult to hold onto, he would become frightened out of mind and seek Sara out once more.

At the end of September, the Bachmans moved out of the Sussman house and bought dead Elam Raber's farm. The price was good. Only problem was, it had no barn. Like its owner, the structure had died a long, slow death. Now, two years after Elam had returned to the earth, his barn had become nothing more than a pile of rubble trying to do the same thing.

Jordan attended the barn-raising, not so much because he wanted to lend a hand, though he did, but he wanted to see how Sara and her fretting husband fared.

Yes, and he wanted to see Emma too.

To his delight, she ran right over when he arrived, though she stopped short of throwing herself into his arms, almost as if she'd run into an invisible wall a foot before him. Just as well, from the looks they were getting. If he were not careful, some of the women would try to protect her from him.

While that would be best for both of them, Jordan simply wasn't ready for it, so he tipped his hat and made for the wood-framed barn.

Right behind Adam, he climbed to the tallest beam,

drew his hammer from the worn leather pouch around his waist and began to nail the thing together—him and about two hundred Amish and, maybe, six other non-Amish, like him.

Beside the clothesline, on the far side of the house, Jordan noticed Sara and Mercy comparing the sizes of their respective bellies. He grinned. They must do that every day; they were together so often.

Around him, hammers made a clamoring racket while most of the women below acted more like worker ants, scurrying to and fro, playing with children, setting tables, laying bright quilts in the grass on such a perfect Indian Summer day. But not a one of them looked as fresh and vibrant as Emma wearing a dress the color of blackberries—one of Sara's Bishop-vexing creations, no doubt.

Adam must have noticed him gazing at Emma, because he cleared his throat and frowned pointedly.

Jordan warmed beneath his collar, looked down, saw the plank he'd left half-nailed and got back to work.

At noon, six hammering hours after they began, the Bachman barn was half done. It would be complete by dusk. Jordan made for solid ground to break for lunch. Lunch, be damned; in the world he'd left behind, it would be called a banquet.

Adam followed the surprisingly hard-working *English* down to the ground. If the fancy man had designs on Emma, he'd best forget them.

"Sara looks good," the man dared, setting Adam's back up.

"I don't need anybody to tell me that," he snapped. "And it was not Sara you watched."

When The *English* leaned close, his grin aggravated Adam the more. "Medically speaking, your wife looks good.

Since I am a doctor and you've been, um, concerned about her condition and all, I thought you'd like to know that she came for an examination the other day and she and the child are doing well."

Adam grunted and went to sit at one of the dozen or so tables, his stomach in knots. Sometimes he forgot to worry about it, and there went The *English* reminding him that his wife might die.

As ever, Sara came to serve him first. "You're not nailing ground floor planks today," she said near his ear.

"Hurts just to think about it," he returned, his smile breaking, even as he tried to glower.

He had always anticipated her approach at fellowship meals with mixed emotions. He wished she wouldn't bring attention to him by teasing him or serving him first. But, if she did not, he would wonder why, and ponder it to death.

These days, he wished she would just lie down and take this time before the baby as something of a holiday, to gather her strength, as Abby used to do.

Adam noticed Jordan and Roman, across the table, watching him, some joke at his expense sitting between them. He bit into a corn cake with a vengeance. In his mind he was taking a piece out of either hide with great satisfaction.

Fortunately, none of the other men had noticed his foolish preoccupation with his wife. They spoke mostly among themselves, though Zeb Troyer teased Sara about her inability to get any closer to the table. By the time she reached the end of its seven-foot length, she had gone back to get more food three times. Adam could tell the way she walked that her back ached again. These days, most nights began with his rubbing wintergreen liniment into it, to her moans of pleasure.

He shifted in discomfort just thinking about Sara moaning.

Zacharius, the idiot too blind to see that she plainly suffered, asked for more corn and Sara turned to fetch it.

"Damn it, Sara, sit down and rest." He shoved old Jake Kicher over with his hips to make room for her. Then he grabbed her hand and tugged her down beside him. "Get your own thirds, Zack. Sara needs to rest."

Everyone stilled.

The *English* and Roman looked at each other, at him, then at each other again. "Alive, and kicking," Roman said, and the doctor chuckled.

"Eat, eat," Adam said to the rest of the staring men. "What's the matter with everybody?"

"They never saw Mad Adam Zuckerman act nice before," Roman confided in a mock-whisper loud enough to draw laughter.

"To his wife, even," one man added.

Sara's face turned nearly as bright as the *ferbudden* dress she'd made for Emma, her stubborn chin rising, despite the fact that she was the only woman at a table reserved strictly for the men. "I can't stay here," she said.

"You can if they go," Adam all but shouted, giving the men a look calculated to shiver them in their big, clumsy shoes.

Some did leave, but not all of them.

"Why don't you go to the quilting bee this afternoon and make sure she has a cushion for her feet," Abe Zook called from the end of the table. "And leave the carpentry to the men."

"Abraham Zook, you nasty man," Sara snapped. "Adam is the one sent you a hundred dollars last month when Irenee needed to go to the hospital in Philadelphia."

"Sara," Adam gasped, shocked to the soles of his feet that she had revealed something he'd told her in confidence.

"Ya," Roman said. "He's the one always gives the most for those in need. He's mad alright."

Adam stood, mortified, unmoving.

"Why is Mommie sitting with the men?" Pris asked Lizzie as the girls approached, unaware of the turmoil about them.

"Because she's fat," Katie said.

Lizzie giggled. "Mommie's not fat. She's going to have a baby."

"My don't want her to die like my other Mommie," Katie said, which made Pris whine and throw herself against Sara.

Adam didn't know who made him madder, Roman and The *English*, the men, Sara, his girls or his rutting self.

If anything happened to Sara, because of his selfish lust, he did not know how he would survive. No, nor the girls either.

One thing he knew for certain. He could not touch her after this baby came and he'd best get used to it. If he knew what was good for him, and for Sara, he'd best not touch her again, starting today.

Chapter Eighteen

Sara realized over the next days and weeks that Adam had withdrawn from her, not only in the physical sense. She felt bereft and out of sorts, unloved, adrift.

Harvest chores kept him outside so late some nights, she was asleep when he came to bed. They never went walking. They never even talked anymore.

Her husband had become moody and snapped at unexpected times. She knew exactly how he felt. She had not only argued with him, she had bickered with her mother-in-law, and once, even, with Emma, though she wasn't sure exactly how they'd managed it. She knew only that they'd parted in tears, the both of them.

There was a lot of making up for her to do, though not between her and Adam, because he kept saying nothing was wrong.

In October, the Hershberger house was struck by lightning and burned to the ground. The aging couple had never had children. Levi had been ailing for some time, though his wife, Sovilla, did well for her eighty-eight years.

Roman invited them to share his daudyhouse with his mother and father. His dead sister's teenage children already lived in the main house with him, so his home and his pocketbook were stretched tight.

Several days after the fire, later in the evening than was normal for callers, Sara heard a knock at the kitchen door.

"I came to collect for the digitalis Doc Marks special-orders for Levi from Boston," Roman said as he came inside.

Without a word, Adam abandoned the farm catalogs spread across the kitchen table and unlocked the tiger-maple desk, where he dipped into the cracker tin of money he kept there.

While Adam silently counted out their contribution, Roman accepted a cup of sarsaparilla tea and a slice of warm Ob'l Dunkes Kucka. "Mm. Good Sara. I think maybe you make better applesauce cake than my mother, but don't tell her I said so."

"How are they all?" Sara asked.

"Mom and Pop are *goot* and they are happy to share their home with people of their years. Levi has aged for losing his own home, but Sovilla has a new spring in her step, just having my mother for company. Pop and Levi play checkers, when neither of them is napping." Roman grinned. "So they play about an hour a day."

Even Adam chuckled.

"But what about Levi, does he do any better? Does the digitalis help him?"

Roman shook his head. "I don't know. Doc says he might need something costs more."

Sara regarded her husband. "Adam, did you give him enough?"

"I did."

"Are you sure?"

Sara could tell it annoyed Adam, her questioning his generosity before Roman, but—

"Leave it, Sara," Roman said.

"Well, how much did you give him?" she asked her husband as she rose and went for the cracker tin.

"Why do you want to know?" Adam snapped. "So you

can tell all our neighbors how much?"

Sara felt as if he'd slapped her in public. She was so embarrassed, she nodded in Roman's general direction and said goodnight.

Not much later, she heard Adam come to bed.

He tried to coax her into his arms, but she refused to be budged. What did it matter? That's about as much as he cared to touch her these days anyway. With her big belly, she disgusted him. With her big mouth, that day at the barn-raising, she had destroyed any trust or caring he might have felt for her. He hadn't touched her in passion in weeks.

"I am sorry," he said into the silence some minutes later.

"For never touching me anymore?" she said before she had a chance to think, then she rolled even farther away. She would not beg. "It's all right. Go to sleep."

"Passion between us hurts you," he said. "This is the way it must be. If you . . . after the baby, this is how we must be. There will be no more children, Sara. If we are still together . . . after . . . believe me, I will be grateful every moment for the life we share."

"A life where you insult me before our neighbors?"

"A life where we raise our children together."

"We are not together. We are as far apart as we were the day I came to deliver Hannah."

"We are the same. That night you flayed me with words; tonight I flayed you . . . in front of Roman, to my distress, and yours. I repeat, I am sorry."

"Sorry you married me."

"If you remember," Adam said, "I had no choice."

"As if I did. So you are sorry?"

Adam sighed. "Being married to you has been both the best and the worst experience of my life. It has been, at times, better than heaven, and at others, worse even than hell."

Sara said nothing more. She could not speak for the sorrow choking her. Her silent tears fell until she slept.

Toward dawn, she sat up and rubbed her back. Adam tried to soothe her with his big capable hand, but despite the depth of her craving for his touch, she pushed him away and rose to don her robe. "The hell is happening now, isn't it, Adam? Too bad we were pushed into marriage so quick. If we had waited, your mother would have arrived soon enough to care for the girls and we would both have been saved."

"If we could arrange life the way we wanted it," Adam said, sitting on the edge of the bed, his voice tired, "we would be God."

"The way you want your life is not with me in it, I think."

"Sara, don't. Come here. Where are you going?"

She had awakened because she thought she heard someone at the kitchen door. And she'd just heard it again.

Mercy's husband stood on the porch. "She is in labor," Enos said. "It's too soon. You have to come. She's calling for you."

"Go get Jordan—Doctor Marks—and tell him to meet me there. Hurry."

Sara went back into her bedroom to dress. "It's Mercy," she said when Adam questioned her.

"Give me a minute," he said.

"Enos is waiting for me. Go back to sleep."

"No, I. . . ."

"It's an hour till dawn and, frankly, Adam, I don't want you, at this moment, any more than you want me."

Licking salty tears from her lips, Sara hurried to the barn

to hitch up her small buggy. She had lied to her husband. Twice. Enos was not waiting for her. And she wanted Adam so badly, she could die of it. But that was not to be considered right now.

Mercy needed her.

An hour later, Sara was certain she could feel every single one of Mercy's labor pains deep in her own womb, in the small of her back, especially.

Thank God her own babe wasn't due for a month and a half yet.

The minute Sara arrived, before she saw Mercy even, she prepared a tea of Gossypium root bark, as she had done during Mercy's last delivery, to induce stronger contractions.

Mercy drank it dutifully, but her labor did not proceed at all as it had done the year before. It blazed a flash-fire trail of agony through her. Within the first half hour, her pains came closer and closer, until they were already a minute apart.

"Seven times I have labored, but I have never felt such agony before," Mercy admitted during a moment of respite. "The pains are ripping me apart, Sara. I am afraid."

Only Sara knew that Mercy was not alone in her fear. Sweat poured down her own brow. "How long were you in labor tonight, before you sent Enos for me?" Lord, she wished Jordan would hurry.

"An hour, no more."

"And before you told Enos you were in labor."

Mercy nearly smiled. "Minutes only."

Oh, Lord. Oh, God. She should have gotten that information from Mercy before giving her the tea. Suppose she'd made matters worse with the infusion. Suppose she'd caused her friend more pain.

Suppose Mercy died.

The thought was not to be borne. Sara thrust it dutifully aside, so she could give Mercy and her twins her full attention.

Twins who would be born a month too soon. "I won't lie to you, Mercy. This is not good. The babies will be small for sharing their nourishment and growing space, and smaller still for coming early."

"I know," Mercy said even as she cried out with pain.

Sara bathed her friend's face and pressed her cheek to Mercy's cool brow. "I wish. . . ." She sighed. "For your sake, my friend, I wish to God I knew more."

"Jordan will be here any minute," Mercy said.

Sara went back to check her progress. "So will one of your little ones. One with hair as pale as corn silk." *And a very weak pulse, if any.*

Mercy gasped a laugh and screamed as she pushed.

The blonde mite of a boy slipped into Sara's hands with no sign of life. Sara sobbed and worked on it for as long as she dared, but the next child that needed help entering the world might have a chance.

She turned her attention back to Mercy, who knew, without words, that the first of the twins had not survived.

The second took a bit longer, which worried Sara. "When did you last feel life?" she asked Mercy.

"I . . . I don't remember."

"Yesterday? Last week?"

"I don't remember," she wailed.

Damn, damn, damn. The child came. Another son. To be placed, as he was in his short months of life, beside his brother . . . but in death.

More labor, but not for the afterbirth, Sara realized with shock.

"A third boy," Sara said, her voice wavering. She held

up the lifeless child, no bigger than the cupped palms of her hands, regarding it through a mist of tears with an overwhelming sense of wonder and loss.

Sara washed and wrapped each babe separately and brought Mercy all three to hold. Crooning, she kissed small fingers, tiny noses, and Sara wept with her.

Mercy ran out of tears.

Sara did not.

She put the babies back in the cradle and helped deliver the afterbirth. It came fast, easy, and in one piece, thank God. Mercy was not bleeding overmuch.

"It's not your fault," her dear friend kept saying, but Sara did not hear nor heed her words.

She had just got Mercy washed, and clean padding placed between her legs, when Enos returned. "The doc's on his—"

He fell to his knees beside the cradle.

"Boys," Mercy said. "I'm sorry, Enos."

Enos turned on Sara. "This is your fault. What did you do? How could you let this happen?"

I don't know, I don't know, Sara kept thinking, but words would not come. She had cost the lives of three babies. She had failed her best friend.

"No, Enos," Mercy kept saying, "it's not Sara's fault," but the grieving man knew nothing but rage.

"Get out," he ordered Sara. "Out."

Sara kissed Mercy's cheek. "I will be sorry until the day I die," she whispered, then she hurried outside, as fast as her clumsy gait would allow, and climbed into her buggy.

When she topped the rise, Sara saw Jordan's fancy carriage climbing Hickory Hill from the valley, headed in her direction. She did not want to be forced to see him. She could not bear to confess her failure. Rather than take the direct route to Walnut Creek, Sara turned her buggy onto Maple Valley Road to go around the town.

She had been a fool to think she could be a midwife. She had all but killed three babies. She could no longer allow herself to risk the lives of the women who might entrust themselves to her care. She did not, after all, possess the skill to be a midwife.

That dream was not meant to be; neither was her dream of having a husband and family of her own. If she kept going, no family would miss her, none of her own, that was.

Adam's family would be better off without her.

Was it only a year ago that she had been so young and so filled with a sense of purpose and invulnerability?

A lot could happen in a year.

Sara tried to concentrate on her driving. She needed not to run the buggy wheels through so many holes. The jostling was killing her. Her back was killing her. She hurt so bad, she had to untie her apron because the strings binding her belly were making her discomfort worse.

Untied, her apron flapped in her face, so she pulled it off, over her head, and tried to stuff it behind her seat. It fell out almost at once and a gust of wind took it and lifted it in the air. Sara reached for it and nearly fell from the buggy.

She stopped and got down, but when she saw the wind carry the apron upward and toward the woods, her sore back reminded her she wasn't in any condition to climb a tree, so she gave up chasing it and got back in the buggy.

Sara started driving again, heedless of her direction, so long as she went far, far away from all she could never have.

Once she had believed she could save every mother and child she tended. She had believed that she could make Adam love his children. "As if he could love anyone." He didn't even love the child she carried with so much hope, until now. She had even believed he would come to love her. Sara laughed aloud, but ended on a broken sob.

"Poor baby," she crooned, rubbing her big belly, ignoring her aching back. "I want you, even if your Datt does not. He doesn't even want me. He only got stuck with me, because the Elders made him marry me. He needed somebody, anybody, to nurse him back to health. He needed somebody to take the responsibility for your sisters off his shoulders."

Sara stopped the buggy. She still found Adam's giving her the girls to be something of a puzzle, the pieces of which she could not seem to fit together, no matter how many ways she tried. Another foolishness on her part, most likely. She mocked herself with a curse and regarded the fork in the road. One road lead back home—well, to the Zuckerman farm. The pike would lead her toward the far reaches of the state, where Ohio met Pennsylvania. She had heard there were several Amish communities in that vast, unknown place.

Sara pushed her hair more securely beneath her bonnet and looked around. The weather was turning. Despite the October date on the calendar, winter was almost upon them, the wind brisk, the air cool. She might have to stop for the night and she had no money for shelter, but the shack where her child had been conceived lay along the pike to Pennsylvania.

Why not take the pike? Join another community. Start again.

She had failed Mercy.

She had failed as a daughter and sister.

She had failed to teach Adam to love. He was sorry he married her. He had his mother and sister now; what did he need her for? Lena and Emma would take good care of the girls. Sara wiped her eyes with an angry hand. Yes, she would miss them. Her arms ached to hold baby Hannah even now, but soon she would have her new little one to fill the emptiness.

"You," she told her restless child, "will know only a complete and willing love, not a half-grudging one. You might have only one parent, but she will love you enough for two, though she will miss your father until the day she last closes her eyes."

Sitting there, looking down that lonely road, Sara knew she had no choice. She could not go back. One parent who loved was better than two, if one of them made a child yearn for what could not be. Better to be content in life than feel as if something was missing.

For the child pressing and turning in her womb, she must go. To relieve her husband of the burden of her presence, she must. As she must to relieve the community of a midwife who could kill.

And she must do it now, before anyone could change her mind, before goodbyes could weaken her determination or tears sever her resignation. She would make this sacrifice for the child she carried, for the family she loved, but did not belong to, and for the people and community she'd failed so miserably.

Mourning the babes who'd died at her hands and would never know the joy of life, Sara turned her buggy toward the road to Pennsylvania.

Her community needed better than a fumbling Amishwoman for a midwife. They needed a book-taught doctor. If they were too foolish to call Jordan . . . well, that was not her problem any more, was it?

Though her people had not embraced or welcomed her

rebelliousness easily, leaving even them was more difficult than she expected. With every mile she placed between them, she mourned. The thought of not seeing those faces, of never seeing her new mother and sister again, made her cry out with the unfairness of it.

She hoped that someday Lena and Emma would forgive her for her part in their arguments. They would be good to the girls, to children of their own blood. Blood made the difference. Lizzie, Katie, Pris, baby Hannah: they were not Sara's blood and never would be, no matter how badly leaving them lanced her heart.

Lizzie would learn to cook fine without her. Katie would still giggle; maybe not for a few days, but giggling was inside that girl, no matter what. Sara worried about leaving Pris, though, and Hannah.

She swiped at her eyes so she could see the road better.

The greatest break in her heart, the one that pained her more than her back right now, was the ache of leaving that big, little boy of a man. That stone-for-a-heart male with his beard of wire and nibbling lips of silk that could turn her to water.

That same headstrong man had made a space for himself in her wary heart and would reside there forever. If she were to be honest with herself, Sara had to admit that the place Adam Zuckerman occupied was very, very big. So big that maybe her love for him had overflowed into her very soul when she wasn't looking.

Silly her, for letting it happen.

For a minute, Sara stopped and held the reins, unmoving, not certain she could go on.

She wanted to go home.

Home to Adam.

To her children. Except, they were not hers.

She could do this. She was strong, and a scrapper, everybody knew it: stubborn, passionate, determined.

If that were so, then why did she feel so much the opposite right now?

Even as she sat there, the air turned to a snap and the temperature plummeted, much like a certain leaf-crackling night about a year ago. The temperature had chilled fast the night she went to deliver Abby's baby.

Her words to Adam still haunted her. She had stood in judgment, foolish, stupid. That girl; that was the one she most resembled now, she thought. Foolish, stupid, weak, afraid. Still stubborn, though, because she flicked the reins and continued in the direction she'd set, away from everyone and everything she loved, for their own good.

Before long, snow swirled around her in tiny flakes. Barely there, but enough to remind her of getting lost in the snow before. She stopped the buggy again. She was not terribly far from home, yet something in her rebelled at turning back. Not just because she was stubborn, but because she simply could not bear to go back, then have to make the same, painful decision another day.

She could not. This was best.

The snow, she saw soon enough, was no more than a flurry, a hint of the future, nothing like the other time. She could bear the chill that was left after it stopped, but what about her child? Could he bear it?

Where had Adam said the shack stood, precisely? At the least, she needed an outhouse. At the most. . . .

Sara pressed her hand to the small of her back. Oh, she did not like this backache at all.

Adam bedded down Titania and Tawny after his trip to the buggy factory, where he'd replaced the reins to his mother's buggy. She'd had them repaired and rebraided so many times, it was a wonder she and Emma had made it all the way to Ohio from Indiana without an accident.

It was a wonder they'd not snapped that night in the snow as he'd searched for Sara. Adam shivered. He never wanted to spend a similar agony of hours again. Even now, bad as the day had begun, he could hardly wait to set eyes on Sara.

He hadn't wanted to leave this morning, but he'd not been able to bear waiting for her to return, and he knew she wouldn't want him at Mercy's, their argument distracting her. He'd needed to keep busy, but the trip to Millersburg had been dull, lonely.

Funny how one journey with Sara and the girls, and one with Sara alone, could change the way a man thought. He didn't like traveling alone any more. He supposed he had to admit that he liked having company on long rides. And not just any company, but Sara with her smiles and laughter, and the girls with their trips to the trees every twenty feet and the kinds of questions that could drive a man mad.

Adam nearly smiled. Imagine Mad Adam thinking such a thing. If Sara were here, he'd take her hand and share the joke.

Damned if he hadn't found himself smiling over some of the girls' annoying questions on the ride home today. Damned if he didn't anticipate a house filled with noise, even Emma's screech when he walked in.

Sara should be back and exhilarated after delivering twins. Lord, he wanted to take her to bed. And she wanted him as much as he wanted her. Was he crazy to worry so about the birth? Was he crazy to deny himself, and her, during this safe time?

Probably.

He raised his head. Perhaps he'd tell her so tonight.

Ah, but how would he bear not having her after their child's birth, if he did not begin the way he must go on?

When he got home, the house was quiet. Too quiet. But for a lop-eared rabbit on a bed of quilts, no one raised their head in greeting. No dinner scents lingered, no supper pans of hot food simmered on the stove to answer the growl in his stomach.

All the times he'd wished for quiet returned to haunt him, and he imagined any number of frightening reasons for the silence.

He cursed. Foolish. His mother and Emma had probably taken the children and—

Was Sara still here, alone? His body quickened at the notion. Adam rolled his eyes over his eagerness for his wife. Then again, what was different about that? He supposed, with the child due in less than six weeks, he'd best be thinking about something else. Still, six weeks was a long time. . . .

He entered their room, hoping Sara was napping and hadn't heard him come in, but his fantasy of waking her with kisses took wing when he saw the empty bed.

He headed for the stairs.

Every single bedroom was empty. The house was empty.

Had she spent all day tending Mercy?

It wasn't till he came back to the kitchen that Adam found the note tucked into the jelly cupboard latch.

Sara is still with Mercy. Took girls to Verna's quilting. Knew you would be hungry. Bread, cheese and cold beef inside. *Mutter*

Sara must have found the note and gone to join them. He went back out for his buggy. Nobody would expect Mad

Adam Zuckerman to show up at a quilting supper. For a minute Adam was uncomfortable with the notion of sitting down with all those women, but then the look on Sara's face when he did—on all the women's faces—was enough to make him anticipate the scene.

Old Verna about swallowed her smacking gums when he walked into her best room. Her look alone would have been worth everything, if Sara had been there.

Emma screeched when she saw him and quit the room, but his mother rose and came to him. "Is Sara all right? I didn't like her backache yesterday. I hope she's not still at Mercy's. She needs to rest. I told her to rest."

A buzz started in Adam's head. His heart, for some reason, took on a tripping beat. The faces of the women around the quilting frame held different expressions: expectant, curious, worried.

Adam took his mother's arm and led her to the kitchen. "She isn't resting. She isn't home." He scrubbed his face with a hand. "I thought she'd joined you, here."

"She must still be with Mercy, then."

"I'll go get her. She shouldn't be trying to drive that buggy with—Why are you worried about a backache?"

Adam could have sworn his mother said, *dummkopf,* below her breath. She shook her head. "Go find Sara."

An hour later, Adam left the sad house of Mercy and Enos Bachman. Mercy had been feeding little Saramay when he arrived. "It wasn't her fault," she said when she saw him. "How is she? I was afraid she was in labor too."

Too? As if she'd slapped him upside his head with a barn-beam, Adam reeled.

Mercy's boys had not survived their birth. Three of them, lost. Sara would blame herself and bear triple the guilt. Adam knew that as well as he knew his own name, and the knowledge chilled him.

He would not allow her such guilt. Self-flagellation, especially over death, could be crippling. Worse. It could make you crave death yourself.

Adam swore but tried to stay calm.

Mercy's boys had been born before ten this morning and dusk drew purple streaks on the horizon even now. Sara should have been home hours before.

But nothing would be simple with Sara, especially with guilt as a dark companion. Where had she gone? Even if she believed she deserved punishment, she would not hurt the child she carried, which calmed Adam a great deal.

At the end of the Bachman drive, he stopped his buggy to think. Sara did not run from her problems. She faced them. But she was not herself these days. The Scrapper who'd faced down Mad Adam Zuckerman was carrying a child. She had turned into the woman who'd wept when she tripped over a rabbit and sent a platter of pigs' knuckles and sauerkraut across the kitchen to splatter the walls and dirty the floor.

Adam urged the horses onward. He could almost laugh again, as he had that night—at the sight, at her fury at him for laughing—if he were not so out-of-reason worried about her.

She had believed, if she were a midwife, that there would be no more dead mothers or babies, which worried him the most. He'd tried to tell her that she shouldn't take such burdens upon herself.

He only wished she'd listened.

Deep down, Adam hoped Sara understood that she could not blame herself for those babies' deaths. She had told him the day Abby died that she was not a doctor, just a midwife. After today, did she still understand the sense of her words?

Just a midwife, not a doctor. Jordan. Much as Adam disliked the man, much as he hoped Sara would seek her husband out first, she might have gone to the medical man in these circumstances. His opinion on the deaths of Mercy's babies would matter to her.

Adam swore and stopped at the side of the road to light and hang his buggy lanterns. While he did so, he thought he heard something flapping in the trees, but it was too dark to see much of anything. He climbed back into his buggy and turned his horses back toward the doctor's house on the far side of town.

Chapter Nineteen

As Adam drove, something ate at him. He felt as if he shouldn't be going to the doctor's. As if he would waste precious time, if he did. And Mercy's question nagged him.

Is Sara in labor too?

Adam turned the buggy around to go back to the Bachman house. He wanted to know every detail of the morning, of the way Sara had left them.

Once there, when he learned what Mercy's husband had done, what he had accused Sara of, Adam wanted to strike the man. Then again, he, himself, had been more than brutal to those around him, after Abby died.

If Sara was safe, he supposed he would someday be able to forgive Enos Bachman.

"She left just a few minutes before Doctor Marks arrived," Mercy had said. "But the doctor said he had not seen her on the road and we thought that was odd. But then he said he expected Sara was not ready to face him with what she would think of as a failure. When he left, he was going to find you, Adam."

Adam had wanted to shout at the poor grieving woman. He wanted to rage because she had not told him all this before. But it was a quirk of their people to keep their business, their thoughts, to themselves. Coaxing was always required when information was sought. He had often been guilty of withholding it himself, most recently from Sara.

He should have explained to her why he could not love.

He should have laid bare his past, his deep secret and great weakness. A woman should know the evil her husband inherited from his father. Sara deserved at least that much. More.

If . . . when he found her. . . .

He turned back to Mercy. "What made you think she was in labor?"

"That backache of hers."

"She's had a sore back for weeks."

"But when it moves low and around to the sides—"

"Labor?"

Mercy nodded.

Adam begged blankets, bread, cheese, and left Sara's friend praying for her safe delivery. Mercy did not blame Sara for her loss, but Adam blamed Mercy's husband for his relentless quest for sons.

Adam caught himself. Lord, he had stumbled into the trap Sara once fell into. Judgment. And he knew better than anyone what could happen, even with the best of intentions. Like Abby, Mercy might whine and beg for her husband's attention. Like Sara, she might drive him wild with her very scent. And in bed, touching him as she rolled into and against him all night long. Despite his determination, Mercy's husband might be no match for her womanly wiles.

Adam loved Sara's womanly wiles. He loved—

He cursed and backed his team up. If Sara had missed seeing the doctor, she had not driven toward town.

When he heard that flapping sound again, Adam stopped the buggy. He took the lantern off its hook and followed the direction of the sound.

It had not been that long since he'd climbed a tree, and yet he found the task grueling, given the fact that his heart raced with fear and worry.

What if Sara was in labor?

Lord this was a tall tree.

What if she were calling his name even now?

No wonder he hadn't been able to see the flapping thing from the ground, it was black.

What if she needed help?

Adam wiped the sweat from his brow. A black cloth. No, it was an apron. Could it be Sara's?

Who could tell?

With no apron, what would she wrap the baby in, if she were in labor and if she delivered it alone, and if she. . . .

Damn it, aprons were all the same, white or black, big or small.

Big? Adam held the lantern over the apron again and examined its pleats, not tucked and stitched, but open to accommodate an expected child. He cursed, jumped from the bottommost branch of the low-slung oak, and nearly turned his ankle. *"Dummkopf,"* he said, returning to his buggy.

He knew Sara didn't go through town and she didn't go home. He took the fork toward the pike, toward the shack where they had made lo—

"Go, go fast," he urged his team. "Run like the racehorses you were meant to be, and don't *dopple.*"

Pray God she remembered shelter awaited in this direction.

What if he lost her because he couldn't get to her in time?

If he broke a wheel, he would kill himself, but better him than Sara. Besides, the wheels were good. He'd checked before he left for the buggy factory, in case they needed tending while he was there.

He was an idiot, thinking about wheels and buggy factories. Sara's very life lay in the balance. One thing he knew for certain: he could not live without Sara in his life. He could not.

She would not die. She would not.

Sara didn't quite recognize the shack, but for a vague memory of her struggle for air and Adam's description of that night. From his words, she had located the near-ruin, praise be. She would tell him later that he gave good direct—

She would tell him nothing. There would be no later for them.

Rubbing the result of that night, crooning her love for the child who seemed to be seeking a comfortable spot—she knew exactly how he felt—she tried to adjust her vision to the dark interior of the one-room wooden structure.

She found a blanket on the floor in the corner, one of theirs, she thought, left behind the last time, and shook it out. It was dusty, but warm. Wrapped in it, Sara found dry enough wood in the lean-to out back, and matches, a lantern—theirs too.

She unhitched her horse so it could graze and forage.

The blaze did not take long to catch. Sara sat on the hearth, her head against the stone, skirts tucked beneath her. She wished she had a mattress, a pile of hay, anything soft on which to lay her tired body and soothe her aching back.

She would move away from the blaze when she warmed.

A long three-quarters of an hour later, an overwhelming sense of relief and gratitude engulfed Adam when he found her in the shack, asleep against the fireplace stones, her cheek pillowed against her hand.

A minuscule ember from the fire sat smoldering on the

blanket in which she was wrapped. He brushed it away and tried to be angry with her for getting herself into this mess. She might have been in grave danger. But he could not help his grin over the wild rejoicing in his heart just for looking at her, safe and sound.

Christmas carols, he heard in his head. Alleluias and angels singing praise to God. Joy, he felt in his heart, as if the world had suddenly righted itself after spinning out of control.

He had not been this happy since. . . .

He had never been this happy.

"Liebchen," he called gently, but Sara did not awaken. She seemed deeply asleep, undisturbed, and did not appear to be in labor. "Alleluia," he whispered aloud before he went outside to get the blankets and food Mercy had given him.

He made a bed for her and she did not awaken through all the jostling she took as he lay her down. He would let her get the rest she so obviously needed, before he took her home.

His heart, when he gazed upon her, curled on her side, relaxed in sleep, expanded to the point of near-pain.

He could not love her, he reminded himself. He would do everything in his power to see he never did, to insure the impossibility. But he could make her life somewhat easier, more pleasant than it had been. Perhaps in time she might come to understand, if he told her everything.

And he would tell her. Soon.

Today when she awoke. Tomorrow at the latest.

Or the next day.

He had all but transferred his anger at his father to her, when she had done nothing but try to show him how to love. She had given him and his mother and sister her patience and caring. The love she gave his girls was open and unconditional. They had become happy, carefree children because of Sara, certainly not because of him. It was a wonder they didn't have nightmares, living with him.

Adam's thoughts were arrested. Sara sucked in her breath, changed position and unconsciously placed a hand to the small of her back. The low keening wail she emitted seemed filled, almost, with despair.

He saw now, in the way the light from the fire fell on her face, that tears had dried on her cheeks, then he found himself looking into the rich green depths of her eyes. Their dark inner circles widened. "Adam?"

"You're in pain."

"It's . . . it's my back, it aches so."

Adam moved his hands to soothe and massage. "Let me ease you."

Before his eyes, her abdomen stretched taut and changed shape even as his fingers worked on the small of her back. Like its mother, their child fidgeted when confined.

"What are you thinking?" he asked, when she closed her eyes almost in ecstasy.

"I am floating on a cloud, hoping this dream will never end."

"I have been called many things—*dummkopf,* mad, bad and mean—but never a dream."

Her smile changed her face and her glow warmed him. "I need to change sides," she said, so he helped her to lie on her other side, the child between them now.

"I think she will be very strong, judging by her efforts to dislodge me from beside you at this moment," Adam said.

Sara's smile widened. "Will he? As strong as you? I can't wait to find out."

Panic caught Adam like a blow. *Please God. I do not de-*

serve her, but let her live to raise her child. "Sara, why did you run away?"

"Mercy—"

"Doesn't blame you. Why do you blame yourself?"

She looked away from him and toward the fire. "I do not want to be a midwife anymore. I cannot, and the world will be the better for my decision."

"And how will four weeping little girls be for your decision?"

"Oh, Adam. Were they crying?" Sara made to sit up.

Adam sighed and urged her back down. "You left them. Of course they will cry when you don't come back."

He lay facing her and put his arm around her to continue rubbing her back.

"You're trying to frighten me."

"Frighten some sense into you, maybe. Somebody has to. Our girls love you, Sara. You are their Mommie. What will they do without you to love them back?"

"They have you. You love them."

"Do not say so." Adam sat up at that and regarded the waning fire over his bent knees. "Do you know what my father used to say as he *punished* us for our supposed faults? He would say, 'I do this because I love you,' over and over again, as he strapped us, or . . . or worse." Adam looked at Sara then, almost afraid to see her revulsion, but he was surprised to find nothing of the sort in her gaze, not even pity, praise be. Only understanding, he saw, and . . . caring. He had to swallow before he could continue. "Love hurts, Sara."

She took his hand, squeezed. "Abby knew, then, about your father?"

"Yes."

"Why did you never tell *me?*"

"What? Reveal my scarred and worthless self to my strong and capable Sara?"

"Incapable, you mean. I am the true failure here. I *know* I am. You simply *think* you are."

"With good reason."

"You are *not* like him. You love your girls."

"Love doles out harsh, painful punishments, Sara. My father proved that. And I am exactly like him."

"No, Adam. You are strong and worthy, or Abby could not have loved you."

Sorrow filled Adam and tears blurred his vision, but it was past time for honesty, so he would not try to hide his feelings from Sara, not anymore. "I knew when I killed someone as good and kind and loving as Abby that I was as worthless as my father said. I have proved it, Sara, time and again."

"The only thing unworthy about you, Adam Zuckerman, is your foolish notion that you are anything like the brute who raised you."

"Do you not see that if I let myself love the girls, or you, or my mother or Emma, I will destroy you all? I beat Butch Redding exactly as my father would have done. Without your intervention, I might have beat the man to death."

"You love Butch Redding then?"

Adam swore but he regarded her with an unexpected spark of hope glowing deep inside him. "What are you saying?"

"That you were protecting Butch Redding's children *from him,* as someone should have protected you and Emma."

"My mother—"

"Failed you in that way, I know." Sara stroked his brow, her touch a blessing. "But in the same way that it is time for

you to realize your own worth, it is also time for you to forgive your mother. She could no more have stopped your father than Jenny could stop Butch. So you beat Butch in
Jenny's place, because he harmed her child. You hurt a
beast, Adam. You could never hurt a child. You planted a
butterfly garden to tell your girls you loved them in the only
way you knew, in the way your mother told you."

Adam searched within himself for the truth in her words.
"That *is* how my mother told me. I had forgotten. She said
the butterfly garden was a symbol of her love and God's
healing."

With the reminder, Adam discovered that he could forgive his mother, and that forgiving others could ease the
darkness of worthlessness inside oneself. But self-forgiveness
was not to be found. "I did not remember my mother's
words, Sara, when I planted the garden."

She stroked his cheek, his beard. "Deep down, you did."

Afraid even to acknowledge the illusive seed of redemption budding deep inside him, Adam moved his arm behind
her again to continue his soothing motion along her spine.
"You are a stubborn and amazing woman, Sara Zuckerman."

"You are headstrong and have amazing hands, Adam
Zuckerman."

He chuckled and massaged in widening circles.

Sara begged for his kiss with parted lips and a forward
movement of her head. Adam groaned and fitted his to the
invitation of hers. Contentment filled him as he slanted his
greedy kiss this way, then that. Awakening. Need. He
should be shot for wanting his wife in these circumstances.

He continued soothing Sara's back as he pulled her
closer against him, as close as he could, given her current
condition.

"You want me?"

"What is so amazing about that?"

"I don't disgust you then, shaped as I am?"

"Disgust me? Are you mad? With your eyes, your scent, your laugh, your very presence, you tease and seduce me. Near or far, in bed and out, smiling or sassing, kissing or scrapping, and especially, big with child, you drive me mad with wanting you."

With joy in her heart, Sara felt the rhythm of Adam's hand at her back change from soothing to passionate. When he reached her upper back, he stroked the side of her breast. She saw need smolder in his eyes, felt him throb against her.

Having wanted him so desperately for so long, Sara unpinned her bodice, just to feel his touch. As he accepted her offer and took suckle, purls of delight shot through her. She had yearned for weeks, and now, finally, she was in her husband's arms. But she was also in labor and she guessed it was about time to tell him, since it had begun to progress quickly in the past few minutes.

"Adam?" She bit her lip and rode out a contraction. "Adam, do you finally believe that you could never hurt a child?"

He pulled away and regarded her blankly.

"Do you believe you could never hurt a child?" she repeated.

"I am beginning to see the sense in your words, but . . . why are you asking now, when—"

"I just want to be sure before—" She gasped.

"Before?"

"Our babe is born."

Awareness hit Adam hard. Sara saw it happen, saw the color drain from his face. "Now?"

Before she finished nodding, he had pinned her bodice

back together. After he wrapped her against the cold, he put out the fire and lifted her in his arms.

"Where are you taking me?"

"Home where you belong."

"I don't want—"

"Yes you do. Stop pretending different."

Just to be contrary, Sara pouted. He was right. Sometime during the last hour, her determination had faltered. She thought perhaps it had happened when she opened her eyes and saw him watching over her, his brow creased with worry.

Besides, she had no strength left with which to stop him.

They were off in a blink. "I didn't know your butterfly horses could go so fast."

"Neither did I, until today."

"Well, slow them down."

"Your problem, Sara, is that you want to control life beyond human ability."

She braced herself for a contraction. "Because I want you to slow your horses?"

"Because you won't admit that only God has dominion over death, not Sara Zuckerman."

She released her breath. "Fine, then Sara Zuckerman does not need to be a midwife."

"Sassy thing."

"Slow down, Adam."

"Can you slow your pains for me?"

"Of course not."

"Neither me with the horses, then." He took her hand. "If you being a midwife is part of God's plan, then you must. And you are meant to be a midwife. I saw that with my own eyes. Open your heart, Sara, and do His work. Whether tilling the soil or delivering a child, we all must."

"If God alone controls death, as you say, it cannot be your fault, then, that Abby died."

"I will not accept that until you accept that it was not your fault that Mercy's triplets died."

Sadness filled her. "In my logical mind I understand your words, but I do not know if I will ever be able to deliver a child again."

"Will you consider it, later, maybe?"

"I will be open to the possibility of remaining a midwife. If only we could find one," Sara wailed. "Where are you going! This is not the way home. I want to go home, Adam. Please, or I will birth your child in this buggy."

"Another mile," he said. "Please try to hold on. Damn it, Sara. Why didn't you tell me sooner that you were in labor?"

"We would not have had such a lovely reunion, if you were worried I would die at any minute."

Adam looked at her in appalled shock. He growled. "If we survive this, I may have to beat you."

"Why Adam Zuckerman, you're not so worried all of a sudden. Why?"

"Abby had not the strength or spirit to welcome me into her arms from the day she conceived. She never, ever, sassed me when her time was near. She certainly never made me want to beat her then. And, believe me, she did none of those things when she was in labor." He grinned and turned back to the road. "Sara Zuckerman, I think you just might be as strong as you say you are."

Sara laughed, then she squealed. "The pains, they're coming quick, Adam. I want to push."

Like a shot, Adam regarded her, the road, her again. "That can't be good." He stopped the buggy.

"Where are we?" she wailed, her head back, her eyes closed in pain.

"Here. We're here. Don't push until I get you inside." Jordan opened the door to his surgery. "I've been waiting for you since I spoke to Mercy."

"Thank God," Adam said, laying his wife on the surgery table, as the doctor indicated.

"Adam Zuckerman, you impostor. You do love me!"

"Sara, hush. Not now."

"Why do you think Adam loves you?" Jordan asked, to distract her and Adam as he removed her under-clothing so he could deliver her child. "Adam you don't have to go. Just take Sara's hand. Sara, try not to break any of his fingers, alright?"

Sara giggled, she gasped and she cracked her husband's knuckles as she pushed. When she knew she had a minute to breathe, she regarded her husband with wonder and answered Jordan's question. "I know Adam loves me because he proved it by putting aside his jealousy of you to bring me here, so you would keep me safe in childbirth."

"Damn it, Sara!"

"Push, Sara."

Sara obeyed. Adam grimaced.

"Almost there," Jordan said.

"I *do* love you!" Adam shouted, almost in defeat. "But damn it, you should have let me say it first!"

"I love you, too!" Sara shouted as their child slipped into Jordan's hands.

"A son," Jordan crowed with a grin and a wink. "And he looks just like me."

Adam barked a laugh and welcomed his son into his arms. "Come," he said, heart full, as the boy regarded him through Sara's eyes. "Come and meet your Mommie."

Epilogue

Though the girls could not wait to see Sara and their new brother, no one was more impatient than Adam to bring them home.

Jordan had insisted that Sara remain in the small bed in his surgery for twenty-four hours, while he made certain that she and the baby were healthy.

Adam did not complain. The doctor had taken good care of them, he saw, and he would thank the man properly, as soon as the lump left his throat for seeing Sara nurse their son.

Jordan left so they could have some privacy and so Adam could help Sara don her new blackberry dress to go home.

It humbled Adam that Sara might have chosen the fancy medical man to marry, but she had chosen him instead, a big, *dummkopf* Amishman.

"I love you," he whispered against her hair as he took her into his arms for the first time in two days. "Don't leave me again, please. Ever."

Sara smiled through happy tears. "I never will. Can we go home, now?"

Within the hour, they pulled up to the front, rather than the back of the house. "What is going on?" Sara asked when she saw all the carriages.

Adam shook his head as he took his bundled son from her arms and helped her get down; then he handed his boy back and walked her up the front walk.

Once again, like on the night Abby died, she stood at the base of the porch steps, and for a long minute she hesitated, overwhelmed by the gifts she had been given, and especially by the cost. But the door to her home stood open in welcome, and inside, she saw, people were waiting.

Sara entered and stopped. In her best room, all but empty of furniture, save the chairs against the walls, sat Bishop Weaver, Roman, Lena and Emma. But on the cleared floor sat a number of women, Amish and English alike, and as many—more—children, babies, dolls even.

Mercy gave her a smile that eased the guilt Sara felt for holding her own healthy newborn. She was grateful Jordan had convinced her the triplets could not have survived under any conditions. Gossypium root bark might actually have given them half a chance, Jordan said, had the boys been bigger or stronger.

As if reading her, Mercy reached out, and Sara took her hand and squeezed it, before she turned to her other guests. "I am so glad to see you all, but what are you doing on the floor?"

"Saramay and I are among the women you helped and the babies you delivered," Mercy said. "Hetty, Lydia and everyone here are your successes, Sara. We wanted you to see how many altogether. Not everyone could come, though."

"The dolls," Adam said, "are for the babies you will never deliver if you do not remain a midwife. Imagine missing all those miracles. Imagine some of those babes' chances, if you are not there to bring them into the world."

Bishop Weaver stood, smoothed his beard and placed his hands behind his back. "That would be a great loss to our district," he said. "Sara, we want you to be our first Amish midwife."

"Please, Sara," Mercy said.

Their *first*, Sara thought, with a mixture of wonder and fear over what she had wrought, but she could not keep from accepting the challenge with a full and grateful heart. When everyone cheered, she had to bite her lip to keep her tears in check.

"But Sara," the Bishop said, his voice carrying a note of censure of a sudden, "mind the color of your dresses!" He raised his arms in supplication, or defeat. "I saw two more that color just today!"

Sara's chin came up. "It's a *good* color."

Adam rolled his eyes.

The bishop nodded and gave her an exasperated smile. "It *is* a good color. But some are not. Come and see me and we will discuss which is which."

Sara beamed and Adam chuckled as he moved aside to reveal their girls, also on the floor. He sat beside them, and Pris climbed into his lap. "We too would be lost without you. All of us," he said, his voice gruff. "All around you, Sara, are people who care about you and need you."

"We love you," Lizzie said.

Despite the color riding up his neck, Adam gave a half nod. "We do."

Sara felt weak with the need to sit, and cry, and kiss everyone at once.

Katie pointed her finger at Sara. "You cannot get away from us."

Pris rose, ignoring her father's "Stay," and ran to throw her arms around Sara's legs and beam up at her.

Everyone rose then, all talking at once.

Lena passed plates of peach kuchen and sand tarts, and Emma filled glasses with cider.

Adam and the girls came to stand beside the chair

Bishop Weaver had vacated so Sara could sit. She kissed each of her children in turn. Even Adam bent forward for his kiss, right there before God and Bishop Weaver.

Then Sara unwrapped the baby and showed him to the girls. "Here is your new brother," she said. "What shall we name him?"

"Sunnybunny," Katie said.

Lizzie shook her head. "Papa said Noah, like your brother, if we got a boy."

Sara looked at her husband, big, bad, Mad Adam Zuckerman, and her heart overflowed. "Noah," she said. "A brother who will play with his sisters in the butterfly garden amid the warmth of their father's love."

About the Author

Annette Blair is the Development Director and Journalism Advisor at a private New England prep school. Married to her grammar school nemesis—and glad she didn't know what fate had in store—Annette considers romance a celebration of life.

Among her career achievements are: a *Romantic Times* Reviewers' Choice Award Nomination, two Booksellers Best Awards, a Winter Rose Award, a LORIES Award, a Book of Your Heart Award, two Laurel Wreath Awards and two Blue Boa Awards of Excellence. She was also a winner in *Affaire de Coeur Magazine*'s 2004 Reader-Writer Poll. She has been a Holt Medallion finalist, an Orange Rose Finalist and an Aspen Gold Finalist.

In bookstores now is Annette's *The Kitchen Witch*, a Berkley Sensations Contemporary, soon to be followed by *My Favorite Witch*. Also available is the fourth in her popular Rogues Club Series, *A Christmas Baby*. Always happy crafting a new romance, Annette loves hearing from her readers, antiquing and collecting glass slippers. *The Butterfly Garden* is her second Amish Historical.

Hartland Public Library
Hartland, WI 53029

DEMCO